THE FUGITIVE'S CONCERTO

JILL CARLSON

THE FUGITIVE'S CONCERTO

Merton Glenn Publishing

Cover design: Stephanie Larson
Cover photography: Terry Carlson
Cover pianists, left to right: Jade Brimm, Aja Stallman, Kaytlen Johnson

The story and characters in this book are fictional. Actual historical dates and locations are presented as accurately as possible.

ISBN-13: 978-0692122617
Library of Congress Control Number: 2018905287

Printed in the United States of America

For Jerry

My best friend

FALL 1944

PROLOGUE 1

NOVEMBER 22, 1944

With a hiss of brakes, the North Arlington Special stopped at Old Dominion Drive and Lee Highway. Only six passengers remained. They watched as a man of slight build, his wispy blond hair straying over one eye, made his way to the front of the bus. He was dressed in U.S. Army fatigues, but he was without cap or jacket. Balancing a small duffel bag, he waited for the final wheezing lurch, then maneuvered down the three steps to the street. On his left arm was a dingy cast, just visible under a shirt that looked a couple of sizes too large.

He watched the bus recede into a dusky haze of diesel smoke, then walked a few yards to a grassy knoll and leaned the duffel against a tree. The wind had begun to sharpen. He drew into himself, pulling up his collar. It was difficult to use his plastered left arm but he managed to unfold a piece of wrinkled paper, shake it to the breeze, and study it for the tenth time since he'd begun this last leg of his journey.

He put the paper back into his pocket, which held eight dollars and a Baby Ruth bar. He calculated that he was nearly there, wherever that was. He had not known his true bearings for some time. All he had on that small piece of paper was an address he'd copied in a USO center.

Everything he had ever loved was gone and he did not know whether he would find anything here to replace them. Neither had there been anything for him on the lumbering troop ship that had docked in New York two weeks earlier. Unless it was Jimmy, but Jimmy had his own life to begin again in Ohio. No, he could not go where Jimmy was going. This destination was for him alone. He picked up his burden and began walking.

Old Dominion Drive curved to the north and was sparsely traveled, even at this time of day. Not many Arlington residents owned cars now, and those who had them usually left them in the garage, especially tonight when they were home saving gas and preparing for Thanksgiving. On this leg of the narrow roadway, there was not much in the way of protective shoulders and a few times he had found cover in the ditch and new pains in his left arm.

Not much farther now. Just put one foot in front of the other.

It had always been his habit to sing in hard times. But nothing would come. Perhaps he would never sing again, never let music beckon to his heart. Yet deep within he felt the old stirrings of cello and violin, of piano and French horn — muffled in their small hiding places — the caves and burrows where his heart's lodestone had always refreshed him with hope.

It was nearly dark and a sliver of crescent moon winked the stars into place one by one. He paused to take it in — this same sight he'd beheld across the ocean. He shifted the duffel to his back and began walking again. Then, sweetly, faintly, the echo of piano keys floated in the crisp twilight. He was sure that he had heard something. There! He stopped, leaning into the sound. Yes! A Clementi sonatina. Opus 36 Number One — the andante section.

"Oh slow down, slow *down*," he muttered. "Andante! *An-dan-te!!*"

As if in response, the arpeggios stopped abruptly and began again, slower now and nearly *andante!* He stood rooted, oblivious to wind and traffic. Where was it coming from? Down that little street? Was that Twenty-Second Street? It was no longer light enough to read the slip of paper. Turning to his right, he kept walking, welcoming the homey atmosphere of thick shrubbery.

He might even believe he was back in France among hedgerows of blackberry and hawthorn and poplar.

He followed the sound, a chord of thrumming tied to his inner being. *Oh, don't stop, don't stop the andante!* Now he was running, not caring that his arm throbbed with each pounding step. But there was no more music — only the soft rustle of early winter wind and his own gasping breath. He stopped and breathed slowly until he felt strong enough to go on.

Suddenly a porch light blazed and two little girls burst from a small house on his left. Their laughter lit up the night, the clatter of small feet thumping rhythm into the sidewalk. And behind them stood the object of his search — looking for all the world like a tiny piece of carved granite, her thinning gray hair caught up in a bun, and one small bony hand thumping the railing.

Eliza Bestor's face melted into a crinkly smile. "Remember, O'Dell — *An-dan-te! An-dan-te!* Hurry now, girls. I promised your mother you would be home before dark!"

PROLOGUE 2

THANKSGIVING DAY 1944

Wisps of leaf smoke swirled up Vermont Street against the glow of the late afternoon sun. It was nearly seventy degrees and the aroma filtered through windows and screen doors and drifted lazily toward the sky. With its tantalizing scent, it touched kitchens already full to bursting with the rich smells of roasting turkey, spicy pumpkin and mashed potatoes.

The pungent smoke breathed safety and all things normal. On this Thanksgiving Day of 1944 every home in the neighborhood had taken a break from uncertainty and fear. Hardly a ration coupon was left as mothers splurged sugar, tea and meat stamps in their headlong efforts to forget the war and gather their families around the table.

Small white banners with one, two and sometimes three or four blue stars graced several of the neighbors' windows. One star for each child, father or brother fighting in strange-sounding hamlets and islands around the globe. One neighbor's window held a blue star for their daughter, but all her family knew was that she was somewhere in the South Pacific. Each soldier was prayed for, hoped for — and all too often buried across the sea and promoted to a golden star on the window. "Missing," some of the early-morning telegrams had said. One word to cover tears, memories, and questions that would echo for generations.

In the middle of Vermont Street Thomas and Olivia Farnsworth had posted their blue-starred banner on the window closest to the front door. Its red-bordered white field, barely visible behind lace curtains, heralded one star for Olivia's army sister, hopefully safe on the West Coast, and one star for her little brother Alexander, who was now three years into directing the slogging traffic of trucks — the convoys carrying K-rations, ammunition and the never-ending paraphernalia of war. Was he somewhere near Belgium? Maybe France. Or Germany. Olivia imagined his journey, the lines on her mental map drawn by the bits of fragmented news broadcast each evening after the children had gone to bed.

Olivia basted the turkey one last time and pushed it none too gently into the oven. It was healing to have good honest work today. She had not wished to sit still too long, imagining what might happen to her brother. She did not wish to think even one more time about their backyard neighbors the Porros, and the telegram they'd received last week. Franklin Porro's big brother would not be sitting at the family table, ever again. The thought flickered briefly that maybe she was not too old, at thirty-five, to go off to war.

Thomas Farnsworth laid a cream-colored dishtowel over the Thanksgiving linen and sat at the side of the table. In front of him were a Bakelite-handled carving knife, a sharpener, and a two-tined fork. He pulled the sharpener slowly back and forth. The knife should respond well and take its edge nicely. Although his back was to the kitchen, he could feel Olivia's tension. He had offered help once. But for now it was best to quietly tackle this one last thing, and then perhaps he would find Kate and bring some music into their day of thanks. Sometimes he wondered whether his own star should adorn the sign in the window. After all, he was only thirty-six and eligible to serve. But his boss had declared him "necessary to the war effort." And here he would stay.

On the front porch, O'Dell and Patti Farnsworth sat waiting for dinner. They'd plunked their feet on the concrete steps of their gambrel-roofed home and from their perch they sat like little queens surveying the sloping lawn and quiet street.

Patti held tightly to their beagle puppy, which squirmed and whined at her feet. "Listen, Dellie. I hear Kate. Oh. Wait. There's Daddy's saxophone too."

Patti hummed to the softened melody floating through screened windows. She could hear the rolling piano and throaty saxophone playing their Thanksgiving favorite — the family's song of gathering, a once-a-year anthem of hope and peace.

Bless this house, O Lord we pray. Make it safe by night and day.

Nine-year-old Patti knew all the words. She always knew the words.

O'Dell turned to her sister. At seven she felt it her duty to stretch up to Patti's skills. She couldn't remember the words, but hummed loudly into the puppy's face.

"Stop it! Don't do that, Dellie! Skippy doesn't like it!"

"Does too!"

"I'm telling Daddy. He's a hunting dog and Daddy said not to spoil him!"

O'Dell shrugged. "Okay. Do what you want, then." She edged closer to Patti and folded one of Skippy's ears, its silky softness rumpling into her hands. "I like it up here, don't you?"

Patti surveyed their neighbors' houses from her high perch. "Uh huh. But I sure don't like it when we have to take the weeds out of this front lawn."

"Yeah. Weeds all over the creeping muddles!"

"Not muddles, Dellie. Myrtle."

"Oh."

Patti turned her head toward Old Dominion Drive, where the traffic murmured like honeybees. "Up here we can see — oh, just everybody!"

Patti snuggled Skippy onto her lap and stroked his back, careful to keep one hand tightly around the leash.

"Let me hold him, Patti."

"Can't. Daddy told me to take care of him while Mother's cooking."

O'Dell scuffed her brown oxford shoes and edged closer. "I won't hurt him. You know I won't hurt him!" She touched her nose to Skippy's, felt his wet tongue on her cheek.

Inside the Farnsworth living room Kate and her father ramped up the volume. Patti began singing again.

Bless these walls so firm and stout, keeping want and trouble out.

O'Dell pulled on the puppy. "I can sing, too, you know."

Patti jerked Skippy's leash.

Bless the roof and chimneys tall, let thy peace lie overall.

"You sing real nice, Patti. Why don't you stand up and do it. And then everybody can hear you!"

Patti stood. She was proud of her voice, so praised by teachers at John Marshall School. O'Dell pulled inch by inch on the puppy's leash as Patti lifted her voice.

Bless these windows shining bright....

"Stop it, Dellie! Quit pulling!"

A squirrel chattered in the poplar above the mailbox at the bend in the sidewalk, whisking her tail vigorously, beady black eyes fixed on the puppy. Skippy strained at his collar and yapped a warning as the squirrel leaped onto the flagstone steps and dashed for the street. The beagle whimpered and jerked, then broke free just as an ancient Plymouth, packed to the ceiling with the Hardesty family, hove into sight, lumbering toward Old Dominion Drive and Thanksgiving at Grandma's.

O'Dell screamed. "Skippy! Skippy! Skippy! No! No! No!"

Inside the Plymouth, the family heard the bump. The car jerked to a stop, tumbling the five younger children together.

The squirrel had made it across the road. Skippy had not.

Bless the people here within, keep them pure and free from sin.

Patti and O'Dell tore down the flagstone steps, onto the sidewalk, nearly tripping each other in their headlong race. O'Dell stumbled and sobbed, pushing ahead of Patti. She would get to the street first. It was her fault! Hers! Hers! Hers! She would make everything good again. She must. She would reach that puppy, hold him, tell him it was all right, feel his warm body in her arms. Her breath rasped loud and urgent.

Between the front wheels, something moved. Slowly, the little beagle scratched against the pavement, heading for the ditch.

Once across the street, O'Dell knew that it was not all right. It would never be all right. The tiny body lay in a tangle of weeds, blood trickling from its side. Kneeling, O'Dell scooped the warm, wet puppy into her arms and carried him out of the ditch, across the street, across the sidewalk and up to the house, her tears mingling with Skippy's lifeblood.

And inside the Farnsworth home, all was quiet.

The music had stopped.

SPRING AND SUMMER
1945

CHAPTER 1

O'Dell lay still, listening to the morning. She always knew by the sounds what time it was, when she should begin the day, dress for school, practice the piano and show up at just the right moment for breakfast. Patti was singing in the bathtub.

Kate was at the piano and soon she would be finished. Then it would be O'Dell's turn to practice. Mother was in the kitchen, clattering pans and dishes in a kind of tippy-tap punctuated by the soft thudding of refrigerator and oven doors. Daddy was quiet. He always emerged at just the right time, ready for work.

But what was that new sound? O'Dell lay still, squinching her toes against the sheet, trying to give it a name. It wasn't a heavy sound but it had a soft rhythm, a steady drip, drip, pause… drip.

As the sun's rays gently filtered through the woods, the tree closest to the window shifted its branches, releasing a shower of soft snow. Now she knew. It was the sound of melting. Last week's storm had not only canceled her birthday party but covered, once more, the wooded glade where Skippy lay buried. It was winter's final blanket of snow, good for hiding what O'Dell did not want to see.

O'Dell closed her eyes. Just a few minutes. She'd have to get up soon. But not yet. She stretched once more, then looked up. A little brown spider lowered itself slowly, inching toward her head. The spider and O'Dell regarded one another in suspended silence.

Slowly O'Dell slid from the blanket. Safely out of reach, she shot up and tumbled to the floor, catching her foot on the iron bedstead. Thomas heard the little yelp and came to her door.

"Dellie, are you all right?"

"Yeah. Just another spider. It's okay." She smiled and looked into her father's face. "I think it looked at me."

Thomas gave O'Dell's shoulder a light squeeze. "Well then, he'd have something pretty to look at, wouldn't he. Think you can scurry downstairs now?"

"Guess so."

A blue jay screamed on its way through the woods, "like a giant letting out its breath," O'Dell thought.

Thomas patted his daughter's shoulder, then straightened. He'd have to hurry, too, if he wanted to catch his carpool. "I hope you're ready to practice, Dellie. Kate's about done, and you'll need to leave time for breakfast. Mother's making pancakes."

"With molasses?" O'Dell screwed up her face.

Thomas put a finger to his lips. "Don't let Mother hear you fuss. We're low on ration stamps."

O'Dell ran her fingers across the banister in a drumming motion and started down the stairs. At the bottom, instead of turning left toward the living room, she peered around the doorway at the kitchen and waited until her mother turned her back and stood at the sink.

O'Dell tiptoed along the back of the kitchen toward the basement stairs and padded noiselessly down the three steps to the landing. In front of her was the tiny powder room and through the window to her left she could see robins building their nest under the porch roof. She turned, clutched the railing and inched her way down the steep flight. A tiny bulb cast a pale light over the washtubs, and under one of them was Skippy's bed.

The floor was cold, and the rough concrete prickled her feet. She shivered as she crept toward the wicker basket. She took a quick look at the stairs, then sat on the floor and let the cold seep into her bones. O'Dell closed her eyes and smoothed the cloth, thinking of the way Skippy's silky ears rippled against her fingers.

She remembered the terrible screeching wheels and the thump. And she remembered the blood. Especially the blood.

On Christmas Eve she had stayed awake until nearly midnight, watching clouds float in the star-decked night. She was sure she had seen Santa Claus skimming the skies with his flying reindeer and she had poked Patti awake. The two of them had whispered and imagined, and it was O'Dell who had the inspiration to beg the old gentleman to bring back their puppy. Anything was possible on this night, and the same robed saint who always climbed down their chimney and stuffed Daddy's long black socks with tantalizing bulges would surely honor their request.

Patti wanted to believe in Santa Claus, especially on this night, and hoped Skippy's sweet face would be sticking out of one of their stockings on Christmas morning. She'd kept O'Dell's secret. No one but Patti and O'Dell knew why the puppy had broken loose from their grip, and Patti would not tell. Not ever.

Slowly, noiselessly, she pulled out the basket, just as she had done many times over the past three months. The blanket, a worn checkered tablecloth, had been neatly folded into eight thicknesses. O'Dell had counted them herself. She fingered the cloth and pulled a corner of it up to her cheek. Then she noticed something. On one corner of the basket was a dark stain. What was it? A shiver of fear crawled along her neck. Quickly she pushed the basket under the washtub and raced up the stairs.

"What have you been doing, O'Dell?" Her mother stood firmly planted in the kitchen doorway. "You should be practicing right now! You'll have to cut your time short, and make up for it after school. I want us to have breakfast together."

"I needed to use the bathroom." O'Dell raced past her mother toward the piano. A solid thumping of her favorite sonatina was what she needed. With it perhaps she could erase the secret stain.

♪

In the high-ceilinged living room, an old upright piano snugged the short wall behind the hall closet. It was visible from the front door and also the east window. It had been lovingly — if not a little roughly — scarred and polished for the past five years.

Kate sat on the piano bench folding her music books into perfect order. "Dellie, I'm going to put my music on the left side of the top. Right here. You and Patti can put yours in the bench." Kate was tall and willowy, and moved with easy grace. Her younger sisters felt that somehow Kate had ascended a higher plane beyond their reach. In six months she would be in high school.

Kate rose to her full height, and with a quick smile she was off, her loafers beating a tattoo up the stairs.

O'Dell slid onto the bench. Then she just sat, listening, her head bowed. "I have to do that," she'd once countered when her mother had told her to quit dawdling.

She could almost hear the piano, even before the first key was struck. Middle C. She tried humming it, groping for pitch. Then O'Dell lightly pressed the ivory, willing the piano's vibration to match the hum in her head. Almost! Now a chord. She struck C major with both hands, bass and treble. Then in sharp staccato the family of chords from C to F, and then G. Up and down the piano she went, faster and faster, louder and louder, first playing the chords, then rolling them into broken patterns.

"Mother do you want to hear that old sonatina again?"

"Yes, then come quickly to breakfast."

This sonatina was O'Dell's favorite. She was queen of the piano while she played its little scales and arpeggios. When finished she clapped her hands together in triumph and closed the tattered Clementi book.

"Breakfast, girls. Hurry now."

O'Dell gathered her books and shoved them into the bench. She was just pulling the wooden fall into place when she heard another tune. Clink, tink, clink, tink, rumble tink, rumble tink. Perhaps it was coming from outdoors. O'Dell ran to the west window and shoved it fully open. The sloping, undulating front lawn showed patches of green myrtle through the melting snow. Near the tulip poplar tree, where the sidewalk took its right turn toward the street, a squirrel sat motionless, studying the clink, tink, clink, tink, rumble. Silence. Tink, clink.

Silence.

Then she saw him.

Some said his name was Bodie but no one really knew whether it was his first or his last name. And no one knew where he lived or what he did after he took his wagon-load of bottles and scraps to the redemption center each afternoon. Short and thin, he appeared even smaller because he walked bent into himself, as if to protect some inner sanctuary.

"Tah… tah… tah…" O'Dell sang the first three notes of Clementi's sonatina with the bottle clinks her accompaniment. She swept her hands from side to side, willing her makeshift orchestra to perform, with herself as the prima donna soloist!

"Dellie, come away from that window." Her father's voice was terrible in its quietness. "You will never wave to that man. Come now. Quickly. Mother has breakfast."

"But I wasn't waving, I was…"

"Come away."

CHAPTER 2

O'Dell gulped her breakfast, hurried into the kitchen with her empty dishes, threw on her coat and raced for the poplar tree at the corner of the flagstone walk. She smacked her lips and made a face. Molasses on her pancakes would keep her taste buds busy until the ten o'clock milk break.

She sat near the poplar and stared at the house next door. She could just see one bedroom window and the French dining doors through gray spindly branches. Maybe if she looked long enough she would see Phillip Berning head out the door. Then maybe he would walk with her. Most days, though, he'd get to his sixth-grade room at John Marshall School before anyone had sighted him.

Phillip lived with his mother Greta and a tall secretive man she called her brother. And their collie Beauford. Phillip's father had died at Pearl Harbor.

The Berning house was a salt-box style, and some said it was too big for the neighborhood. It was three stories tall, stark white with black shutters. It made a peaceful face, O'Dell thought. It could glare fiercely in the afternoon sun, but at eight thirty-seven this morning it seemed half asleep.

O'Dell closed her eyes and thought about that face. She wondered what it would say with its mouth open, what it would hear if tuned to the morning.

Slam! Ten-year-old Patti vaulted onto the sidewalk, cap in one hand, bookbag in the other. "Get yourself goin', Dellie! I'll race ya!" She flew across Vermont Street, jumped the ditch and was into the brambly woods before O'Dell could leap into action.

The two sisters vowed never to travel Wakefield Street alone. That was where third grader Eddie Johns lived. Even fourth graders like

Patti shuddered when he appeared. The shorter but more tortuous route up the wooded hill meant braving scratches and slushy snow as they climbed through backyards and over fences in a beeline shortcut through Vernon Street, then to Wakefield and Twenty-third.

At Twenty-third Street there was group safety. But no cover.

Leaning against a stout sycamore at the edge of the woods, O'Dell clutched her side and gulped big mouthfuls of air. "Stop. I don't see the posse."

Patti crouched and worked her way toward the street side of the sycamore. "There's Eddie. See? He's down by those blackberry bushes. And he's got his dog with him." No one wanted to get near Rusty, whose snarling bite was quick and legendary.

O'Dell snorted. "Well, we can't... Wait," she hissed. "Look over there, behind that green house. See Marsha? She's got Bobby and Gracie. C'mon. Quick."

Happy with their precision timing, the two girls glanced back at Eddie, now just a block behind.

Eddie examined a forsythia bush for robins' nests, pretending not to notice the girls. Rusty had bolted home in response to a shrill command from Mrs. Johns.

O'Dell pressed Patti's hand. "I like it when we have adventures together. Don't you? It's like... just like... music."

"It is?"

"Yeah. It's like when the violins play first, then all the little musics butt in to help."

"So who are the violins, Funny Face?"

"We are."

Patti nudged O'Dell with her shoulder. "Good secret, kiddo. But hey, don't tell anyone. They'll think you're a goofus." Patti snorted a quick laugh and jerked O'Dell's arm as they ran for the posse.

Now it was just a short trek past two crossing guard stations — one at Old Dominion Drive and the other at Twenty-fifth, where John Marshall Elementary School took up the whole block with its three stories of worn brick and regimental windows. Flat as a bull-dog's face, its front had no indentations, no place to stand in the rain. You went from street to steps to inside the door, then chose a small flight up, or a longer flight to the basement where a shortage of wartime space had put second graders into a plywood enclosure near the auditorium. O'Dell and Patti galloped up the front steps and raced for their classrooms.

"O'Dell, come to my desk please."

"Yes, Ma'am."

"Run over to Mr. Brown's room and give him your wet socks." Mrs. Foster folded her arms across a plump bosom, her lips compressed into a scarlet line. She relaxed her arms and wagged a finger. "Did you step in the mud again?"

"Yes'm."

Mrs. Foster sighed. "Run along to the furnace room, then. And get some dry socks."

It was worth a scowl from the second-grade teacher to get a trip to the furnace room where Mr. Brown had his little kingdom. Everyone called him Brownie but they got few words in reply. The janitor never said much and rarely smiled. He moved slowly, head bowed. But there was a warm constancy about him, a calming presence — like rich, slow music.

The furnace room was warm and clean and without embellishment except for a gray metal desk and the framed photo of a young soldier. Ducts and pipes jutted like tree-limbs from the black coal furnace. Hanging on the pipes were neat rows of white, tan, brown and black socks. Brownie always knew whose they were, and kept a running inventory for wet little feet. Teachers suspected he bought his own supply.

"Here you are, missy. Get those socks and shoes off and give them to me." His voice was flat but soft and comforting. While O'Dell tugged on her wet knotted shoestrings, Brownie ambled to the furnace and inserted a metal crank onto the grates and commenced rattling and shaking. In the cave-like room the commotion began with small brittle jerks and clanks which soon enveloped the ductwork, until the stone enclave rang with what O'Dell called "soldier feet." Upstairs and down the basement hallway, every classroom was put on hold as each child stopped to listen.

"Now then. What's this? You've got a speck of blood on that ankle, child."

O'Dell jerked like she'd been stung. "No! It's not blood. She looked down and shook her head slowly from side to side, strands of hair brushing her face. "No!"

Brownie turned, lit his pipe, and rummaged in the top drawer of his desk. O'Dell sat rigidly on her chair, breathing heavily.

"Well then, just hold your sock ready while you look at the picture of my son, there on the desk." He crossed the room and knelt by the chair. In one deft motion Brownie had slipped a Band-Aid on the little cut. O'Dell inhaled sharply. Her eyes narrowed while she pondered this fresh assault on her trust.

"I think you're better already. Now, on with the sock. And here are your shoes." Brownie headed for the furnace. "Get those shoes on and be off with you, child. I have work to do."

O'Dell shuffled down the hall for a few feet, then stopped to listen. It was cool and ghostly quiet. Every child was in a classroom.

She went slowly, tracing her fingers against the smooth painted walls. The more she walked, the more she was in command of her space again. She felt quite alone yet deliciously independent. Somehow the brief interlude away from her classmates had poked into her soul with adventurous thoughts much like a balloon is pricked by tree limbs — daringly in flight, yet imperiled by danger.

Her footsteps slowed as she approached the auditorium. She stepped quietly toward the scarred brown table tucked in the corner, where her classmates' jackets and boots lay in mounds.

O'Dell walked to the corner. She'd never been alone near the coat table, and certainly never alone while it was stacked with children's clothing, books and homework. It was cool and soothing in this quiet room of browns and grays. She had it all to herself. And today something on the table gleamed. A silver quarter lay among the mounds of coats. Someone had forgotten to take milk money to Mrs. Foster.

The silver glinted invitingly. Just twenty-five cents. No one would miss it. Casually she looked around and pretended, even though she'd seen no one, to casually swipe her hand across the table as if checking for dust. Deftly she pocketed the coin, then entered the classroom to find twenty-two children quietly filling their notebooks with math problems. Would that quarter make a bulge in her pocket? She covered it with her hand. Mrs. Foster held her with a commanding frown and suggested she get busy copying from the board.

Somehow this type of quietness was different from the safety of Brownie's little kingdom and the anonymity of the ghostly anteroom. It hung like a pall. O'Dell squirmed and glanced first left then right. She caught Mrs. Foster's eye and quickly looked down. Then she saw Ricky shuffling to the front of the room. There was a mumbled exchange with the teacher.

"Children. Eyes forward." Mrs. Foster clapped her hands for attention. "Ricky has lost his milk money. He thinks it may be in the auditorium. Have any of you seen a quarter that does not belong to you?"

That does not belong to you… to you… to you. The echo of those balloon-pricking words got louder and louder inside O'Dell's head. But she would not, could not, open her mouth. No. Not in front of her classmates. Never.

CHAPTER 3

At home that afternoon O'Dell busied herself with hiding things once again. She shivered with anticipation. She'd tried very hard, and nearly succeeded, in tamping down her conscience. The silver quarter lay nestled in her underwear drawer, unseen and unrepentant. And now she had another secret — a hiding place for tonight's backyard game.

Thrushes and robins called out their sleepy messages as evening shadows lengthened over the Farnsworth backyard. Spring came early to northern Virginia and the windows were flung open to the late afternoon warmth. Nearly all of the snow had melted, leaving tiny puddles and mushy lawns. Not a breath of a breeze stirred, and the woodsy smells of sassafras and damp leaves filtered through the open windows.

At six o'clock the girls gobbled their supper, hurried through the dishes and raced outside. It was Friday and Kate had her game planned for the neighbor children — an evening of hiding in the woods. Nine had gathered so far. Veronica, at six, was the youngest, with Trudy and Kate vying for seniority at fourteen. They'd come after supper in twos and threes to the Farnsworth backyard in high expectation of a kick-the-can marathon. It would end at dusk — the time when it was hard to find your opponent, the time when daytime gave all of its rights to the darkness.

Two days ago O'Dell had located the perfect hiding place. No one would find her. She needn't burst out of the woods in a mad dash to kick the can and free the prisoners. She would wait it out in her perfect spot. She hadn't told Patti, and that had tweaked her conscience. But Patti nearly always won, she told herself. No reason to tell Patti. Not this time.

The Farnsworth backyard lay in a roughly elliptical shape that stretched from north to south and was just wide enough for a badminton net. It began its blend with the wooded hillside on the east and also on the north, where a double clothesline sported two white sheets. At the south it narrowed a bit until all that was left of the grass-filled yard was the path to Phillip's house. And beyond the path, more woods.

"Who wants to be *it?*" Kate asked. No one volunteered. "All right, then, let's do tiger toes. Line up." She placed herself in front of the assembly and began the chant as she pointed fingers at first one, then another: "Eenie meenie miney moe, catch a tiger by the toe." No one ever knew how many words she planned to put into the chant, so no one could figure out ahead of time how to avoid the tiger's bite. This evening Kate was in full cry and had listed the tiger's homeland, his ancestry and favorite foods before her finger finally rested on ten-year-old Franklin Porro.

"Franklin's it! Go over there by the window, Franklin. Remember, no peeking. Trudy, you kick this time. And kids, you can go into the woods but just halfway to Upton Street, or into the front or side yards. But you can't go inside the house or garage." Kate set a Van Camp's pork and bean can next to the sunken back porch.

Patti waved her arms. "No, not there, Kate! The robins are under the roof. You'll scare them."

"Okay, Patti Robin. Here, then." Kate moved the can closer to Phillip's house. "Ready, set… turn your head and *count*, Franklin!"

Thunk! The can hurtled toward the laundry line and caught the center sheet amidships.

"Stop. Stop," Kate yelled. "Patti, help me take down the wash." Carefully they brought the two ends together from the first sheet, matching corners the way Mother liked it. Then the second sheet was carefully folded and squared.

"I'll take them." Olivia Farnsworth walked briskly to the line. "You should think of these things before you start your activities, Kate. See the mud on this sheet?" One speck lingered from the can.

"I'm sorry." Kate handed her the sheets and watched her mother go into the house. Somewhat subdued, she turned to her little audience again. "*Now* we're ready! Okay, Franklin. Kick it again!"

Thunk! Ka-tunk ka-tunk. Eight children scattered like ants. O'Dell raced down the steps into the sunken porch and crouched below the cinder block rim, waiting until everyone headed to the woods or the front yard.

"Thirty-two, thirty-three." Franklin pushed his forehead against the house and continued to count in a sing-song voice. Still time.

Now! O'Dell crouched low, skittered out of the porch and headed into the deepest part of the woods between her backyard and Phillip's. Dense bushes tore at her trousers and shirt, but the biggest nuisance was the occasional branch that whipped against her face. Ahead she could see Phillip zig-zagging along his chosen path. He, too, had a favorite place built with saplings in a crude lean-to. Of course he knew that Patti and O'Dell could find it. They had even helped him build it.

About two hundred yards from the house O'Dell spotted her hideout just as Franklin shouted "fifty" and ran to fetch the can. O'Dell leaned against her secret tree, the grandfather of all white oaks. Obedient to some inner timing, it once again sprouted pale budded leaves. Thomas Farnsworth said this tree could be as tall as a hundred feet, and perhaps five feet across, yet easy to miss because it was crowded into the thickest part of the woods. O'Dell leaned against the tree as if considering her next move. She looked in every direction, then listened. No movement. No sound.

Some creature had dug a wide burrow under the oak. The shallow tunnel sloped down about three feet, then continued horizontally under the base. It was time for O'Dell to decide. Would she brave dampness and wee beasties for the sake of the game? All factors pointed to readiness, including the bushy branch she'd dragged here yesterday for camouflage. She'd even planned her battle dress: long trousers, long sleeves and a bandana head-covering. But still she hesitated. How would it feel to go underground in the wet earth? She knew the sounds and the feel of her own little world. What would it be like down there? O'Dell took a deep breath. She would go in, but just partway. And that would have to do.

It was a lot harder than it looked. First she poked along the tunnel with a long stick. It seemed empty except for a faint tink that sounded like glass. If anything was alive in there it would have to be very small. She backed in, her belly scraping over moss, twigs, dead leaves and slimy dirt. When only her head was above ground she pulled the branch on top where it scraped and tangled her hair. All things weighed, she could manage this.

After her breathing slowed, she became more attuned to the woods. She could hear a squirrel chattering farther up the tree and could imagine its tail twitching in annoyance. She heard twigs snap some distance away, then a shout from Franklin and a race for the can.

Ka-thunk! Someone got to the can before Franklin, and the counting and the shouting began all over again.

The distant sounds from the Farnsworth backyard were beginning to take on a dream-like quality, like echoes of some other time and place. They were not in O'Dell's world anymore. It was almost peaceful under the tree and she began humming softly. Just last week their mother had brought home a surprise gift for the children: a 78 rpm recording of *Peter and the Wolf*. O'Dell had leaned against her father's knee while the family listened. She'd imagined Peter, his grandfather, the duck, the cat, the bird, the hunter and the wolf. Each was represented by a different musical instrument. Wouldn't it be fun, she thought, to see all the characters run through the woods, just as they did in the symphony!

O'Dell was especially taken by the wolf's theme. She began to hum. "Da-da-da-da da da *dum dum dum* da doooo." She loved the mellow, rich tones of the French horn, and she drew out the long "doooo" with her childish vibrato.

"Hm-hm-hm-hm-hm-hm…" The answering voice floated faint as a bumblebee. O'Dell could feel the adrenaline shooting through her stomach. Did she just hear an echo of the wolf's tune? Phillip! That sneaky squirt had found her!

"Phillip!" Her sharp whisper floated on the air. "I hear you!"

Nothing. Then, a soft mushy movement on wet leaves, as if someone were testing for balance. A long pause.

"Phillip?"

Another step and then another. Quieter now, until the sound was swallowed by the trees.

O'Dell's piano teacher had said that silence was just as important as the piano notes. "Silence makes you wait, and waiting gets you ready for the best part." With her small bony hand Miss Bestor had tapped the piano, her little bun bobbing on the back of her head. "O'Dell," she'd said, "what is the best part of *your* music?"

The absence of sound in the darkening woods was as chilling as the humming and footfalls had been only moments before. The silence was sucking the air out of her body.

"All-the-all-the-outs-in-free-ee!" The game was over. Kate was yelling for her. "Dellie, c'mon. You win! Everyone's here!"

So it hadn't been Phillip. O'Dell wanted to fly from this subterranean nest but she could not. She was one with the earth. Her crying welled up inside her but found no escape. Now the footfalls were back —heavier, faster. No soft mush on leaves now, just the flat slapping of shoes and heavy breathing. O'Dell buried her head in her hands and squeezed her eyes shut. But the darkness behind her tightly closed eyes was worse than the heavy twilight.

"No-no-no-no-no! Don't do it, don't do it, don't do it!" she whimpered.

A rough hand grabbed her shoulder and O'Dell looked with relief into Phillip's eyes.

"Dellie! For Pete's sake! You gonna lie there all night?"

"Patti?"

"Hmm?"

"Can I sleep in your bed?"

Patti grunted and moved closer to the edge. "Okay."

O'Dell slid under the covers and lay quietly, letting the comfort and warmth of the double bed soak into her body. She pulled the crisp sheet and light blanket under her chin. Across the room a bulky roll-top desk was just visible, and beyond it the faint outline of the north window. She could hear heavy splats of rain on the hickory branches that drooped against the window.

"Patti."

"Yeah?"

"What if there wasn't anyone left, like if your parents weren't there. What if there was no one left to, you know, to punish you when you did something wrong?

"I don't know. Maybe you could just figure it out for yourself."

"Mm. Maybe."

"Did you do something wrong, Dellie?"

O'Dell lay quietly.

"Dell-*leee?*"

"Yeah. It's, you know, it's..."

"Oh c'mon Dellie, just *tell* me!"

"I stole some money, Patti." There, she'd said it.

Patti turned sharply and propped herself up. "You *what?*"

"I took a quarter that belonged to Ricky. It was just on the coat table and no one was looking." O'Dell squirmed at Patti's heavy breathing. She couldn't see her sister's face but imagined Patti's frown. "And then the teacher asked if someone saw it and I didn't say anything. And oh, Patti, *I couldn't! I couldn't!*"

Patti settled back against her pillow and both lay silently, with only the patter of rain to stir their thoughts. "Well, just think about it, okay? Just think about it!"

"Okay, okay."

O'Dell rubbed her eyes.

"You crying, Dellie?"

"No. I mean, yes. A little. Not much. But Patti, There's something else."

"Oh please. I'm too sleepy to talk anymore!"

"Patti, did you know where I was hiding?"

"Huh uh."

"Well, I went to that big oak tree Daddy always talks about. You know, the one he says is just hunnerds of years old."

"Not hundreds, Dellie."

"Well, anyway, *old!* Did you know there's a big tunnel underneath the tree?"

Patti was more awake now. "How do you know there's a tunnel?"

"I was hiding in it."

"Oooh Dellie, how did you stand it! Weren't you scared?" Patti shuddered.

"Not at first." O'Dell turned to face her sister. "I had it all figured out." Relieved, O'Dell quickly told Patti what she'd bottled up since planning her outfit. "Didn't you see I wore long pants and long sleeves and a bandana? I knew if I could get into that tunnel, then no one could find me. Not even Phillip."

They both lay still, listening to the rain.

"Patti, there was someone else in the woods."

"Of course there was! Phillip, for sure. And then there was Madeline Morrow, and I think I saw Veronica go that way too."

"Yeah, but…" O'Dell fumbled for words. "There… I think there was someone right by me and he was humming the same thing I was humming and then he walked away. And Patti, it didn't sound like one of the kids!"

Patti turned and balanced on one elbow, her brown hair sweeping the pillow. O'Dell could feel her frown. "Dellie, are you foolin' me? Because if you are…"

"I'm not. Cross my heart and hope to die." There was a fumbly swish on pajamas as the pact was sealed.

"Who do you think it was?"

"It was someone who knows music, Patti. I hummed *Peter and the Wolf.* You know, the wolf thing, and he just hummed it right after me!

Patti repeated the tune. "Like this?"

"Yeah. Just like that."

"Did he say anything? Or maybe come closer?" Patti yawned and turned toward the west window. "Whoever it was certainly didn't mean to hurt you, Dellie." Another yawn. "I don't think I can stay awake any longer. Wanna go to sleep now?"

"Please don't go to sleep."

"I have to. I can't stay awake."

"Well, g'night then, Patti."

"Night, Dellie."

The rain was heavier now, its percussion beats drumming the children to sleep.

CHAPTER 4

The next morning dawned with special brightness. O'Dell, back in her own bed again, breathed deeply of the new morning and watched puffy clouds scooting across the sky against a crisp breeze. Such a day was tailor-made for a fresh start. If there really was a mystery man, he certainly did not belong in this pure daylight.

She hurried downstairs. Mother was calling.

"Patti! O'Dell! Come quickly, girls. Listen." Olivia slipped a handkerchief into her purse, then reached out to smooth Patti's hair. "Daddy and I are going across the street. Mrs. Morrow's father died last night and we're taking her a pot of soup. We'll try to be back in an hour. Patti, you clean up that mess you made in the basement, and O'Dell, please tell me — what is it you need to do that you did not do yesterday?" Thomas and Olivia regarded their daughter with expectant frowns.

O'Dell blanched. A dark kaleidoscope of doubt whirled in her brain. Someone found the quarter. Someone from school called. What did they know? What should she do?

"I don't know," she whispered.

"You need to practice. You skipped your time after school, so you will need an hour this morning." Olivia pinned her little green hat in place, careful not to disturb the two rolls of loose brown curls that swept back from her temples.

Relieved, O'Dell flipped the conversation into safe territory. "Where's Kate? Doesn't she have chores?"

"She spent Friday night with Gretchen. You know that. She won't be home for half an hour." Thomas cast a look at O'Dell, his lips pressed close. It was a look she knew. The absence of sound.

The screen door clicked shut. O'Dell watched her parents cross the street. Then she whirled with relief and grinned at Patti. "Wanna play catch?"

"Dellie! We only have a few minutes. You get in there on the piano or I'm telling Mother!" Patti thumped down the basement stairs.

O'Dell knew Patti wouldn't tell Mother. She walked to the window by the piano and pressed her nose against the glass. A line of red and yellow tulips had begun to blossom near the woods, and beyond that the garden plot, all ready for planting. She'd often wondered whether a garden on the slant would make water run downhill and empty on the grass. "No," her father had patiently explained. "That's why we have grass strips between the rows. That keeps rain from pushing the dirt downhill. It makes the water go into the ground instead of forming little gullies."

Patti knocked on the pipes and hollered from the basement, her voice all echoes and muffles. "Dellie, you're not practicing!"

"Oh poo!" Dellie didn't want to practice all those new pieces. She pulled out the week's assignments, then slammed them on top of the piano and sat fuming. She straightened. The Clementi sonatina, that's what she'd do! She was in a hurry to finish practicing and fumbled her way through the first part. Then came the andante portion. "Slo-w-ly, dear," Miss Bestor would say. But O'Dell loved the triplets and couldn't stand playing them like a clodhopping old horse. Soon she was racing through the first line so rapidly that she muffed the trill. "How does that go," she whispered to herself. "Deedle deedle dee, I think."

Patti would know. She'd played it last year. O'Dell clumped through the kitchen and started down the basement stairs with her music book. At the first landing she paused. Once again she would have to face the washtubs and Skippy's basket. She determined not to look in that direction.

Descending into the dim cellar was like entering another climate. Cool quiet air enshrouded her like a mantle. It was always that way in the quarried-stone cellar. Summer or winter, it didn't matter. That blanket of cool air stayed the same.

The interior was dimly lit with hanging sixty-watt light bulbs. One bulb hung in the center by the stairs, another over the washtubs on the north end, and the third held sway over Daddy's neat assembly of shelves and workbenches on the south.

In this secluded place, odd things happened. Once they'd found a flying squirrel hunkered in the corner beneath the small, crank-out window. The squirrel's webbed arms were folded, his brown eyes large with fear.

Under the stairs stood a crock. Last year it was full of fermenting root beer, smelling of yeast and sassafras. The year before, Daddy had filled the crock with dirt and embedded eight turtle eggs he'd found in the woods. Nearly too late they discovered that his "turtle" eggs had produced baby copperheads.

Past the washtubs, beyond Skippy's bed, stood the door to the empty garage, a testimony to their lack of transportation. Two years ago they'd sold their 1936 Chrysler in a patriotic gesture to the war effort.

Near the center squatted the giant coal furnace, which Daddy shook down each night in cold weather. The girls rarely heard it clunking except on Christmas Eve, when everything was magical and no one slept. It had not been many weeks since O'Dell was sure she'd seen Santa Claus riding through the midnight clouds, ready to answer her plea for Skippy.

O'Dell squinted. She couldn't see very well in the dim light, and all was quiet. Where was Patti? Ha! There she was, next to

Daddy's workshop, reading *Swiss Family Robinson* in *Classic Comics*. "Uh oh, Patti. Now *you're* not working!"

"Listen to this, Dellie. They were shipwrecked on this little island and the boys all had their own guns. Even the little brother. Patti's eyes widened. "Oh boy! I'd love to go shooting, wouldn't you?"

"Lemme see." O'Dell scootched close to Patti and soon their two heads touched as they were absorbed into the story.

"Hey. Don't turn the page yet. I wasn't finished." Patti jerked on the book.

O'Dell looked up suddenly. "Wait, Patti."

"I said, don't turn the page too fast!"

"No. Not the page. Listen, Patti."

A soft thud. The door? Shoes?

"Patti, don't move," O'Dell breathed. "We can't let Mother and Daddy know where we are. Pretend we're not here."

Quick steps trotting to the kitchen. Stopping. More steps, this time to the top of the stairs.

"Patti, O'Dell! You down there?"

Patti and O'Dell exhaled with a muffled whoosh and a giggle. "Oh it's just Kate. She won't tell."

"Just Kate, huh?" She looked at her two sisters and frowned.

"Don't tell on us, please Kate?"

"Okay but you owe me one." She trotted down the stairs and sat on the bottom step. She leaned forward, her chin cupped in her hands. "Dellie, did you play your Clementi a little while ago?"

O'Dell sensed a trap. "Yeah, I did, and I played it just right, too."

Kate was thoughtful. "Maybe not exactly like Miss Bestor told you to, though. Right?"

"Aw-w, you weren't even here, Kate!"

"No, I wasn't here. But… I heard it. On my way home."

"You heard it? How?"

"Someone was singing it. And it was only those parts you always play."

Patti leaned forward. "Who, Kate?"

"I don't know. I couldn't see anyone. But it sounded like it was coming from behind the Kiplinger house."

The girls waited for the rest of the story.

"But it was so perfect. And it was kind of soft. And beautiful. So very beautiful." Kate looked as if she might cry. "I've never heard anything so peaceful."

The screen door thudded softly closed.

"I think it's Daddy," whispered O'Dell. She and Patti were frozen to their chairs.

"Girls!" Thomas stood at the top of the stairs. He took in the scene with one glance. "Patti, do I see a comic book on that chair?" He paused, but not long enough for an answer. "You will put it away and commence cleaning. Kate, go to the kitchen and help your mother. Dellie, did you practice?"

"Well…"

"I thought so. There will be no trip to the movies tomorrow afternoon. The Glebe Theater will just have to get along without you."

"But Daddy, it's *A Song to Remember!* It's about Chopin!" O'Dell could surely win this battle. Her father loved Chopin.

"We will talk about it later." Then his voice softened. "And please say something to Madeline and Lydia. They lost a grandfather, you know."

The three girls glanced at each other, stricken. They hadn't given a thought to their two playmates across the street.

♪

After lunch Thomas stood in the hallway a moment, sifting his principles. The girls had disobeyed. He had spoken. Yet he longed to experience *A Song to Remember*, and tomorrow was its last day at the Glebe Theater.

He could always think better while playing the saxophone. The cool metal under his hands, the mouthpiece responding to his tongue and lips, the honeyed notes vibrating against his chest. He would play first, decide later.

Thomas walked briskly to the hall closet and knelt beneath the winter coats. He slid the scarred black case across the floor, placed it on the piano bench and snapped it open. Inside, the gleaming saxophone lay cool and mute.

Thomas stood very still for a moment. Then he ran his forefinger reverently around the edge of the bell and lifted the silver instrument away from its frayed satin bed. He'd bought it from a college friend and taken it back to the farm the year before he married Olivia.

His three brothers thought he was a bit strange in his musical tastes. Saxophones were born for jazz, they'd said, but Thomas preferred Mendelssohn, Chopin and the hymns he'd sung as a boy. He lifted out the small neck-piece and dabbed the cork end with pure lanolin — a Christmas gift from his neighbor. The little jar had come with the tag: "A nubbin of mutton from Morton."

Next he inserted the neck into the saxophone body.

Now the silk sachet packet of wooden reeds. He gently aligned one of the reeds with the mouthpiece, then screwed it into place with the metal ligature.

Kate stood in the hallway, watching her father. She studied every move, waiting for the right moment. Not too tightly on the ligature. Now his hand would reach out for the gray neck-piece, loop it over his head and snap it onto the back of the saxophone.

"Do you want me to play something, Daddy?"

Thomas took a soft cloth from the case and ran it over the pearl keys, the neck and the bell, knowing full well that the instrument was in pristine condition.

Kate moved a step closer. "I could play *Who is Sylvia*."

Thomas kept wiping.

"Or maybe *The Lost Chord*."

"That would be nice."

CHAPTER 5

O'Dell sighed. Could she wish and wish for something she wanted, and would it come true? Could she wish really really hard to go to the theater this afternoon? Maybe. Just maybe. But maybe she was being punished for not practicing and for stealing the quarter. *And* for Skippy.

She leaned on the dining room windowsill. Mother was in the kitchen and O'Dell thought it safe to take another peek at that silver coin. Most of the time she left it buried in her drawer but this morning she'd tucked it in her pocket. Cautiously she drew it up to the light and examined it. Maybe the pictures on the coin would give her a hint about what to do with this badge of misbehavior. On one side sat a princess who looked over her right shoulder. She held a flag and the whole scene was ringed about by thirteen stars. *I'd like to be that lady,* she thought. On the back, a fierce eagle looked like he was going to eat a big ribbon, and in his feet he clutched some arrows.

A slow movement caught O'Dell's eye and she lifted her face to watch the Hardesty family on their way home from church. They always walked right up the middle of the street on Sunday mornings, parents in front, the six youngest children behind. And following at a distance, nineteen-year-old Maggie Hardesty. Now at nearly noon, they were making the trip back down. Maggie was quiet, as she always was when walking with the family. But in that sliver of time between light and darkness on weekday evenings, Maggie could be heard at the south end of Vermont Street as she sang her way home following a day of work in the city. O'Dell always stopped at the sound, shivering with the glorious, audacious beauty of it.

"I do it so I won't be scared," Maggie had once confided to Kate. "I sing as loud as I can, and it fills my insides with courage."

O'Dell took particular notice of little Tina Hardesty. Her straw hat was yellow with a pink ribbon. That was O'Dell's favorite mix of colors. It spoke of sunshine, and even though her mother had told her once that "pink and yellow crayons do not go together," she longed to absorb those colors into her very being.

"Mother, why don't we ever go to church?"

Olivia moved briskly around the table, setting knives, forks and spoons onto the crisp white sheet she used as a tablecloth. "We don't have to go to church in order to be good, O'Dell."

"Are we good, Mother?"

Olivia walked to the window, a cream-colored plate in each hand. She looked thoughtful for a moment. Then her face clouded. "You need to stop asking questions about things that you know nothing about."

"But if they..."

"Come help me in the kitchen, O'Dell."

On Sunday the eighteenth of March, 1945, a uniformed usher took two hundred and fifteen tickets from patrons of the Glebe Theater — five of them from the Farnsworth family — for the last showing of *A Song to Remember.*

The theater was six weeks old and still had that new-car upholstery smell. It was a near twin to the theater in next-door Alexandria, and soon had a patronage eager to find a movie house in its own neighborhood. It was the first in Arlington to boast of air conditioning, and on this muggy spring evening a banner declared: "Ten Degrees Cooler Inside."

O'Dell tingled with excitement and nearly sprinted toward a bank of cushiony, gray-upholstered seats. Olivia laid a hand on her shoulder. "Slowly, O'Dell. Daddy goes first."

O'Dell stopped. She wanted a seat away from her mother, who had no tolerance for fidgeting. She would hang back, maybe sit on the outside. But no, her mother hung back also, meaning to occupy the aisle seat and enclose her little family in parental security.

"S-s-st! Dellie, in here!" Patti motioned with a wave of her hand.

"Are you sure you two can behave yourselves?" Thomas leaned forward, surveying the placement of his three daughters. "Kate, maybe you should sit between them."

"I think they'll be all right, Daddy." Kate was just where she wanted to be — close to the end of the row where she could steal quick glances at a group of junior high classmates who came in a noisy bunch and sat near the front. She was also ideally positioned to slip out and buy a Bit O Honey bar, and she wasn't about to budge.

Thomas turned to Patti and O'Dell. "When the movie starts, no talking." He had been lenient with the girls. They could attend the movie, but no shenanigans. Somehow he must atone for his lapse of discipline.

The big clock on the wall ticked forward to three fifty-eight.

The lights dimmed slowly as the plush red velvet drapes swept open.

Looney Tunes! The theater erupted in applause as Bugs Bunny's crafty mug zoomed out of a whirling jumble of red circles. Oh, he was clever! Inside of two minutes he had Elmer Fudd bemoaning "that wascally wabbit" while Dellie and Patti exploded in giggles. Olivia smiled and patted her hair. Thomas' lip turned upward.

"Could I have one of your Tootsie Rolls?" O'Dell whispered to Patti.

"Didn't you get anything?"

"I forgot. Daddy, can I go get something?"

Thomas handed her a licorice stick. "Sit still, Dellie. No more trips to the lobby."

It was dark, but Thomas knew she was making a face.

O'Dell wondered how those cartoon people did that whangy-whirly music at the beginning and end of *Looney Tunes*. Maybe she could try it on the piano. If she could just hear it once more. But the cartoon was finished and the theater grew dim again as the drapes were pulled closed. Kate shifted for a better view of her classmates. Behind her two women wished they had more coupons for sugar, *since it's Lucy's birthday*, and someone nearby spluttered a tight little cough.

"Daddy, is…"

"Sh-h-h-h."

Plush red velvet drapes swept back once more, leaving pale, sheer curtains. The glow from the screen was mistress now. It beckoned every head and bade them welcome the lady of the torch.

Now the sheer curtains were slowly pulled open and *Columbia Pictures* announced in lilting script that *A Song to Remember* had just begun.

"Oooooh! Cornel Wilde and Merle Oberon," whispered Kate as she read the list of actors. But it was awhile before her favorite appeared on-screen, because twelve-year-old Frederic Chopin took center stage for the first half hour, bouncing his way through sonatas and family discussions about his future.

By the time Cornel Wilde appeared as the adult Frederic, Kate was ready for him. "Lovely," she breathed.

O'Dell gripped Patti's hand when Chopin plunged into his first polonaise. "Oh my goodness, my goodness. Watch him! Watch him do that, Patti! How does he *do* that!"

"Remember when Milton Collins played it at Miss Bestor's recital? I think he was just as good," Patti whispered.

Thomas reached out and tapped both girls on the backs of their heads. Patti and O'Dell grew still, and for the next hour they were totally absorbed in Chopin's life — his disappointments, his possessive girlfriend, the ravaging illness. And always Frederic at the piano, with intricate trills, bold octaves and plaintive whisper-notes born of pain and longing. O'Dell gripped Patti, who was too wrapped up in the intensity of Cornel Wilde to realize that she was actually offering a Tootsie Roll to her little sister.

O'Dell sat taller and taller in her seat. Chopin's mastery of the keys spoke to something deep inside her. *It's where... where I'm supposed to be,* she thought. *I must do that. I must.* Even in the darkness and two seats away, Thomas felt the steel in his daughter's will. Something responded within him, and he knew that he wanted what she wanted, just as he yearned for all three of his girls some heaven-sent purpose. He felt a teardrop forming and quickly fumbled for his crisp white handkerchief. He was ready to do battle. He was ready to be the knight in shining armor for his family.

But he was not ready for the blood. Frederic Chopin was dying. Red drops fell on the piano keys, changing the scherzo from crashing crystal waves to discordant death knells. Thomas stiffened and glanced at O'Dell. He willed her to relax and reached for her hand.

A long whisper-groan emanated from O'Dell's throat. "Daddy... Daddy... no... he couldn't. Do something. Oh, Daddy *do something!*" She began sobbing quietly, hugging herself and rocking back and forth.

Thomas lifted O'Dell out of her seat and held her tightly. Perhaps he could quiet her. But the sobs grew louder as a slow murmur rippled through the audience. Heads turned and soft shushing sounds grew.

Briskly, Olivia marshaled the girls. "Come. Time to leave. "Patti. Kate. Quickly now."

"But it's not fin…" Patti held back.

"Don't argue."

The tight little retinue filed along the dim aisle, the mournful bars of Chopin's final concert accompanying their retreat.

"Thomas."

"Hmmmm…"

"Thomas, we will have to do something."

Kate awoke to the sound of their murmuring — low voices, barely discernible. She strained to hear the words, but something was pressing on her arm, and it had gone all numb and tingly. She turned and came face to face with her little sister, sound asleep in the comfort of Kate's shoulder. She wasn't sure how she'd wound up with O'Dell in her bed, and even less sure what to do with her. Gently she pulled back her arm and shook it until the circulation pricked like needles. Then she was still once again, concentrating on the voices.

"Thomas. *Please.*"

Kate heard shifting, the creak of springs. She lay very still, focusing on her south window and the sliver of light from Phillip's back porch.

"Olivia, we've been all through this before. It will take time. Dr. Nabor says…"

"I know very well what Dr. Nabor says, Thomas."

"All right, then. Let's go back to the beginning."

"And where would that be?"

"We both know where that would be. Dellie saw the accident. She was right there. She carried that bloody dog out of the street, up the stairs and into the front hallway! He died in her arms."

There was a long pause, and Kate wondered if her father had simply taken refuge in silence.

"Yes. In her arms, her two bloody, bloody arms." Olivia's voice trailed off.

"Well, don't you see. It's only natural that Dellie might blame herself for Skippy's escape."

Kate struggled to find a more comfortable spot, but O'Dell's head was pressing on her shoulder again. She strained to hear more as her father's voice changed — more comforting, his common-sense tone — the one he used when the girls were arguing with each other. "All right, so now she may be terrified at the sight of blood, but Dr. Nabor says many children go through that."

"*Who!*" Olivia's voice was icy sharp. Kate could almost see the scowl and feel her mother's pent-up rage. "Do you know anyone who's ever gone through that?"

Silence. A slight rustling and low creaking.

"She's not getting over it." Olivia's voice quavered. "It's been over four months, Thomas. Four months!"

"Remember your brother's last letter? He said he thought he would never again be able to endure the sight of blood."

"And..."

"And he is enduring. He is surviving."

"But Alex is twenty-nine years old, Thomas, an army captain. O'Dell is… is… a *child!*" Olivia muffled a sob and began weeping quietly.

"Well." Silence from Thomas for several seconds before continuing, a bit sharply, this time. "All right, then! The least we can do is remove that little icon from under the washtubs!"

"Icon?"

"Yes. Skippy is gone and O'Dell should know it too. Get rid of that basket!"

"Oh Thomas, it's not…"

"I'm sorry, Olivia. I'm sorry." The springs creaked again. Now Kate knew that Daddy was comforting Mother, had put his arms around her. But where would Kate find comfort for O'Dell? For herself? The weeping continued, and the oldest Farnsworth sister was alone with her little burden.

CHAPTER 6

The whole room seemed gray this morning. Like a heavy fog that seeped under the windows, then out from under the closet door. The sheet felt heavier — another weight that O'Dell could not control, and the blanket had lost its comfort. The bright morning would not come for O'Dell.

She tried to remember the hours before the mist. Somehow she'd wound up in Kate's bed last night and had been carried by her father to the bed where she belonged. She'd felt his gentle hands rubbing her back until her eyes closed against the darkness, where once again she was gripped with dreams.

There was mist in the dreams, too. And blood. She was back once again across the road, picking up her pet. Walking back up to the house. At the car again. Starting over, and over, and over. And always she remembered: it was not Skippy who had escaped, but Dellie who had made Patti let go of the leash. Skippy was dead because of her. But she must not tell. Could not tell. No, not ever.

The door clicked open. "Dellie?"

"Hmm?"

"You okay?"

"I dunno."

"Can I get in with you?"

O'Dell lifted the blanket and moved over.

"Why did you do that yesterday, Dellie? What's the matter?"

O'Dell pressed her hands into her eyes. "Why did he have to die, Patti? Why does everyone have to *die!*"

"It was just a movie, Dellie." She waved her hand in a little circle. "And… and even though Daddy said we all have to die sometime, for you and me it's not for a long time."

"Maybe. But maybe it would be better if I did die now."

Patti turned her head sharply and glared at her sister. "Don't die, Dellie. I forbid it."

"Well, okay."

Patti reached for her sister's hand. "This little piggie went to mar…"

O'Dell shrugged loose. "It won't go away."

"What won't go away?"

"The blood."

"You mean Skippy?"

"Yeah. He… you know… he won't stop bleeding."

"Oh."

They nestled together, listening to the morning clatter. Patti should be practicing right now and she wondered why there were no sharp commands from the kitchen.

Patti nudged O'Dell. "Know what Phillip told me?"

"What." O'Dell was a little miffed that Phillip had told Patti something. Phillip was older than both of them, but in her heart she claimed exclusive rights to his friendship.

"If you don't like something, punch it." She sat up, swatting the air.

"Like… how do I punch something I can't see?"

"Like *this!*" Patti grabbed her pillow and whopped it on her sister's head.

"You little…"

"Didn't like that, huh? What about *this?*" Patti whopped again.

"No. I don't like that one bit. I just like *this!*" O'Dell swung her dense feather pillow against Patti's mid-section.

"Ooof! Okay. You want war? You got it, sister!"

Thomas took a step back from his daughter's closed door, carefully easing his slippers, heel to toe, against the polished parquet, heading toward the stairs.

In the eerie silence of the Farnsworth home on Monday March the nineteenth, nothing was as it should be. Olivia was afraid of the usual morning sounds, and she would do nothing to start them. Patti was probably asleep but this was one day Olivia would not bring her down to the piano. She would not invite her husband to breakfast or set the table for five family members. If the morning began its normal cycle, she was sure that once O'Dell showed up, everything snug and comforting would yield to some dark splotch.

Kate had skipped piano practice, gulped her orange juice, slogged too quickly through her oatmeal, and sprinted for the bus twenty minutes before the appointed time. Yes, Kate had felt it too.

Thomas splashed warm water over his beaver-hair brush, then poked it into the white shaving cup. Yes. Action. This was good. Lather his face, scrape off the whiskers, don shirt and tie. A brisk walk to the carpool stop, then a day full of the kind of crises he could manage. Funny, he thought, as he twisted his face to get the razor just right, that mapping a strategy to curb foot-and-mouth disease in the nation's livestock industry was more peaceful than trying to figure out what to do with his daughter's fears, his wife's anguish, the pockets of pregnant silence.

Sometimes the weight of raising three daughters in this season of war gave him piercing headaches, and he would retreat to a corner of the living room that was not shrouded in Karastan carpets. He would lie on the floor, face down, unavailable to the four people he was supposed to protect. The cold hardness yielded a strange kind of comfort, where he could be alone in a house of clattering feet and unfinished melodies.

CHAPTER 7

Each new day had brought a modicum of healing. Slowly, slowly, the movie appeared to have been forgotten. The Farnsworth household lay in peace this first Sunday of April, where the only sounds were bird-calls and the familiar "tink-a-tink" of Bodie's wagon.

In the middle of the night O'Dell had crept again into Patti's room, and at sunrise they deciphered the morning sounds together. The tink-a-tink was as old as earth, as new as bright pennies. Every morning, the same. Tink, tink, tink-a-tink. The wagon of old bottles, metal and rubber.

The girls lay under the covers listening to Bodie. They knew better than to run to the window, and still better not to wave. O'Dell turned to her sister. "Patti, whaddaya think Bodie does with those bottles and rubber and junk?"

"He takes them to a special place for the soldiers."

"What for?"

"I don't know, but I think they just make more airplanes and tanks and things from them."

"But why does he have to do that? Doesn't he have a real job? I mean, Daddy just brings money from work."

"I don't think Bodie works, Dellie."

"Picking up bottles and junk is work."

The two sisters chattered softly together for a few minutes and then they heard Olivia clattering pans in the kitchen. Daddy opening the front door to get the Sunday paper. And the Bottle Man.

"Oh phoo, I don't care." O'Dell rushed to the window and threw up the sash.

"Dellie! Don't! You know what Daddy said!"

O'Dell leaned out the window.

Patti whispered in panic. *"Dell-ee!"*

"Sh-h-h. I'm just looking. Wait. He's stopping."

Bodie bent to examine an Orange Crush bottle. He held it up to the light, checking for cracks. He was facing south, his left side toward the Farnsworths' front yard — toward Patti's window.

"Patti!" O'Dell's whisper was more an intake of breath than a word. "Oh, Patti, look!"

Patti tumbled out of bed and stepped to the window. "What?"

"Look at his left hand."

"Oh-h-h Dell-eeee." It was a long, drawn-out whisper.

Missing from Bodie's left hand was his fourth finger — the "ring" finger. The stub was about an inch long, a timid companion to the four elegantly tapered fingers. Gently he placed the bottle in the wagon, grasped the handle and began his slow trek south. He stopped suddenly and bowed his head. Two moments. Three. And slowly, while the girls froze in horror, he lifted his face and beheld them both. A half smile touched his lips, but was quickly gone, giving the girls an indelible memory of grief-filled eyes framed in strands of wispy hair.

From the kitchen came the familiar call: "Breakfast, girls."

Patti turned a questioning face to O'Dell. "But, it's Sunday. Why is breakfast so early?"

"Wait. *Wait,* Patti!" O'Dell was standing against the wall now, moving her head barely close enough to peek outside. "Look who's there."

Phillip had suddenly emerged from the thick trees of his front yard. He was gesturing in quick little jerks. The Bottle Man stood rock still for several moments, then moved closer to the trees and laid his hand on Phillip's shoulder.

"Oh, what's he saying, what's he *saying!*"

"Sh-h-h! Be quiet, Dellie!"

Phillip reached into his pocket and pulled out a wad of something and began peeling what looked like slips of paper — one at a time. He glanced quickly at his house, then gave the papers to Bodie. As silently as he'd appeared, Phillip melted into the landscape.

"I think it was money, Patti. I think Phillip gave him money."

Olivia had dressed the table in white linen, had polished the silverware until it shone. Six daffodils in a small china vase sat on the precise middle fold of the tablecloth. Jelly glasses filled with orange juice graced every table setting, and beside each of the girls' plates there was a package and a tiny wooden lamb all fluffy with sheepskin.

O'Dell picked up her lamb and nestled it beneath her chin. She let the fuzzy wool tickle her cheeks. It's wise little black face seemed to come alive in her hands. Patti held hers, ran one finger along the fluff, then set it down. Kate left her lamb on the table, nudging its wooden legs slightly nearer to her plate.

"Open your present, Patti!" O'Dell wiggled and bumped until her mother reached under the tablecloth and gently prodded her leg with a fork.

There was something soft and pliable in Patti's gift. She squeezed it a little, then pulled on the silky blue ribbon and gently folded back the white tissue. Murmurs went up from the girls as

Patti lifted out a white slip adorned with two inches of lace trim on the bodice and hem. Olivia glowed, as she always did when conferring gifts.

"Oh, thank you, Mother!"

"It's from both Daddy and me, dear."

"Thank you, Mother and Daddy!" Patti carefully folded the slip and wrapped it again. "Now you, Kate."

Hers was a tiny unwrapped box, etched in gold. Kate pushed her thumb against the lid and slowly propped it up. Inside, a silver ring topped with a turquoise stone lay embedded in black velvet.

"It will go with my turquoise scarf! Oh, it's *beautiful.*"

Thomas smiled at his daughter. "I brought it home from Mexico last month, Kate."

Slowly Kate took the ring and turned it to the light, then slipped it carefully onto the fourth finger of her left hand. Patti's and O'Dell's eyes widened as they exchanged knowing glances. *The ring finger.*

"It's your turn, O'Dell." Thomas pushed the big box, lightweight and square, closer. O'Dell stared at the gift, wondering why hers was so big. Slowly she pulled the narrow green ribbon, then tugged at the lid. Tissue obscured the mysterious lump inside.

"Open it, open it!" Patti urged.

O'Dell smoothed back the fragile paper. "Ooooo! It's like music, Mother! It just makes music!"

"Put it on, dear."

O'Dell hopped up and ran to the hall mirror. "Oh! *Oh!* Pink and yellow, pink and yellow, pink and yellow!" With the straw hat in place she tried fastening the wide satin ribbon.

"I'll do it, Dellie." Kate stood behind her, expertly looping and tying and then stepping back to let her sister see the full joy of the glorious thing on her head.

It was one of those moments of perfection that could not be planned, could never be held, but Thomas knew it would sustain him, that somehow it would protect the family in some inexplicable way. "Take it off now, O'Dell. You can put it on again when we go to church."

Kate and Patti turned puzzled eyes toward their father.

O'Dell stared hard at her mother, who was busy setting toast, eggs and milk on the table. "I didn't think… we…"

Olivia kept her eyes on the platters. "It's Sunday April the first. Don't you know what day that is?"

"It's April Fools Day," Patti and O'Dell crowed.

"It's also Easter. Daddy and I just think it would be nice to go to church. O'Dell and Patti, I have set out blue jumpers for you to wear. The bus will be at Lee Highway at nine-thirty."

O'Dell hated riding on a bus. There was no music to the belching, grumbling beast as it stopped to board passengers. There would be no music when the bus rumbled up, or when she mounted the steep stairs in a jumble of people and hoped the hiss of air brakes and the lurch of the vehicle would not distribute them in frantic piles before they got to their seats.

But today, O'Dell did not mind. She had her new straw bonnet with the pink sash, and while the bus could not sing to her, she could sing to the bus. She could sing to the whole world, as long as she wore her pink and yellow hat. Joyfully, she turned to her mother. "May I sit in front with Phillip?"

"How do you know Phillip's going to be on the bus, O'Dell?"

"There he is right there." O'Dell pointed across Lee Highway to Vermont Street.

"Don't point, dear."

"But I see him. He's with his mother and that man."

"You mean her brother, Grandon Tolson."

The family could see the bus coming from the west while Phillip and his mother and Grandon hurried from the north.

O'Dell patted the seat beside her. "Sit here, Phillip."

Gratefully, Phillip sank down on the cushion. "Thanks, Dellie."

"Where are you going, Phillip? To church?"

"Miss Bestor asked us to go to the YWCA and check out the auditorium. We'll have the piano recital there." Quickly he assessed O'Dell's jealous narrowing of eyes. "It's not that special. She just knew we'd be in the city today. Then we'll go to Loew's Theater to see *Casablanca*." He paused, flexing his muscles. "Wish we could take in a Senators game. I got a bat from them last time."

"You mean that time when someone got mad and threw it?"

"Yeah, it has a chip in it but I don't care." He smiled mischievously. "Now it's unique. And that makes it mine." He snapped O'Dell's bonnet. "But you're all dressed up. I'll bet you're not going to the movies."

"Mother said we're going to church."

"Where?"

"I don't know. O'Dell shrugged her shoulders and let out a

sigh. "I love sitting up here. You can see everything, and oh, the noise isn't so bumbly."

"Bumbly?" Phillip chuckled. "Well, I like sitting anywhere but back there with my… with my uncle."

O'Dell turned her head.

"Don't turn your head, Dellie."

"Why? What's the matter?" But she knew something was wrong. Even her hat could not sing the tall, slump-shouldered man away from his scowl.

"He's not who you think. He's…"

"What?"

"Nothing."

The two sat quietly for a moment. Phillip smiled, and turned to his little neighbor. "Dellie, do you know how many cylinders a bus has?" O'Dell started to open her mouth, but Phillip continued. "Okay. A small car has six cylinders, and the biggest ones — I saw a Lincoln Zephyr last week that had twelve cylinders. So how many does this big bus have?"

O'Dell could see the glint in Phillip's eyes. She sensed a trap, but had no idea how to get out of it. So she said the first thing that came to mind. "About a hundred?"

Phillip laughed his grown-up laugh. "No. It has six."

"*Six!* You're kidding me, Phillip."

"Yeah, really. The cylinders are just bigger, that's all."

"Oh."

Phillip and O'Dell sat comfortably in each other's presence as they passed through Cherrydale. She rummaged in the big pocket of her jumper. Yes, the woolly lamb was nestled safely. But also in that pocket was the silver quarter, which hadn't been quite so heavy when she'd shoved it in there an hour ago.

"There's the bank where I have three dollars," O'Dell offered. "Daddy said it has to sit there for a whole year." But her smile melted quickly as she touched the coin, where it was nearly burning a hole in her jumper.

"It's kind of strange looking," Phillip said, "that bank building and the grass around it. See? It's a triangle right in the middle of the highway."

O'Dell fingered the satin ribbon on her bonnet and tried humming. It could not be heard over the growl of the bus with its belches and lurches, but deep inside, she could feel the music. She thought it would be enough. But it was not. The quarter in her pocket had no music, only dull, unforgiving metal.

Patti leaned forward and squeezed O'Dell's shoulder, then pointed to the right. ROSSLYN HOME OF ORANGE CRUSH read the big sign near the bridge.

They both thought of Bodie, and were silent.

Phillip's face was turned to the aisle when O'Dell palmed the quarter from her jumper and slipped it into his coat pocket.

CHAPTER 8

It was called The Church of the Presidents. But Olivia reasoned that if senators, generals and presidents would be welcomed at the New York Avenue Presbyterian Church, then so would the Farnsworths.

The family alighted from the Metro bus on Thirteenth Street fifteen minutes before services were scheduled to begin. Olivia and Thomas, undaunted by the long line of saints awaiting entrance, herded their family into the throng.

At ten twenty-eight, three sisters and their parents finally gained entrance to the building through a side door flanked by wrought-iron fences. While they were not in time for sanctuary seats, they were gently told they might just be able to squeeze into an ante-room and listen through mounted speakers.

"This must be the Lincoln Parlor," Olivia whispered as they were ushered to their seats. "Look. There's Abraham Lincoln's picture on the wall, above that red sofa. Straighten up, girls."

O'Dell patted her jumper pocket. The little woolly lamb, whom she had already christened Stardust, lay sleeping upside down. She peeked around her father at Kate, who sat primly facing forward, her left hand against the white pages of the open hymn book. The turquoise ring sparkled.

The chairs were just wide enough and they were crammed tightly, but O'Dell didn't mind. She loved the feel of her father's wool suit against her arm. She settled back with a sigh of contentment and stared out the narrow window. She could just barely see the feet of those people who still hoped to gain entrance, if only to stand somewhere and hear Peter Marshall thump the pulpit and speak with the ring of heaven in his Scottish brogue.

The mounted speakers came to life with a rumble. Someone, somewhere, was playing the mammoth pipe organ with plenty of bass pedals and all the stops pulled out. The speaker boxes were not quite up to the task, but something of the brass and silver majesty of that kingly instrument shuddered into the room and welded the inhabitants into one, vibrating community. With a clicking of shoes and unfolding of skirts, forty-four churchgoers rose to their feet and sang as one.

Christ the Lord is risen toda-ay; A-a-a-a-lay-ay-loo-oo-ya!

Clutching little Stardust, O'Dell opened her mouth. She couldn't read all the words on Daddy's printed program, but it didn't matter. She just patted her bonnet and let the ahs and oohs well up from the depths of her soul. It didn't matter whether she could sing. It just mattered that she had a song. Next to her, Patti trilled harmonic thirds above the melody. O'Dell would ask her later how she did it.

As briskly as it had begun, the music ended, and the forty-four settled back into their chairs.

Someone was reading, O'Dell knew, because there was a bit of droning sing-song. It was all about a lamb led to the *slotter*. The lamb in that sing-song story didn't talk, didn't open his mouth, just like her little lamb. Carefully she pulled the lamb out of her pocket, enclosed it with both hands, and transferred it to her lap. With one finger she stroked its dark little face. "Stardust, you be quiet now."

Thomas touched her arm, then pulled back. O'Dell knew she must be more careful. On and on went the voice. Then silence, and a bit of fluttery shuffling came through the speakers.

Voices, and more voices, as the choir's anthem stirred in liquid sound. *All in the April evening, April airs were abroad.* It was a rich, sad melody sung by endless, far-off souls. "Maybe hunnerds," O'Dell whispered.

The singing continued. *The sheep with their little lambs passed me by on the road.* O'Dell's head jerked up. She turned to the window and tried to imagine all of those little lambs and their mothers walking down that very street. Then, the music took a frightening turn. The lambs were crying, with a "weak and human cry." O'Dell brought Stardust slowly toward the curve of her neck, hiding him with both hands.

When the choir began repeating the melody, O'Dell no longer heard the words. She had begun her own song. She patted her bonnet and started to hum with those "hunnerds" of voices. Softly, softly. Don't get Daddy's attention.

Patti whispered to her mother. "I have to use the rest room." Olivia looked stricken, then gained her composure and glanced around quickly before rising and taking the two younger girls by the hand.

"Come Patti, O'Dell." They squeezed through the tight rows to the door. Then, on and on down the silent, cool hallway to the ladies' room. Inside were fresh lilies and linen towels. The creamy marble countertop was reflected in the walled mirror. Cherry-wood stall doors swung open without a sound, and clicked shut with a whisper. A young woman with an apple-blossom scent breezed in and washed her hands in two quick motions. Her heels tapped a staccato rhythm back to the entrance, then faded into a soft pad, pad, pad on the dense carpet.

Outside in the hallway again, Olivia's face brightened with a conspiratorial look. "Let's take just a glance into the sanctuary, girls. We'll have to find the stairs, then go up to the balcony."

"But they won't let us in the balcony, will they?" Patti hung back, uncertain. "They said all the places were full."

"We will wait for the opportunity. People always come in and out of doors. We can just look for a few seconds, then go back downstairs."

Patti and O'Dell exchanged secret glances and made an instant decision: they would be perfect little ladies so Mother would not change her mind. Sometimes their mother was a child, full of fun and mischief, like sunshine suddenly peeking around thick dark clouds. The two sisters intended to play in that sunshine as long as it lasted.

The balcony stairs were indented into an alcove, the walls of their ascent graced with all things old: portraits of ministers, presidents, wealthy contributors. Olivia whispered, then made shushing sounds, then whispered again. "Slowly, quietly. Follow me. Sh-h-h-h."

O'Dell barely touched the carpeted stairs, yet she was sure that every footfall was like the thump on a bass drum. Patti followed, trying not to breathe. Once at the top, they were faced with a long blank wall. At one end was a narrow door. It was simple and white, with no adornment. It spoke of barriers and secret defiance. Olivia slowly and quietly cradled the handle, and there it rested while Patti and O'Dell grew dizzy from holding their breaths. They bowed their heads low, as if to shrink themselves from detection. They waited for their mother to act.

From the other side of the door, the muffled thunder of Doctor Peter Marshall's baritone swelled and receded like waves on a beach.

Olivia turned the handle slowly, slowly, and pulled. One inch. Two. Through the tiny opening to the balcony they saw the backs of several dozen parishioners. They didn't move, exactly, but here and there was a nod of assent, a turning to a companion, a relaxed smile. Patti was sure she'd heard a little chuckle.

The Reverend Marshall's brogue was no longer muffled. It was clear as ice, as powerful as iron. "If a man has a hundred sheep, and one of them goes astray…"

O'Dell reached into her pocket and clutched her little lamb.

"Doesn't he leave the ninety and nine and go into the mountains, and seek that which has gone astray?"

The three interlopers stood riveted behind the partly-opened door. Olivia's hand still grasped the knob. The girls huddled together as if clutching the sides of a rocking ship.

"He is not a God sitting on a gilded throne high up in the heavens, but a God walking through your front door and mine."

Olivia still had the doorknob in her hand plus a new, thorny concept of the God whose closeness she had always measured in miles, not inches. She was a bit frightened of this God who might walk through her front door. She preferred an enthroned deity — one on whom she could gaze from afar. She had put one hand on Patti's shoulder, in readiness for turning her girls back down the stairs. But then she paused.

"In that new tomb which had belonged to Joseph of Arimathea, there had been a fluttering of unseen forces, a rustling as of the breath of God moving through the garden."

The Reverend Dr. Marshall was coming to a close, but Olivia could no longer process new words. She was still figuring out what to do with a God who might come straight into her house. She closed the door and corked this brave new thought so tightly into her head that she was surprised to hear the organ's deep golden voice on the other side of the wall. It swelled and trumpeted and vibrated from the top of her head down to her ankles and made the back of her head tingle. She'd barely recovered from this captivity of her senses when the full choir and three hundred parishioners flung their voices into the sanctuary, willing it to breach windows and rafters and hover in a protective canopy over the dozens of people sitting in folding chairs on the lawn.

Both girls leaned into this wild, abandoned melody which rose and fell in freedom, just the other side of the wall. They'd never heard such singing.

Crown Him with many Crowns, the Lamb upon His throne.

O'Dell's fingers dug into her pocket and locked around her little friend. A song about a little lamb! But why would he sit on a throne? Just a tiny lamb? She'd seen Dr. Nabor's lambs at her farm. They were so helpless, always upsetting their milk buckets and galloping into all the wrong places. How could a lamb possibly wear crowns and sit on a throne?

Awake, my soul and sing.

O'Dell thrilled to the prospect of letting all that rich music run like a golden river inside her soul, up one side and down the other.

Patti felt the bold, wild desire to sing, and Olivia was beyond shushing her. How could she!

Olivia turned to her daughters as the music came to a close. The sun that had peeked around the clouds of their mother's face had stayed bright and warm. Perhaps it would follow her home.

CHAPTER 9

Olivia was almost cheerful, a feeling she'd rarely experienced since the beginning of the war. Surely hanging sheets on the line in the early afternoon sun, with the brown speckled thrush singing its heart out, was the closest she had come to peace in a long time. The lines eased from Olivia's face and she smiled.

O'Dell sat near the end of the clothesline, making mud pies, her bright chatter like a soft drumbeat. The two older girls were still at school, but first and second graders were relegated to mornings-only this week.

O'Dell wondered if she could dig to China, like Franklin Porro had said. With her big spoon she dug deeper and deeper.

Olivia turned to watch. "I think you have dug far enough, O'Dell. I'd like you to fill up that hole."

"Yes, Mother." O'Dell stopped and let her spoon fall to the ground. She felt in her pocket for Stardust. The wool was a comfort to her and she brushed him against her cheek.

"Mother, who can wear a crown?"

Olivia pegged a clothespin onto a sheet and turned around. "Well... kings and emperors, for starters."

"And princesses and queens too?"

"Yes, dear."

O'Dell returned the little lamb to her pocket and began scraping dirt back into the hole.

Olivia bent to the basket for one of Patti's pinafores. The sun warmed her hands, and surely these sheets would be dry before supper.

"Mother, how can someone wear *many* crowns?"

Olivia straightened and regarded her daughter. "Well, maybe a queen might have a special crown for the throne, and another one to wear on other days."

"Can a lamb wear a crown, Mother?"

"Where did you hear that?"

"They were singing it Sunday at church. Didn't you hear it?"

"I will have to think about that."

O'Dell finished scraping dirt. No use asking her mother to explain. This was a shutting the door answer and there was nowhere else to go with questions. "Can I play in the front yard now?"

"*May* I play."

"May I play."

"Yes. But listen for my call."

There was a spot in the front yard at the end of the driveway that O'Dell had always thought of as hers. Shielded by lacy bushes, she could see everything — and even though it was just possible to be seen from the house, she always felt hidden. She took off her shoes and socks, laying them carefully aside. The earth smelled old and mysterious, but the air had freshened from the evening's rain, and it curled around O'Dell's feet in little caresses. She studied a patch of bare ground which was just short of the sidewalk. Here at the end of the driveway, the retaining wall stopped abruptly and at its narrow end the joining of two little streams gave O'Dell just what she wanted — the makings of a small puddle. It should be easy diggings here!

She fumbled in her jacket for the big kitchen spoon she'd used in the backyard, then began digging. Slowly, one scoop at a time, the little indentation grew. When she knelt to her task, O'Dell was nearly hidden by ferns and the gray smooth stones that Thomas had used to cloister three budding azalea bushes.

Happily she continued her digging, scooping and squishing, until a very sizable mud hole rewarded her work. As she worked she hummed her Clementi, galloping through the first portion, then slowing down for the andante section the way Miss Bestor had taught her. O'Dell was so happy today that even obeying her music teacher brought her joy.

He was behind her before she heard him coming. The wagon was empty, and no ting-clink-a-tings had heralded his arrival. O'Dell continued humming, gradually becoming aware that her higher melody was now joined by a man's soft voice. She whirled with a little gasp, then plunked down squarely into the mud hole.

"I am grieved to have startled you Miss." The words were strangely accented, with a curious formal twist. *Like kings would talk,* O'Dell thought.

"Oh! I was… I was just getting ready to sit here, actually."

"You prefer an adobe throne?"

"A what?"

"You have a vast array of foliage and concrete — even this retaining wall — for your comfort. Why do you choose mud?"

"Well, it was just an accident, I guess."

"O'Dell!" Mother's voice was sharp as razors. "Come in! *Now!*"

The Bottle man pulled away quickly, his empty wagon rolling smoothly north. O'Dell stood and watched him go, her pinafore dripping, shoulders slumped. Why couldn't Mother and Daddy like the Bottle Man? He was always polite, and as quiet as he could be with a wagon load of metal and bottles, and besides, he was a friend of Phillip's and that certainly made him all right.

She gripped her spoon and scraped the mud off the front and sides of her pinafore. No use. She was ready for a bath and her clothes needed the Bendix washer.

"O'Dell Constance Farnsworth! You are covered with mud! Just look at you! Mud from top to bottom!" Olivia faced her daughter, who stood dripping just inside the back door. "I didn't think it was possible to be covered with so much mud!"

O'Dell wished her mother would stop saying that. She knew she was covered with mud and didn't need anyone to tell her. She wanted to scurry up the stairs and fill the tub and get it over with. "Mother, do you want me to leave my clothes outside the bathroom? Or maybe take them off here?" The more cooperative she was, the better.

Olivia's eyes flashed. She felt a hot boldness rising up. There was an unknown man talking with her daughter and she would not have it! Surely O'Dell knew better! All of the girls had been warned. She fumed in silence and decided not to wash those filthy clothes. She would not hang them up piece by piece on her pristine laundry line.

"Come with me to the washtubs, O'Dell. You will remove everything that you are wearing and wash them by hand in those sinks." Calming a bit, she steered her daughter down the basement stairs, her voice softening. "I will draw the water for you. Run get that little stool by Daddy's work bench and when you've taken off those dirty clothes, you can cover yourself with this old towel. I am going across the street for awhile, but Kate just got home and she will be in the kitchen."

Olivia turned the faucets and dove into her favorite therapy: good, honest work. The water gushed strong, warm and loud, washing her thoughts with purpose. The tub full, she hurried up the stairs.

O'Dell scurried for the stool and ran back to the tubs to begin her penance. It was slow work peeling off her wet muddy pinafore, socks, shoes and underwear, but finally they lay in a sodden mass at her feet. They looked smaller, somehow, than when she had put them on this afternoon. She wrapped herself in the old towel.

She was glad Skippy's basket was gone. Now it was cleaner in the dark recesses below the tubs, with nothing to remind her of that guilty day. She threw her muddy clothes into the deep water, hopped up on the stool and watched each garment sink slowly to the bottom. Mother had filled the tub with warm water and it felt good to plunge her arms up to the elbows. She hummed a bit of her latest piano piece, Schumann's *The Happy Farmer.* O'Dell loved the chords in the right hand and the jaunty way the melody looped from top to bottom with the left hand. Surely the farmer was skipping while working. But how could he do that, with a horse to guide and the plow pushing hard into the ground? Hadn't Daddy said that farming was slow, plodding work?

With her bar of Ivory soap she rubbed and scrubbed, squeezing and plunging each piece up and down to chase the suds. She twisted and squeezed, saving the pinafore until last. It was a big piece to handle but O'Dell grunted and leaned into the job. First the ends, now the middle.

Then she felt it. A bump in the pocket. And she knew what it was without looking — her precious lamb. *No no no! Not Stardust! No!* She loosened her grip and opened the pocket and into the deep dirty water the lamb tumbled slowly, becoming one with the darkness.

O'Dell began wailing. The towel slipped off her back and fell to the floor.

"Dellie! Dellie what is it!" Kate darted down the stairs and ran to the tubs. Surprised to see her little sister unclothed, she grabbed the old towel from the floor and draped it around O'Dell's shoulders. "What's going on!"

"Oh Kate! He was in my pocket and now he's gone! He's drowned! Oh Kate, do something! Do something quick!"

"Who's gone, Dellie?" Kate had begun shouting to override her sister's sobbing. Then she took a deep breath and spoke more softly. "Dellie, please tell me who you mean. *Who* drowned?"

O'Dell leaned over the tub, her eyes closed. She poked the water with her index finger, harder and harder, the little splashes soaking into her towel. "In there! My little Stardust! *In there!*"

"All right, all right. I'll get him, I'll get him. Just move back a bit." Kate rolled up her sleeve and plunged her arms deep, swishing slowly. First, a limp sock, then the pinafore, then another sock and finally underwear. "I don't feel it, Dellie. Are you sure he's in there?"

"He was in my pocket! He's drowning, he's drowning!"

"All right, all right… let's see." She fished along the bottom and brought up a very soggy, limp lamb. Quickly she rinsed it under the faucet. "Now, Dellie, let's wrap him in the corner of your towel. Okay, there, now, I'll just squeeze a minute."

O'Dell wiped her nose on the other end of the towel and hiccuped the last of her sobs.

"Well, he doesn't look so bad, Dellie. I think we can fix him."

"But Kate, the sheepskin's peeling away from his body! And now all of his bones will show!"

"Hmmm. Well, I'll tell you what. Let's go upstairs and set Stardust on my window ledge. There's a nice warm breeze and he'll be dry in no time. After we glue him back together, and when the wool dries, well, *then* we can decide what to do." She turned to her little sister. "Dellie, this will be our secret, okay? I won't tell Mother and we can just fix this ourselves."

O'Dell looked at Kate with shining eyes. "Okay."

"I'll drain the tub, Dellie, and you run upstairs and get some clothes on. I'll be up in a minute. And hurry! My, but you look like a little tweedhopper. Don't let anyone see you!"

"Dellie, sh-h-h... Come here quick! Mother's in the basement ironing." Kate pulled her sister across the hall into her own bedroom and led her to the window, where a hint of late afternoon sunshine and warm breezes washed the room in early spring softness. Stardust sat on the windowsill, his straggly wool drooping.

But there was a definite improvement from an hour ago, and O'Dell lifted her little lamb off the windowsill and smoothed his coat.

"I'm going to glue down the sheepskin, Dellie. Here." She fished a tube of airplane glue out of her pocket. "When he's completely dry this little fella is going to be a different lamb!!

O'Dell lifted him to her face and felt for the old softness. The wool had a scratchy feel, but the lamb looked so forlorn and lost that her heart melted. She would make him right again. She must. "Can I help you do that, Kate?"

"If we're both together at the right time, Dellie, but let's do it while Mother's busy."

"Yeah. She's already mad enough over my clothes."

Kate winked, took the lamb and set him on her dresser. "And don't worry, Dellie, I'll take care of him. But right now I promised Mother I'd fold laundry in the basement. She has the radio on and my favorite program is coming up in five minutes!" The graceful tapping of her loafers receded down the stairs. O'Dell practiced making funny faces in front of Kate's mirror, then went in search of Patti.

♪

Something was burning, but Olivia could not grasp what it was. All around her was dampness and dimness and high-pitched crackling voices. They just kept talking and talking and Olivia just wished they would stop so she could see what was burning.

There it was. The smoke was right under her. Perhaps it was her hand. Should she move and get help? The iron. The hot iron. It was burning Thomas's shirt and she studied it with curious detachment. She should move that iron, stop holding it. That's it. Stop. Everything was stopped. Perhaps she should stop too.

The President was dead. Today, Thursday, April the twelfth, Franklin D. Roosevelt was dead. That's what the crackling radio voices had said. But it could not be true. It could not. Must not. Alexander was not home. The Russians were almost to Berlin and Alexander, her little brother, was not safe, was not home.

Kate dropped the laundry basket and rushed to her mother's side. "Mother? Mother, what is that! Mother! *Move away from there!* Oh Mother, what's happening? What should I do!"

Olivia's thoughts and mumblings floated up from a deep cavern somewhere. "Kate, would you, perhaps... throw some water on that shirt?"

Kate jerked the cord from the outlet and raced to the washtubs where sheets ballooned in grayish water. *A scoop. A scoop. Quickly. The scoop.* Kate darted back to the ironing board and splashed water on her father's shirt — the new one with French cuffs.

"Mother. Please. Come upstairs. I'll help you." Kate didn't like this new place she was sliding into. It was too much in the middle. First her little sister on one side, then her mother. Kate in the middle again. But if it was duty they were looking for, she would do what she had to do. If she could just figure out what that was.

♪

"Kate, what's the matter with Mother?" O'Dell hung back, uncertain. Should she help? Would it be best to hold onto her mother or just wait? Mother's face was all funny and sagging. Not smiling. Not frowning. O'Dell wished she would frown, be in control. She reached out and fluttered one hand on her mother's back. Olivia waved her away.

Kate gestured to her sister. "Take the books off Daddy's chair. That's where I'm taking her." But it was more of a walking alongside. Not one of taking. No one had ever been able to take Olivia where she did not want to go.

Olivia backed up to the chair, glanced downward with a look of wonder as if to question the fact that indeed there was a chair in the room. Then she settled heavily as a little poof of air escaped from the cushion.

"Bring me that picture of your Uncle Alexander, O'Dell." Mother's face had stopped sagging. But still there was no frown, just a heavy emptiness.

Kate moved over to the piano and carefully lifted the framed photo. "Here. Here it is, Mother. Do you want me to hold..."

"I'll hold it."

Kate shuddered quickly, then lowered herself uneasily into a ladder-back chair by the wall. She stared at O'Dell, willing her to be quiet.

Olivia studied the portrait of her brother. As a teenager he had always smiled with a mischievous, debonair expression. But in this picture Alexander had already tasted battle, and had faced the camera with the depth of war in his short young memory.

Olivia ran one thumb over the plain wooden frame, starting at the top, then sliding softly down the sides. O'Dell had seen her touch Patti that way, smoothing her hair and then her sleeves, finishing with a little flex of index finger and thumb.

Olivia sat still, hugging the portrait. "Run along, girls. Kate, you warm up last night's soup. O'Dell, you set the table. Your father will be home soon." Olivia had frowned at them both. Their little world was coming back into balance.

In the kitchen Kate found the barley soup, still in its kettle, on the bottom shelf of the Frigidaire. She placed it on the stove, stirred it once, then turned a knob.

O'Dell gathered the dishes from the dining room cupboard and began setting them with soft little clicks onto the bare table. She set each one on its edge first, then lowered it carefully. Every once in awhile she stole a glance into the living room, where only Mother's legs were visible. Her feet were shifting and sliding on the Karastan carpet in little scuffs. O'Dell set the dishes down and slowly began tip-toeing across the waxed hardwood floor in the hallway. She would not go far enough to show her face, but she must find out why her mother was whispering to herself. If she put heel to toe, lifting and placing just right, and going over and around the boards that creaked, she could get to the corner by the closet and maybe hear something.

Olivia was still rubbing the wooden edges, faster now. "Go in the house and wait for me," she mumbled. "Let me take your place." O'Dell heard a tiny catch of breath. Was she crying? Then Olivia sat very still, staring across the room as if she saw something that puzzled her. Now there was no movement. The feet were still, the fingers at rest. A long shuddery sigh came from somewhere deep inside her mother. Then, the absence of sound.

O'Dell turned and made her way back to the dining room carefully but with added urgency and whispered to Kate: "Mother's getting up."

Thomas wasn't very good at comforting. At least, his efforts to comfort Olivia were like trying to prune a prickly hedge. But something had to be done. The nation was reeling from the sudden death of the president, and in his own home, he could see that Olivia felt it the most keenly of all. Well, this had been going on for a day and a half now. What they needed was something definitive.

Yes, that was it. He would meet the crisis head on with one of their special radio evenings. Complete with hot chocolate. He would commandeer Kate and Patti for kitchen duty.

At supper he offered the invitation. The radio program would feature personal glimpses of the president's death. And even though the funeral was still two days away, tonight their local radio station had promised a collage of recordings honoring President Roosevelt.

Seated on chairs and cushions, the Farnsworths waited for the Philco radio to warm up. Finally, a mellow voice floated into the living room.

Thomas put a finger to his lips. "Quiet, girls. It's Edward R. Murrow." Thomas was proud of his fellow alumnus. Although the two men had graduated from the same college in the same year, they had never met. Murrow served as one of Europe's main war correspondents, while Thomas stayed home monitoring the nation's meat supply. Two kinsmen a half world apart.

Tonight, the broadcast began with a replay of Murrow's announcement from across the ocean. But it was quickly followed by an announcer in Georgia, where the president had died. Death had not come at the White House, but at Warm Springs, where the president had been resting.

The story continued: "As the cortège drew into the drive and halted, the sad strains of an accordion played *Going Home*. It was Graham Jackson, a Negro, who had played many times for FDR and the hundreds of others there. Bareheaded and with tears running down both sides of his face, he stood in front of the group and paid his last homage. And as the cars started again slowly, driving around the semicircular drive and on toward the station, Jackson swung into one of the president's favorite hymns, *Nearer, My God, To Thee*."

O'Dell sat on the floor quietly leaning on her father's knee. Death again. She wondered how it must have felt. She wished she could have seen that accordion and pressed the black and white keys. O'Dell fingered her little Stardust, who had made a remarkable recovery. His wool was fluffed out, though the dinginess and straggly ends of each little puff bespoke his trauma in the washtub. Kate had glued his hide more securely, and although there was a bit of stiffness around the edges, he was her own little lamb again.

Patti lay on her stomach, winding a small thread from the carpet, humming slowly in her sweet soprano.

Kate set down the tray of cookies and hot chocolate as the hymn wound to a close. She looked at her mother with apprehension. But Olivia was serene, her hand on Thomas's arm. O'Dell and Patti were quiet. Light had faded gently from the living room, and it seemed to Kate as if the departing sun had left behind a remnant of light for each face. She took in the family scene, almost as if it were a painting. The colors were mellow, joining each other at the edges and flowing into peace. She relaxed. All looked comfortable, even in the midst of this national sorrow. They were all together, unified for the next step, no matter what it was. They would be all right.

Thomas turned a knob on the Philco. The soft "click" snapped into their repose. Now it was just the family, each digesting the words of the announcers, tucking them away for safekeeping. Perhaps Sunday evening they could tune in again, for accounts of that morning's funeral procession.

"Olivia?" Thomas took his wife's hand. "I think it would be good to sleep, don't you?" Olivia smiled weakly at her husband, said good night to each of them and walked toward the stairs.

Thomas turned to the children. "Hop to it, girls. Time for bed." If the evening wasn't exactly the way he'd hoped, it was getting closer. Even the death of a president could not dim the light that had begun to make its home in Olivia's eyes. Mother was smiling, and each of the girls smiled back.

CHAPTER 10

May. Time for flowers, overcoats dumped on the sidewalk, rain and more rain and the last busy days of school. President Truman had quickly recovered from the shock of being thrust into the last stages of the global conflict, and it looked as if the ravaging war years might end at last. The rhythms and sights and sounds in the Farnsworth home were much the same, yet a tangible spirit of hope and purpose was planting its roots into the family. Andante had moved to allegro.

Even Bodie's wagon moved more briskly.

On this Saturday, a whole new crisp morning stretched open with the sun. O'Dell savored the last moments between sleeping and waking, then remembered. It was the dreaded "creeping myrtle" day. She tumbled out of bed and headed for the kitchen. She collided with Patti, who was flying down the stairs. "My ride's here! Bye!"

"Why's Patti leaving? She didn't have breakfast!" O'Dell had a strong sense of justice and it galled her when Patti or Kate did not hang around long enough to participate in the sweet togetherness of family chores. Even worse, this day had the promise of a double marathon. The undulating lawn's creeping myrtle, true to its name, had crept upward in a blanket of purple blossoms. But then, so had the weeds. The whole family, minus Patti this time, would skip Saturday morning radio. No *Let's Pretend* or *The Lone Ranger*. They'd dive headlong into the damp foliage before mid-morning sun and humidity tested their family resolve.

Olivia sprinkled salt on her grapefruit. "Patti's in the Glee Club. Every spring they go to Richmond for the state competition. Don't you remember last year, O'Dell? Come to the table."

O'Dell remembered. Same Saturday. Same creeping myrtle. She clumped into her chair, made a face and filled her mouth with oatmeal. "Creep," she muttered.

The response from her father was swift and sharp. "What did you say, O'Dell?"

"I was just singing. *Creeping myrtle, creeping myrtle, brother John, brother John.*" Quickly she mumbled new lyrics to the old French tune.

"O'Dell, take your dish to the kitchen. Go upstairs and brush your teeth. And when you come down, you will be ready to pull weeds." Thomas finished his white tea in two gulps and left the table.

"Dellie, don't toss the weeds back into the myrtle. Put them in your big apron pockets, like this." Thomas stuffed a green wad into the cloth bag he'd slung over his shoulder.

"But the weeds scratch, Daddy! There are red stripes on my arm!"

Thomas stiffened. Had she pricked her skin? The scene at Glebe Theater was still fresh in his mind, and the unanswered fear was always under the surface.

"They scratch everyone, Dellie." Thomas stood quickly and caught Olivia's eye. "How about some lemonade, Mother?"

"Yes. That would be nice. Kate, come and help."

"What're you doing, Mister Farnsworth?" Phillip suddenly materialized under the poplar tree.

O'Dell spoke up loudly. "It's really fun, Phillip! There's all these flowers, with neat bugs that no one's ever seen before." Olivia,

Thomas and Kate paused in fascination. Here was a new stratagem from their little eight-year-old.

"What kind of bugs?" Phillip was a young entomologist. Anything with more than four legs had heavier pulling power than food and drink.

"Wel-l-l. There's, um, bally bugs."

"You mean those little gray creatures that roll into balls when you touch them?" Phillip was already down on his hands and knees in the myrtle, pulling back the leaves.

"Yeah. I think I saw one under that weed. But you'll have to pull it up to see."

Olivia turned sharply, suppressing a giggle. Oh, but it felt good to laugh again. She grabbed Kate's hand. "Lemonade, remember?"

Phillip caught one of the bugs and put it onto his flattened hand.

O'Dell grinned at him. "Wow. You got a bally bug!"

Phillip gave her a patient look. "Actually, this is a crustacean, in the same family with lobsters and crayfish."

O'Dell tried her own brand of patience. "These don't live in the water, Phillip."

"But they do live in moist surroundings, Dellie. Look. See how wet it is underneath this weed stem?"

"I can't see, Phillip. Pull up the weed."

"If we can get this little crustacean to hold still for a minute, we could count its legs. I think they have seven pairs." Phillip's and O'Dell's heads were nearly touching. "Yeah. There. See? Fourteen legs!" He smiled in triumph and moved the creature next to his face. "Hey there, Mister Isopod!"

"Oh, get another one, get another one," O'Dell crowed. "Pull another weed so I'll have one to talk to!"

Thomas stepped toward the children. "You need to get back to work, Dellie. And Phillip, please excuse us. But if you want to join in, here's a bag."

"No thanks, Mr. Farnsworth. Mom's waiting for me to clean out the garage."

O'Dell sighed and began stuffing her apron again.

Humidity and fatigue pushed the morning toward lunchtime and by twelve o'clock a soggy family was all too ready to pause for chicken sandwiches and celery sticks.

"Can I eat down by the sidewalk?" O'Dell waited, her apron still fastened securely.

Olivia paused. "Well, I…"

"You should say *may I*," Kate interjected.

O'Dell made a face.

"All right, O'Dell." Olivia had her mind on other things, and eating by the sidewalk was not one of them.

O'Dell sprinted for the driveway and jumped off the retaining wall, her sandwich tucked securely into a napkin, her apron full of weeds. She sat near the sidewalk, careful to avoid the drying mud hole. From her pocket she examined the weeds one by one, then chose a white clover which she held up to the light. She noticed for the first time its creamy white center with the pinkish hue. *Pink*. This was just right, and its stem was wiggly enough for the job. She separated out six clovers and began twisting them.

The evening air had begun to settle in lazy cold pockets when Patti stepped from the neighbors' car. "Bye, Madeline! Bye, Mrs. Morrow!"

O'Dell was waiting on the front porch. "You missed it, Patti."

"Missed what?"

"The Iso-poos." O'Dell flipped her hair back and perched on the top step.

"Iso what?"

"Oh, it's just some bug that Phillip found. You know, the ones that curl up when you touch them."

"You mean bally bugs?"

"Well, yeah, I guess you could call them that." O'Dell jumped up, tired of trying to outsmart her sister. "You hungry? Race ya to the kitchen! Betcha want some toast." They let the screen door close with a bang. "Hey! What'd ya sing? Did ya win?"

"Did *you* win," Olivia corrected.

"Did you win," O'Dell repeated.

"We came in second."

"Patti, that's wonderful." Olivia's face and honey-brown hair caught the late afternoon sun filtering through the dining room curtains. Her smile was relaxed, almost happy. The two girls regarded her solemnly. Their mother did not smile much. But something had made her childlike today. They wondered what it was, so they could make it happen again. Their parents stood close together, as if they had a secret between them.

Olivia's smile lit up the room. "Girls, listen. I have something wonderful to tell you: "The war in Europe is over. Alexander is already in New York!"

"So soon?" Kate asked. In her fourteen years she'd been accustomed to waiting for just about everything.

Thomas smiled at his daughter's perception. "The Army wants him back in the States right away so he can manage supplies at the Brooklyn Terminal."

"Uncle Alex? Coming here?" Patti and O'Dell hopped up and down, then grasped hands and whirled each other around the living room.

"He's bringing his French bride and they'll be here in two days. He just called."

"Oh, who is she? Who is she?"

"Danielle. He met her in southern France last summer."

"Mmmmm. Romantic," Kate murmured.

"Patti and Dellie, you girls will have to sleep together while they are here." Thomas put his hands on their shoulders. "Think you can handle that?"

♪

The three girls polished, swept, helped with the baking, made beds and scrubbed bathrooms, all without being prompted. By nightfall Olivia was nearly worn out from their cheerfulness, but at least they had proffered real help.

That was the tempo of the day. But by early evening the sisters had shown no signs of slowing down. From the kitchen came echoes of splats and splops as the three girls threw wet dish cloths at each other.

"Ow! Hey!" Patti turned at just the wrong time and was arrested broadside with a sudsy rag. But Patti had inherited her mother's strong arms and fired a wet missile directly at the back of Kate's head, demolishing her hairdo.

"You nuthatch! Quit it! We have to finish the dishes or we'll be here all night!" Waiting for just the right moment Kate soaked the dish cloth and pretended to go back to scrubbing greasy pans. Suddenly she wheeled, stared at Patti, then threw the sopping cloth directly at O'Dell.

"Ow! Au-au-au-gh!! Stop it, Kate!"

A knock on the wall turned the three little warriors into statues. "Girls, that is enough." Daddy's voice was never loud. But it closed the door on their fun — like iron grating.

Danielle smelled like a hot-house gardenia. She babbled a mixture of English and French with escalating speed, saying "oui" and "thank you" and "merci" as she clung to Alexander, her lips glowing deep pink.

Alexander stood radiant and handsome in his captain's uniform, a lopsided grin planted on his face. He glanced from Olivia and Thomas to the girls, silently begging their approval.

"Ooo! Tu es très sweet," Danielle cooed, pinching Patti's cheeks. "Et tu," she said, rounding on O'Dell, "tu es une petite *doll!*"

Kate had fled after the first round of kisses. Olivia's smile, so radiant earlier in the day, was etched permanently onto her face, which now looked ready to shatter.

Thomas took charge. "We have your room ready, Alexander. First one on your right." Then, to Danielle: "I took your suitcases upstairs. Please let us know if you need anything."

Olivia seized the advantage. "Breakfast is served at seven o'clock. And I hope you will not mind the sound of piano in the morning. The girls must keep their schedule, so they will go to bed now." Her smile began to droop but she finished with a hug for her little brother and an experimental peck on both cheeks for her new sister-in-law.

"Oo la la! Très bon!" Danielle floated up the stairs on a drift of scent, her new husband in tow.

♪

The sun was halfway up the sky as Danielle chirped at Olivia in the sun-soaked kitchen the next morning.

In the living room, O'Dell sidled up to her uncle. "Would you like to see my crowns?"

Alexander fixed a steady gaze on his little niece. He knew her propensity toward practical jokes. Just this morning Patti and O'Dell had exchanged the contents of the salt and pepper shakers to celebrate last month's April Fools Day.

"Your crowns?"

"Yes. Lots of crowns. They're for my lamb." O'Dell smiled happily, then shyly took her uncle's hand. "They're outside."

"Outside. A lamb. Good place for it," he muttered.

She took his hand and led him down the front concrete steps toward the poplar tree, then turned right and continued the descent on sloping uneven steps until they reached the sidewalk.

"I thought they were near the house," Alexander ventured.

"They are! Just a few more steps." She pulled hard on his hand until they reached the juncture of retaining wall and sidewalk. "There!" she beamed.

O'Dell reached into her voluminous pinafore. She pulled forth her dingy little lamb. "See? I got Stardust full of mud but it was okay because I washed him."

Alexander waited. He knew his niece. More was surely forthcoming.

"Yeah, and then he was really ugly and his bones showed."

Alexander knew about bones showing. He'd seen plenty of it.

"But Kate dried him and glued his hide and let him dry some more and I thought he would look better with crowns." She held up the lamb for inspection. "Don't you, Uncle Alex?" She trusted her uncle the captain. He knew everything.

Alexander waited a moment. If he played along as if she were doing some more April Fool jokes — if he laughed at her and was wrong — that brilliant smile would disappear from his niece's face and she might never trust him again. But perhaps she was not joking. What should he do?

"Show me," he said.

O'Dell began singing her new theme song. Every word had seared itself into her brain the first time she'd heard it. The majesty, the soaring ecstasy of those three hundred voices at the New York Avenue Presbyterian Church had spoken deeply to her in those thirty seconds before her mother had closed the door.

Alexander strained to hear the words. A dim memory floated into his head. Where had he heard them before? It was clear that O'Dell was positively joyous over them. He folded his arms and regarded his niece with affection. Nothing in war had made sense except for the bright shafts of endearment which had sneaked up on him in the worst moments of fatigue and hunger. There was the child in tatters shyly accepting a bit of chocolate; an enemy soldier who lowered his gun and let him escape; and Danielle — childish Danielle — whose incessant chatter had been balm to his soul when she'd taken him into her bullet-strafed home.

"Would you like to see the crowns, Alexander?"

"I would. Yes."

"Here. Hold Stardust."

A startled army captain waited for the next move. O'Dell pulled back the azalea bushes and found her nest of wilted clover crowns. Her breath came quickly as she examined them one by one, picked the one with the most life, and nestled it lovingly onto the head of her dingy little lamb. "Do you think he would look better if he was sitting on a throne, Uncle Alex?"

Alexander regarded his niece with tender affection. "I think there are some things too mysterious for understanding, O'Dell."

CHAPTER 11

Sometimes Olivia whistled. Not often, but when she did, it made you want to stop what you were doing and store it up for later. It was a glorious warrior sound that seemed out of keeping with the woman's proper bearing. But this morning, Olivia was whistling. She'd had breakfast with Alexander, and they'd both talked with their sister Elsie on the West Coast.

Alone again in her kitchen, Olivia had whistled the favorite tunes they'd sung as children and rejoiced that everyone would just stay put for awhile, far from the clutches of the war machine.

Danielle was catching up on her sleep in readiness for their trip to the Brooklyn Army Terminal, where Alexander would work with postwar military supplies. Once again the kitchen was Olivia's base of operations, her little kingdom, and she was glad to have it back. It smelled triumphantly of Bon Ami, and not of gardenias.

Thomas heard Olivia's whistling and smiled. Now that the house was emptying out, he could find purpose in his favorite tasks of cleaning and organizing. This day's work was just like any of his other Saturday projects, as far as the rest of the family was concerned. But to chance visitors there was something strangely unsettling about the display in the living room.

From the northeast corner to the southwest, internal parts of the piano were laid out in symmetry and purpose across the Karastan carpet. Some notes on the old upright had sounded a bit fuzzy to Thomas, and a good cleaning was always the first step toward perfection. A thorough mechanical challenge could clear the mind for this father of three. In such an overhaul he would have both the beginning and the end points planned before he started.

He had removed the piano's action and dissected it, aligning each hammer with its corresponding key. The yellowing ivories and faded black keys grinned up at him as he worked. Carefully he finished numbering each hammer — from their smaller pads on the treble hammers to the larger ones at the bass. Nearby, his trusted oil can with its long spout stood waiting.

Edgar Morris the piano tuner had remarked later that he did not know how such foolishness had ever resulted in an instrument which could be described as a piano, but then he did not know Thomas James Farnsworth as well as he knew the insides of grands and uprights.

Thomas was humming happily, carefully wiping each hammer with a chamois cloth, when he felt, rather than saw, a faint shadow. He knew someone was at the screen door but thought perhaps one of the girls had paused to watch him work. Then he heard a soft groaning. It wasn't a little girl's voice. It was a man's cry. He could not leave the felted hammers quickly, or he would lose his place. Quietly he rose from his knees and turned just as he heard light footfalls on the concrete steps. The sound that followed was all too familiar. It was a tinkling wagon load of bottles receding south.

"Daddy, who was that?" Patti lingered in the hallway. "Was it Madeline? She said she'd come over today."

Thomas sighed and compressed his lips. How could he explain to children, or to himself, for that matter, what there was about that man with his wagon full of junk. The nameless little fellow was always hovering. Never breaking the law, mind you. Just continually on the edge of something disturbing. Suddenly, his Saturday work had lost its glow and purpose.

As if reading his mind, Patti posed a question: "Daddy, how do you know when someone's breaking the law? I mean, I know you may have to hit someone or stab someone or even shoot someone. But what if they just kinda pushed you? Madeline says Eddie Johns always pushes her and I said she should tell the teacher but she doesn't want to."

Thomas rolled the polishing cloth into a wad and considered. "Well, suppose you were just walking down the street and someone bumped into you without meaning to. That's not breaking the law. But suppose he kept doing it and kept doing it. You'd know it wasn't an accident about the third time."

"So what would you do about it?" Patti had great faith in her father's judgment. He'd spent long nights studying law, and the children had piled into the family sedan to fetch him after classes. It was a bit of a stretch to explain to their friends why a veterinarian needed a law degree, so usually they didn't try. No matter. Daddy was smart in all the right places, and that's all that counted.

"Well, Patti, that would be called harassment."

"So what would you do about it?"

"First you'd want to figure out why the person is harassing you. And if you could do so without endangering yourself, try to work it out with that person."

"I don't think that would work with Eddie."

"Hmph. Well, it's a bit different with children, because adults are supposed to look out for you. But adults who are being harassed can hire an attorney and bring suit."

"Like clothes?"

Thomas's mouth twitched. "No, it's a lawsuit. The person doing the pushing would have to hire an attorney or get one appointed for him, and both he and the one he pushed would have to go to court." He paused. "Unless of course it could be settled privately, and this kind of thing is usually settled out of court."

Patti took a moment to ponder. Then she lifted her head in joyful surprise. "Madeline's here! Thanks, Daddy. Bye."

Thomas did some pondering of his own. Harassing. Was that what the Bottle Man was doing? Or was it just his imagination? He would begin documenting.

♪

O'Dell walked halfway down the block, then looked back at the house. *Mother didn't say I couldn't go down the street, and she's busy with Uncle Alex. And Daddy's too busy to ask. I can still see my house and Veronica's house isn't that far away. I'll just go a little bit… just to see where Bodie turns the corner. I need to know where he goes next.*

She stepped a little farther, then saw Veronica waving.

"Dellie! C'mere!"

Uh oh. She was in for it now. Veronica was only six years old but with a grownup sense of the mysterious. She had scientific answers for many of life's puzzles and was more than ready to join in all kinds of things neither of them would have done on their own. Just last year Veronica had gamely accompanied O'Dell in running away from home, a one-hour venture that had ended in the woods near a little cabin filled with dark-skinned, cheerful people. After a meal of pudding and apples with this surprising family, the little girls had returned home, chagrined that no one had missed them.

Veronica bolted into the street and grabbed O'Dell's hand. "Hurry! Come see my new Oz books! She dragged O'Dell up the flagstone walkway and into the kitchen. Laughing, they tore up the back stairs to Veronica's room.

O'Dell loved this bedroom. It's south-facing window, covered in organza curtains, filtered light into this childhood haven that always seemed to be full of sunshine. On the creamy carpet, dense and cushiony for little girls' feet, were two dolls, a toy car and a pair of pink pajamas. The sparkling white shelves were home to toys and books that O'Dell could only dream about. And closest to the door, two bright new books stood like sentinels, just waiting to be held: *Ozma of Oz* and *The Patchwork Girl of Oz.*

Veronica stood on tiptoe, eager to please her friend. "You can take one home if you want."

O'Dell lifted *The Patchwork Girl of Oz* and caressed the smooth cover. She heard the faint snap of the newly opened hardcover as she thumbed into the first few pages. "Can I take this one?" She hugged it to herself. But before Veronica could answer, a rolling, rumbling cascade of piano notes startled her and she nearly dropped the book.

"Oh, that's Daddy. Wanna watch him play?" Veronica took O'Dell's hand and pulled her down the stairs.

The untamed, luxuriant notes fairly swooshed up the stairway, sweeping them into the living room. The piano had come alive, as if wound with a key. Roland MacDowell was sitting — no, commandeering — the piano to his will. Boogie. Wild boogie that rumbled inside O'Dell and yanked her like a marionette.

"Daddy. Here's Dellie," puffed Veronica. O'Dell did not move.

"Well, well," boomed the man at the piano. "What have we here! Sit down, little lady, sit down." He patted the bench and moved to his left. "Sit. I'll teach you some boogie that'll curl your hair."

"Oh no. I can't. It doesn't. I mean, I don't know."

Veronica's father trumpeted a laugh. "Afraid of a little boogie? Here. Just hold your hands like this." He curled his left hand along an arpeggio C chord, then slipped into an A, but added the mysterious B flat at the top. He hip-hopped along the notes faster and faster, then stretched his hand to broken octaves, using the same notes. "Think you can do that?"

"Well, I..." Then she heard it: the blessed, blasted whistle. Thomas Farnsworth's whistle could set dogs howling, grandfathers' teeth rattling, and mothers scrambling to evict any Farnsworth child on their premises. Thomas was the only father in the neighborhood who could spike beyond 100 decibels with his homeward commands. Cupping his hands, he blew between his thumbs, raising and lowering three fingers until he had a nearly perfect Tarzan call. His three daughters had begged him not to do it, but secretly they were proud of their neighborhood watchman on the wall.

O'Dell bolted. "Gotta go! See ya later, Veronica!"

Roland MacDowell grinned. "She wants to learn," he murmured. "Yes, and I'll show her how."

Veronica was confused. Wasn't her father's piano playing the best in the world? How could anyone not think so? She sighed and scooted onto the bench. "I'll play with you, Daddy."

Behind a row of hawthorns on Vernon Street, Bodie paused. He too was captivated by the boogie. But he would put it on a leash until it flowed across the surface of his mind and dissipated into an irretrievable puff. Bodie was looking for something deeper — something more lasting than plinking bottles and unthrottled pianos. He would find Phillip.

Upstairs in the Berning home, Grandon Tolson settled into his swivel chair. Its worn and cracked leather conformed to his frame, and spoke of permanency. He was just where he wanted to be — in the den with the door closed.

Grandon did his best work alone. Spread before him on a long oaken table were his new coin collectors' album, a metal ammunition box of newly acquired treasures — and a numismatic encyclopedia of rare coins.

Next week he would retrieve his Nineteenth Century collection from The Numismatic Society in Washington, where he'd taken it for evaluation.

Above the table was a framed photograph of Grandon's Pearl Harbor shipmates. Laughing and carefree, they'd gathered for their last Kodak picture behind the railing of the *USS West Virginia.*

With his fountain pen Grandon had circled the face of the only friend he'd ever had. Everyone else had learned to avoid the scowling Grandon Tolson. But Mike Berning, with his pugilistic cocky grin, gave as good as he got — had insisted, with jabs, laughter and punches, that Grandon like him too.

Mike had a man's name — not like *Grandon*, which always sounded like some kind of piano.

In the swooping fiery Japanese attack, there had been no last goodbyes, no friendly punches to the shoulder. Mike had gone to the bottom of the harbor, in the coffin of the *West Virginia.*

Mike's grin reached into this spartan room, taunting him with memories.

To the left of this photo there was once an old snapshot of Mike, Greta and Phillip. But Grandon had replaced it with a newer print of Greta and Phillip — with himself in the middle, his arms around them both. For awhile, this threesome had been his family. But lately Phillip and Greta had gone to skulking in the shadows. Just out of reach.

He studied the faces for a long time, then shifted. He favored his left hip, where several pieces of *West Virginia's* hull had refused to yield to the surgeon's knife. That errant bunch of steel was keeping him out of the war — away from his need to avenge Mike. He frowned, his dark eyebrows beetling into a canopy.

He swung his chair around, listening. That infernal Bottle Man had stopped right in front of their house again. Grandon limped to the window and scanned the sidewalk. Nothing. Yet he knew Phillip was somewhere in the trees. And what did they do together, in their secret whisperings? What did they always seem to be passing back and forth?

He would check later. But not yet. He turned back to his album.

CHAPTER 12

Kate was awake. She'd been jolted out of a lovely, hazy dream at precisely 2:25 Monday morning. Now the Westclox read 3:10. Outside it was gray-shadowy with clouds drifting across the moon in jagged rifts. No light on the neighboring porch, just a dim glow from an upper room. But there was muffled noise, and lots of it. As if coming from a deep well, the sound crept up to her dormer window.

Who was yelling? Was it Phillip? Now a female voice. Or was it Phillip wailing? But Phillip never wailed, did he? And the dark threatening shout. Deep and hateful. So very quiet minutes at a time — an eerie tone pushing against Kate's eardrums, making a kind of whooshing sound. The uncle? Yes, it had to be Mister Tolson.

But what should she do? Wake Mother and Daddy? They had worked so hard yesterday, and Mother had another stomach ache. Let them sleep. She'd figure it out. She had to.

O'Dell shadowed the doorway. "Kate, c'n I come in?"

"Mm-hm." Kate lifted the blanket.

"I'm scared of that fighting, Kate."

"Me too." Patti appeared, rubbing her eyes.

Kate sighed. "You two get in the bed by the window. There's no more room here." She knew they'd start squirming and chattering like baby squirrels.

But tonight their voices were muted, their breathing full of jerky snuffles, their toes restless under the covers.

"Kate."

"What."

"Didn't that sound like glass breaking?"

"I don't know."

Patti went to the window.

"Patti, stop!" O'Dell's whisper was urgent. "Get down!"

"They can't see me. It's pretty dark in here. Wait. Now there's a light in the kitchen and someone is walking past the window. I see… oh, they're closing the drapes."

"Don't you get it?" Kate whispered. "They saw you, Patti! Now go to sleep and we'll figure this out in the morning." She turned to the wall. But she did not close her eyes.

"Kate. *Kate!*"

"I'm coming, Mother."

"Time to practice. You'll miss the bus."

Kate sat down heavily, rubbed her hands over her face, and lifted her music from the top of the piano. Open the assignment book. Scales, arpeggios, chords. Practice, practice, practice.

No. None of that. This morning she needed something else. A magnificent disruption of schedule. She needed rinsing. She needed to be wrung out. Kate got up, opened the piano bench and found Sindig's rippling Norwegian masterpiece: *Rustle of Spring.* There. Lift hands. Begin.

In the kitchen, Olivia paused. She knew Kate had strayed from her assignment. A knock on the wall was needed and she lifted her hand briskly. But as the sweet notes washed over her, she let her hand drop. Olivia had heard the voices too, and it sounded like breakage from long ago and far away. Yes, she needed rinsing too.

♪

O'Dell could not believe it. Phillip was yards ahead of her, had not waited near the woods when she yelled, did not turn his head.

"Phillip! Phillip, wait up." Coat open, book bag flapping, O'Dell huffed after her friend.

Phillip stopped but did not turn. His shoulders were hunched, head bowed. "Dellie, not now. *Please.*"

"But..."

"Not now." Phillip lifted his head, began sprinting for the woods. O'Dell scrabbled and clawed her way through brambles and vines, over jagged rocks, up the hill and across Vernon Street. More scrabbling, more rocks. Tears splashed on her book bag and her left knee had begun to throb.

There. Through the leafy branches. A boy running on Wakefield Street. Now she could catch him! Good smooth sidewalks, no Eddie in sight. She flung herself into the chase.

But once on Wakefield, O'Dell could not see Phillip. *Gone. Vanished.* He could not have run that fast. O'Dell leaned against a hickory tree, taking in huge gulps of air. "Oh, Phillip!" In her pocket she caressed the woolly lamb. But it was not enough.

Then she heard it. Tink, tink, tink. But with more clatter. Not on streets or sidewalks, but on the uneven ground that descended sharply from Wakefield's westward curve, into hardness and scrabble and little shrubby bushes. The rough pathway to the Settlement. O'Dell shuddered. She'd heard about the people living down there; had even seen smoke ascending lazily from some unknown depths. "Those people" could not be seen from the road. They were swallowed up in brush and steep descent. Everyone knew it was best to avoid them.

"Hey smarty pants! Wait up!" Patti and Veronica chugged through the path, breathing heavily and laughing. Lydia and Madeline were close behind.

Patti frowned. "How come you ran off? Didn't you see us waving?"

"I was looking for Phillip. He's not here. I think he's down there." She pointed.

Patti stared at the worn path where O'Dell pointed. "He wouldn't have gone there." She paused uncertainly. "*Would* he?"

"But he must've. First he was right in front of me and then he just... disappeared." O'Dell's voice trailed off.

"Those people came over on boats, I think. No one knows who they are." Veronica's voice was full of confidence.

Patti sidled up to O'Dell. "Don't talk about this to anyone, you hear? Just come to school. I bet we'll find Phillip in class. He just took a detour, that's all." Patti and the other three girls clattered along Wakefield Street, leaving O'Dell behind to listen and to wonder.

Mrs. Foster was not pleased. Arms folded across her purple-swathed bosom, she inspected O'Dell with a knowing glance. "Take this note to Mr. Brown, O'Dell. And when you return, you may copy the spelling list from the board."

O'Dell tried not to grin. Mr. Brown's cozy den was exactly where she wanted to be this morning. She didn't have to read all of Mrs. Foster's handwriting to know what the note said. In a few cryptic words its message was airtight: "Clean up this child and return her as quickly as possible."

♪

"Brownie?"

"Hmmm?

"Have you seen Phillip?"

Mr. Brown paused, pretending to find clean socks and a shoe brush. "Do you mean today, child?"

"Did he come to school?"

"Yes."

"Is he… is he all right?"

"He will be, I expect." Brownie gave her the socks and brushed the dirt off one of her shoes. He pulled up his metal chair and slipped O'Dell's scrubbed shoe onto her foot, holding it a moment.

"O'Dell?"

"What?"

"You are his friend, yes?"

"Yes."

The other shoe was put into place. Mr. Brown straightened, smiling wistfully.

"Tell your parents about him, O'Dell." He searched her face and found what he was looking for — a flicker of resolve.

"Now. Go." He walked across the room and pulled out the Hoover vacuum.

CHAPTER 13

It was good to be alone again, hanging laundry in her own back yard. The children were safely at school, and now there was time to breathe. But a backward glance revealed that she would not enjoy solitude for long.

Olivia watched her neighbor's slow walk across the grass. Greta Berning's auburn hair, usually in a tidy sweep, hung loosely across her face. The diminutive woman seemed to shrink as she walked, as if trying to become a child again. The aging collie Beauford clung to her side, stealing anxious looks at his beloved mistress.

Olivia finished hanging a sheet. She'd already practiced what she might say to Phillip's mother — sometime. But here was Greta in obvious distress. What kind of words does a person use for *this!*

"Oh, you're busy with laundry, Olivia. I can come back." Greta waved a Pyrex measuring cup. "I've just come to ask if you have any sugar. We're out of coupons and it's Grandon's… my brother's… birthday, and I…" The container lowered abruptly to her side. Greta bowed her head and shuddered one deep sob. "Dearest God, Olivia, you do not know. You just do not *know!*"

"Come into the house, Greta." Olivia took her neighbor's hand, leading her like a child. She paused an instant, then offered an invitation which would have shocked her children. "Beauford can come too." Indeed this dog clung like flypaper and it would have precipitated a howl of abandonment had he been left on the porch.

Olivia was not used to this. Quick and purposeful, she felt awkward having to measure each footstep and make it flow in tandem with slow, tender comfort. Her skirt touched Greta's, then began to swing with it as if they'd been wearing one garment.

"Sit here, Greta." The green chair again. Olivia had often sat there wondering whether her little brother would come home from the war. Now Greta sank into the deep cushions, wondering whether war had come to her home. Beauford sat very close, his white muzzle resting on Greta's knee.

Olivia pulled up a ladderback chair and reached for Greta's hand again. It was cold, and she didn't like the feel of it. Should she let go? She wanted something more to do than wonder how to hold hands with her neighbor. "I will fix us some iced tea. Do you like lemon?" Oh dash it all, asking about lemons. *It just would not do.*

"Please, Olivia. I don't need anything to drink. I just need you to listen. I'm afraid that if I don't say it all now I will never say it." Greta straightened a little and smoothed her skirt.

"Mr. Tolson is not my brother." Greta paused, willing Olivia to look upon her in kindness.

"I began to think that he was not, Greta."

"Yes. Well. Indeed he is *not!*" She spat out the word with such vehemence that Beauford pricked his ears and whined. "It was a decision I have regretted every day for the past three years. I can't… I mean I don't really know how it happened, Olivia. After Mike was killed at Pearl Harbor, everything was just one big muddle. And when I didn't have anyone to turn to, Grandon stepped in to help."

Greta leaned back, closed her eyes and sat still for a moment. "Mike and Grandon worked at the Munitions Building on M Street. The War Department has some offices there too — well, you know all that — so it was a good place to get an inside look at the armament buildup. They knew a lot more than most people. Mike always knew things." She smiled, remembering. "He had an adventurous spirit and I never quite knew how to handle that!

Well, one day he told me that he and Grandon were asked to spend a year at Pearl Harbor, and look into the Navy's readiness. They'd be stationed on the *USS West Virginia*." Greta covered her eyes and for a moment Olivia thought she might be crying.

Greta straightened and wiped her eyes in one brisk motion. "I knew there was no sense pleading with him not to go. We had a nice house in Falls Church and a good inheritance from my father. He knew... well at least he *guessed*... that Phillip and I would be all right. And so..."

Olivia waited. Beauford settled his head on Greta's lap.

"I never liked Grandon... there's always something... *hidden* about him. But he was polite to me. At first. And in the beginning he was nice to Phillip. Well, he just kept asking how he could help me... and one day... it was..." She stopped abruptly and entwined her fingers in a wringing motion. Beauford gave them one swipe of his tongue and nudged her until she smoothed his head. "It's okay, Beauford."

Greta raised her head slightly, looking into Olivia's kind face. "Last night..."

Olivia nodded. "Yes."

"Surely you heard us."

"Yes. Yes, we both did."

"Grandon found an old Liberty quarter in Phillip's jacket pocket. Along with some money. He accused Phillip of stealing from his wallet and from his coin collection. Said he'd been watching him for weeks."

Greta began to sob quietly, burying her face in her hands. "Olivia, I don't know how many 1870 Seated Liberty quarters Grandon had... I mean... he doesn't like me to go into his den, so I couldn't..."

Beauford cocked his head and whined, then wobbled to his

feet. He let out a hoarse bark and walked stiff-legged to the door, which opened with a whoosh and a clatter of feet.

"Mother, Mother! Patti's all bandaged and Eddie's dog bit her when we went back to school after lunch and Mrs. Lansing told her to come home early and I could come with her." O'Dell stopped to catch her breath. "Will she have to go to the doctor? Mrs. Lansing said she would and she..."

Olivia had risen suddenly, hoping to head off the thundering advance of her two daughters. O'Dell looked with surprise at the occupant of her father's special green chair. Both mothers seemed unable to respond.

But Olivia soon recovered. Finally, a crisis she could dive into. "Patti, let's take a look." Olivia pulled the edge of the bandage while Patti winced. "Well, it's not bleeding through, so there is plenty of time to get this fixed properly. But I think you should see Dr. Nabor just to make sure." Olivia lowered her head in thought, then fixed her eyes on Patti's face. "Do you think you could go alone in a taxi? It's just two miles down the road."

"Oh Mother," Patti wailed. "I can't go alone!" Then she brightened and grabbed O'Dell's arm. "She can come with me! She doesn't even have to leave the waiting room. Please, please, Mother!"

In the half second before O'Dell responded, Olivia felt a twinge of fear. If she let O'Dell go with Patti, here were all the triggers that could pluck her youngest daughter into a wailing mess. Dog bites, blood, taxi, doctors — the proven formula for meltdown! And in front of Greta!

"Oh could I, Mother?" O'Dell pleaded with shining eyes.

Olivia drew in one sharp breath, then ran to call Dr. Nabor and a taxi. If the wailing began, it would not happen in her already crowded living room. Let Dr. Nabor deal with it. Suddenly it seemed like a gift from Heaven. Yes. Let Dr. Nabor actually *see*, for once, what they were dealing with. Or were they dealing with it? It was all a bit surreal, this little daughter whose moods switched on and off like a lamp.

♪

"Well, lookit these two pretty young ladies ready to go to town! This is my lucky day!" The Checker Cab driver doffed her hat, spilling a mass of brown curls. "The lads aren't home from the war yet, so it's up to us women to do the drivin'! Hop in, girls. Name's Marge. Let's boogie!"

O'Dell scooted in next to Patti. The seats were hard and cracked, the old Plymouth rattling and gasping.

"Yep, can't get new cars til all the boys are home," Marge hollered over the chugs and clinks. "But this old gal can burn rubber! Oops, better not say that. I have to keep to thirty-five. Saves tires and gas, you know!"

"Patti," O'Dell whispered. "She said *boogie*." If this was boogie, with the discordant clinks and rattles, she was liking it less and less. "Do you like boogie, Patti?"

"Yeah, sometimes. I mean, Miss Bestor doesn't like it, but she said if she can make us play those Anton Reicha fugues then what's the matter with boogie!" Patti giggled, remembering the ancient piano teacher's frown and the way her little bun released straggles of hair when she was riled.

Marge boomed over the rumbles: "You say *fugue*? That's a funny word for music! I think it means 'running away' — at least that's what my brother says. Donny tried to get me to play them but I didn't like all those little notes bumping into each other!"

Marge swerved to avoid a downed tree limb. "I play the piano a little bit. You gals play?"

"Yes. We both do," Patti answered. But she needn't have said any more, as Marge immediately resumed her chattering. "Your mom said you're goin' to the doctor. That old dog take a bite outa ya?" She didn't wait for an answer. "Yeah, when I was a kid I was bit bad. They had to chain up the dog, find out if it had rabies." Her face loomed large in the rearview. "They gonna keep the dog that bit ya?"

O'Dell had begun drawing into herself. All this talk of wounds and rabies was discordant, pinging on her head. Why had she said she'd go with Patti! She pushed into the seat as far as she could, then wiggled and looked at the passing treeline on Old Dominion Drive. Cliffs dense and verdant seemed to rise straight up from the curb and she felt the terrain closing in. Suddenly she leaned forward, opened the window and thrust her arm into the wind. She felt she would suffocate in this new prison of medical chatter.

"Hey! Don't do that! You'll get yer arm knocked clean off! Boy, then you *will* hafta go to the doctor!" Marge laughed and revved the complaining taxi to forty.

Patti glanced sharply at her sister, who was turning pale. Quickly she dove into safe territory. "O'Dell, do you think Dr. Nabor would let us come to her farm again and see all the animals?"

O'Dell brightened. "Last time I fed a baby lamb. You know, the one with the bandage on its tummy." She chuckled at the memory. "He just came right up to me and I thought he was going to yank that bottle right outa my hand!" Sunny memories tiptoed into her mind, mixed now with the echo of bleating lambs and mewing kittens. She sighed and nestled into Patti. Stardust was safe in her pocket.

♪

"Here ya go girls! I'll be back in an hour! Think I'll grab me a malted." Patti and O'Dell alighted uncertainly from the back seat and pushed the door shut. The rattly Plymouth blasted a cloud of sooty smoke and merged onto Lee Highway.

FRANCES NABOR M.D. GENERAL PRACTICE AND PEDIATRICS, declared the sign on the glass door. Patti and O'Dell took great comfort in reading it slowly, examining the chipped white letters. They took their time over each word, seeking to stall the inevitable.

"Ladies first," boomed a kindly voice. A tall man with amazingly long arms reached in front of them and opened the door. "I believe you just go around this corner." They traversed a dim hallway and soon began to smell the faintly antiseptic air of the clinic. The passageway opened into a comfortably plain room filled with an assortment of straight and stuffed chairs. Against one wall sat a young mother with her sleeping infant. The man with the long arms joined them. Several seats over, a teenage boy with a cast on his arm looked up.

Behind the desk, a starched unsmiling nurse beckoned Patti. "You're the one with the dog bite? Shouldn't be long. Just have a seat."

"Does it hurt, Patti?"

"Not much." She settled back against the cushions. "I wish we didn't have to wait."

"I wish we weren't here at all." O'Dell was beginning to regret her plea to accompany Patti. She squirmed, kicked her feet a couple of times, then picked up a magazine. *Readers Digest* was a month behind the screaming victory headlines of April and May. There wasn't much to catch Odell's interest, until she saw *Zoot*

Suits That Save Sailors' Lives. "What's a zoot suit, Patti?"

"Huh? Here, let me see. What in the world? Maybe sailors wear them and it saves lives. I dunno."

"Oh."

"Patti Farnsworth." The starched lady stood with clipboard in hand. "Please come with me." Patti looked imploringly at her sister but the nurse was one step ahead of her. "You're O'Dell? Wait here please." But the "please" was not an "if you please." It was a command.

O'Dell slumped. Then she began studying others in the waiting room. Why did all these people have to wait for Patti, she wondered. They were there first. The mother smiled and beckoned with one finger. O'Dell moved closer and the mother pulled back a coverlet from her sleeping baby. "It's okay. You can come close. He's not sick. We're just here for his first checkup." She smiled at her husband, and paused to let O'Dell have a better look at the tiny mite with the red face. "His name is Broderick."

"Broderick. I've heard that name," O'Dell offered. "But I don't know anybody called that."

The mother smiled brightly. "Don't you think that's a fun name?"

O'Dell opened her mouth to answer but was suddenly arrested by a muffled cry from the next room. "Scuse me. Gotta go!" She trotted over to the closed door and heard Patti moaning. "Oh don't *do* that! It *hurts!*"

O'Dell pushed the door slowly. It opened without a sound. The nurse and Dr. Nabor were facing away. The doctor paused, waving a pair of gauze-wrapped blunt scissors for emphasis. "Patti. I am sorry this hurts. But we must make it bleed. When you came in here, your leg was barely bleeding. This is a deep wound and we don't want it to get infected, do we?" Dr. Nabor relaxed a bit and smiled at Patti. "Surely your father has told you that there is no true healing without blood."

Patti wiped her tears, shook her head, then narrowed her eyes in a glint of defiance. "Well then, just *do* it!" She squinched her face while the nurse held her hands and Dr. Nabor continued her gentle digging with the alcohol-soaked gauze. O'Dell watched as blood seeped in little rivulets down Patti's leg. The nurse wiped them quickly as the doctor kept digging.

O'Dell stiffened. "No… no… no… *no*." Her whispers grew softer and softer — until the only sound in the room was a little thump.

The youngest Farnsworth daughter lay crumpled on the floor.

CHAPTER 14

O'Dell?

"Mmmm."

"O'Dell, I'm going to put a pillow under your head."

The face above her was that of the starched nurse, who was all sweetness and fragrance of lavender now. The little girl melted into her light touch.

"Here's a warm blanket for you, and Dr. Nabor would like you to take a sip of this water, please."

O'Dell sipped, sputtered and coughed over the strange taste. The starched nurse, whose name was Marianne, wiped O'Dell's mouth with a white cloth.

"Where am I?"

"You are in Dr. Nabor's office. You can go home in just a few minutes, but we thought you might like to lie down while you wait for the doctor to finish bandaging your sister's leg." She gave O'Dell a little pat on the shoulder. "I will turn down these lights a bit. The doctor will come in to see you in just a few minutes. Oh, and Patti is doing so well, dear. She is a very brave girl."

The room dimmed slightly, with little musical murmurs of voices just outside the door. O'Dell moved her hand over her shirt and there was a moment of panic when she could not locate her little woolly lamb. But soon she found it beneath her shoulder. Yes, he was there, and she stroked the well-rubbed matted wool. She was getting a little sleepy, and she seemed to be sinking ever so slightly into the horsehair couch.

It was hard to see everything in the room, but directly across from her was a painting in a large gilt frame. She squinted, trying to bring it into focus. Something white. An animal sitting on a big rock? She concentrated very hard in the dim light. Yes. Now she could see. It was a very big lamb. She frowned, holding tightly to the woolly friend in her pocket.

As she focused, her eyes widened until she'd absorbed the whole picture. A coldness gripped her. Perhaps Dr. Nabor took care of animals, too. The lamb had *blood* on it. Was there no end of seeing blood everywhere? O'Dell shuddered. She lay very still and squeezed her eyes shut. She would not look. No, she would *not!* She waited, then began relaxing a bit and soon she opened her eyes a tiny slit and peeked again.

Slowly, her eyes adjusted to the dimness and she began to examine bits of the picture that she had not noticed before.

Maybe that's one of Dr. Nabor's lambs that was hurt, she thought. The lamb, resting on a big gray rock, was staring straight at her. And on its side was a very large red stain in the white wool. It looked as if it had been badly hurt. But the lamb did not seem the least bit upset by the injury. He was looking straight ahead. He was looking at O'Dell. There was a fierce gladness in his eyes. And did he just wink at her? Surely not.

"Do you like this picture, O'Dell?" Dr. Nabor walked to the sofa and sat on the end of it.

O'Dell startled. "Oh. I was just..." Her voice trailed off and she tried to think of something else to say. She studied the face of her family doctor. It was plump and always a bit red. Her salt and pepper hair was pulled back tightly, but one strand hung past her ear. It was a grandmother kind of face. Still, she was a bit afraid of this woman who could poke and prod.

"Is that lamb one of yours?" O'Dell said in a small voice. "Did you, I mean, how did you *fix* him?"

Dr. Nabor smiled and stared long at the picture. She did not answer for a few moments, and then her voice was so soft that O'Dell nearly missed it. "That is not someone I fixed, O'Dell. That is someone who fixed *me*."

"Oh." It was awfully hard to think. She took another long look. The lamb must not be well yet, but he looked at her with such joy that O'Dell was drawn into the picture.

Dr. Nabor chuckled softly. She hoped that in all good time she could tell her little patient how this Lamb kept her going at the very core of her being. She did not often share the beauty of her secret. Somehow, she thought, being a doctor meant you could not take advantage of a sick person's vulnerability. But then, this was different. This little patient needed more than bandages or medicine. She needed the Lamb.

"O'Dell, I was afraid of blood once."

O'Dell's eyes widened. "You were?"

"Yes. And I was also afraid that someone would find out what I had done, something I did not want anyone to know. And O'Dell, it was making me very sick and very afraid. I wonder, O'Dell, whether you are ever afraid someone will find out something about you."

It was quiet. So very quiet. It hurt, this new quiet. It swirled around the room and lit up the picture and caused O'Dell's heart to thump and bump wildly. But then a fresh courage welled up within her. Some hidden music played its golden tune of hope and trust, and helpless as she was, lying prone on the couch, she was curiously emboldened.

"Dr. Nabor," she whispered. "I stole some money." There! She'd said it! She could not wish it back or erase it or tell Dr. Nabor to forget it. Now it floated, waiting to be captured and held like a lost bird in a storm. A couple of minutes went by. Neither spoke.

Suddenly O'Dell sat up and leaned on one elbow. She said the very thing she had never spoken aloud. "And I killed our little dog!"

Dr. Nabor closed her eyes a moment, then took O'Dell's hand. She put her other warm hand on top and enclosed it gently until her little patient leaned back into the pillow.

"You do not need to tell me everything about it, O'Dell. I will keep your secrets. But you must not keep your secrets from this Lamb. You must find out his real Name and then tell him all about it. Because, O'Dell, this Lamb can wipe your blackboard clean, and it will be as if you never stole the money, never hurt your dog. This Lamb of Heaven can do something even better. He can cover your fear of blood with his own blood. He can..."

Suddenly Dr. Nabor remembered an old hymn from her childhood. She had not sung it in a long time and perhaps she would get the words wrong but she would try. She had never thought of herself as an especially good singer, but she did often sing — to her children, to her sheep, her cats and dogs and rabbits. Of course she could sing! Of course! She would do it now!

She cleared her throat and looked at the picture for courage, then hummed a few notes to get her bearings. Very quietly she began: *Are your garments spotless, are they white as snow, are you washed in the blood of the Lamb?* Her voice trailed off and she began humming more and more softly. She turned toward her little patient.

O'Dell was asleep.

CHAPTER 15

"Mrs. Farnsworth? Dr. Nabor here. Yes, Patti did very well. I'm afraid I had to be a little rough on that bite. But she is a brave child. I sent instructions home for keeping it clean and changing the bandage. I know that you are always very careful with such things, so I am not concerned." She paused and cleared her throat. "But I kept them both a little longer because I wanted to tend to O'Dell."

"O'Dell?"

"Yes. We had a little… incident here." Dr. Nabor heard a sharp intake of breath and hurried to explain. "O'Dell came into the exam room unannounced and watched me treat Patti. Apparently it was too much for her."

"Yes, we have been meaning…"

"I gave O'Dell a very weak dose of laudanum and had her lie down on the couch in my office. While the nurse was caring for her, Patti told me a little about your struggles."

She waited a moment. No answer from Olivia. Dr. Nabor continued. "Perhaps the one dose of laudanum was enough. I do not believe in extensive use of such remedies for little girls."

"And then?"

"And then if you would like my help, we can talk some more." Another pause, another silence. "Are you agreeable to this idea, Mrs. Farnsworth?"

"I will talk with Thomas. For now, I am agreeable. Thank you Dr. Nabor, for caring for our girls. I am most grateful."

"Of course, Olivia. Of course." Dr. Nabor lapsed into the familiar first name. Perhaps now there would be closer ties.

Frances Nabor had always wondered why she automatically called the Farnsworth parents by their last names. None of the other families drew her into that rigidity. With five children, two sheep, three dogs and six cats plus uncounted rabbits on her little suburban Washington farm, Frances had never been comfortable with the formality she was taught in medical school. For goodness sakes there was a very needy little girl in the Farnsworth family and she intended to do all that she could for her.

But she would wait awhile before talking with them about the picture in her office. Somehow it seemed best to sit face to face when holding up the Lamb of the Universe.

Marge had never had a fare like this one. Two little girls, one of them bandaged, the other woozy and pale, huddled into the back seat of her clanky Plymouth cab. She'd found an old blanket in the trunk, had tenderly wrapped it around the two of them. She checked the rearview frequently, then double-checked by turning around so often that Patti feared for their lives.

"We'll be home in no time, girls. No need to worry. It's a beautiful day. I'll take care of you. Just hold tight." Oh dear, she was babbling again. She never used to babble. But non-stop chatter filled in the dark chinks of her days, waiting for her brother Donny to come home from the war.

She revved the old metal bucket to fifty. Who cared if anyone saw her. She'd just do it. Just do it. This whole messed up war, with no way for Marge Newsome to do anything about it. Well, today she would do something. Even if it was making her old rattletrap shoot past the government speed limit. Yes sirree! Yes sirree!

In the back seat Patti huddled with her sister. "Dellie? Dellie are you okay?" No answer. But O'Dell sighed and melted into Patti, who moved her arm tentatively around the little shoulder. It was a new place for ten-year-old Patti, to be comforting and not teasing or playing or simply sitting or walking side by side. O'Dell murmured softly and did not move.

What should she do, Patti wondered. Maybe she could sing really quietly. That had always helped her think through things. Her glee club director had said Patti could sing those intricate classical tunes with amazing accuracy. It was fun to see just how far her young voice could stretch. She hummed a few notes to get her bearings. Maybe something from *Peter and the Wolf*. She had fallen in love with it, just as O'Dell had done when they'd listened to their mother's gift that winter. Each character in this classical masterpiece had his own signature tune and she relished Peter's the most. His melody had an invitingly wide array of stringed instruments, something Patti had always longed to try. Perhaps a viola next year.

She cleared her throat and began skipping through Peter's happy tune, hardly daring to sing past a whisper. "La la, da da ta ta," she sang softly, sinking into the music, willing it to wrap around O'Dell and bring her back to that pepper-and-sugar sister of happier days.

Inside O'Dell's foggy world, something sweet and bright tapped like summer rain on a bedroom window. She could feel Patti's arms around her and imagined it was Olivia. And it was good.

Thomas came home to a different world than the one he'd left. His briefcase lay untouched by the piano and he and Olivia talked sotto voce in their bedroom. Kate was put in charge of the kitchen, Patti was urged to sit with her leg propped up, and O'Dell had been hustled off to bed immediately following a hasty supper of Spam and toast.

"Come in the kitchen, Patti, and keep me company," Kate asked. "I'll bring in one of the dining room chairs." But once in the kitchen, Patti did not feel like talking, and Kate sudsed and scrubbed quietly, all too aware that she was again the odd one out, wondering what she should do. Dishes. Always dishes. She'd begin there.

"Patti, what was it like going without Mother in the taxi?"

Patti brightened. "Gosh, Kate, you should have heard the driver! She was a little unbalanced, I think. Patti had just discovered the word "unbalanced" and loved the way it rolled off her tongue.

"Unbalanced, huh? Like what, Patti?"

"Well, she… oh, I don't know. Not really unbalanced, Kate." She sighed and stretched and got out of the chair. "Ya know, I think I'll go to bed now. Maybe Dellie needs me."

"Night, Patti."

"Night, Kate."

Now Patti would be right where she wanted to be — hidden behind the bathroom door. She knew just how to open it slightly so she could kneel on the cold tiles and hear Mother and Daddy talking. She was sick of being left in the dark. Just last week she'd pulled the radio under the covers and listened to *Suspense* but had to turn it off when she'd heard her parents mounting the stairs. This time she meant to hear her parents' story to the finish. And most likely that whispered conversation would rival *Suspense*.

CHAPTER 16

Laudanum. Did you say *laudanum*?" Thomas repeated the word and then all was quiet for so long that Patti wondered whether her father had gone to sleep.

But in a few moments, Thomas resumed. "I've used it with farm animals, Olivia. In carefully administered doses it is a muscle relaxant and sedative. I've seen a belligerent horse calm down quickly." There was a pause. "But we were taught not to use it too liberally or for long periods. Always, we were told to balance efficacy with caution."

Patti wished her father wouldn't use such big words. Efficacy? What in the world was that! Maybe she could crouch a little closer to the bottom of the bathroom door, and that would put her just inches away from her parents' room. She pressed her knees against the tile floor. It smelled of Bon Ami cleanser and Squibb toothpaste.

Patti heard her mother sigh. "I don't like the laudanum idea, but I don't think Dr. Nabor intends to use it unless we ask her to. Perhaps we should work with her for awhile. I'm just plain tired of this. Just plain tired." Olivia sighed again.

"She did seem quite peaceful at the dinner table, didn't she."

"Yes. Peaceful. And sleepy. And that concerns me. Sleep is good but not drugged sleep, Thomas." A shifting of weight brought the creaky bedsprings alive.

There was a little mumbly whispering before Patti could hear her mother's voice again. "I talked with Greta today."

"Oh?"

"Yes. Greta and Phillip are in deep trouble." Her voice lowered ominously. "Mr. Tolson is not her brother."

"Well, I suspected that, didn't you? He doesn't look at all like her. I always thought there was something wrong."

"Thomas, he has been hurting Phillip."

Patti caught her breath. *No, no, no! Not Phillip!*

Thomas's whisper was sharp. *"Wha-a-at?"*

"Yes, he thinks Phillip has been stealing from him. The other night in all that shouting, he was slapping Phillip — said he'd stolen money from his billfold and rare coins from his collection. Greta said the biggest theft, according to Grandon, was a very expensive coin. Something like a Seated Liberty quarter, I think."

Patti could practically feel her father's frown and the steely resolve in his eyes. It swelled her with heart-hungry satisfaction. *Action. Yes!* Patti narrowed her eyes.

Tink tink tink. Patti heard the concert approaching from the south, mingling with early morning birdsong. Now the wagon must be at the Kiplinger house. She heard the wagon pause as Bodie lifted Mother Kiplinger's generous contribution of metal scraps into his wagon. When the tink-tink began again Patti knew he would soon be at Phillip's. She waited eagerly, willing him to emerge in front of their own yard. She waited. But no more tinks. Another few seconds. Silence. It was Saturday and so lovely to stay in bed for a few minutes longer. But that "non-tink" silence rattled in her brain. Where was he?

She pulled back the crisp sheet and touched the linoleum floor with her toes. Dampish. Drat! She'd left the window open all night to the rain. Patti yawned and came closer to the screen. Drops of water were trailing along the netting, and a finch darted into the ash tree just in front of her. She scanned the street. Where was he? Where… oh! Just visible through the feathery Japanese maple near the street. Bodie was fumbling in his pockets for something. He was talking to someone — someone who was hidden beyond the tree.

Suddenly she had to know, *must* know who was beneath that tree with him. Then, Bodie moved back a couple of steps, and there was Phillip. Surely no one could see the two of them from Phillip's house, not through those thick trees. Still, Patti gripped the windowsill in a near panic. "Don't move, Phillip, don't move," she mumbled. She raced on tiptoe to O'Dell's room. Adroitly side-stepping the creaky boards, she silently opened the door, pulling it gently closed behind her.

"Dellie… you awake?" She whispered as loudly as she dared. Patti knew she shouldn't waken her sister. Let her sleep, was the house rule this morning. But she could not wait to share the low-down on Phillip. She knew Dellie would help her solve this puzzle!

O'Dell turned onto her back, smoothing the hair out of her eyes. "Yeah. I'm awake. What time is it?"

"Don't worry about that. It's Saturday. Mother said not to wake you up."

"Then why did you?"

"Oh never mind that. Listen, Dellie. We've got to do something about Phillip!"

O'Dell wrinkled her brow. "I know. Brownie said we should tell our parents."

Patti was deflated. For hours she'd had juicy tidbits to relate, and Dellie knew it all! "Okay, wise guy. What do you know?"

"I just know that Phillip wouldn't look at me on the way to school a couple of days ago, and I think he went down that hill where all the strange people live, and I think… oh, Patti I think

Bodie was with him because I heard his wagon right after Phillip disappeared." She paused for breath, watching Patti's eyes glow. "I asked Brownie if Phillip was going to be all right and he said he hoped so and that someone should tell our parents and then the dog bit you and I just didn't."

"Is that all?" Patti couldn't wait to unload her gossipy dump truck.

"Whaddya mean, is that all! That's a lot, Patti!"

"Well, listen to this." Patti told her everything she'd overheard from under the closed door the night before. Right down to the rare coins and the Seated Liberty quarter.

The Liberty quarter! O'Dell's face got very white and a creeping coldness traveled down to her toes. She seemed frozen to the bed. All that soft comfort of a cozy sleep, the protective sinking into the mattress was gone. And now that bed was hard and unforgiving — a prison cell. She lay very still.

"Dellie what's wrong?" Now Patti was really alarmed. O'Dell had begun crying. "Oh Dellie, don't worry, I'm sure Mother and Daddy will be able to fix everything!"

"No... no... no. They can't fix *this!*" She buried her head in the pillow and sobbed out her breaking heart.

"Do you want me to get Mother, Dellie?"

"No! I do not! "No," she whispered. "*No.* Oh if only... if only *he* was here!"

"Who, Dellie, who?" Patti snatched at this crumb of help. Perhaps she could go and fetch someone to make it all right again, just as it had been in the taxi yesterday.

"Dr. Nabor said there was someone I surely know, Patti! Someone who's the only one who can fix me! But I don't... I don't know where he is!" And once again she buried her face in the pillow, her body contorted with new sobs.

"Phillip?" Patti whispered to herself. It didn't make a whole lot of sense, but she would grab the first thing that might help. She would go down to the street. She would disobey her parents and walk right up to Bodie and Phillip.

"Wait here, Dellie. I'll be back in a minute."

Grandon Tolson stood at Phillip's bedroom window, assessing the little scene that emerged now and then from behind the trees near the sidewalk. In his hand he gripped a metal object so tightly that it left a crease in his palm. The Liberty quarter, so precious in Grandon's collection, so condemning when found in Phillip's pocket. And where did all that cash in his other pocket come from? Surely Phillip must be stealing from him, the master of this house.

His heavy eyebrows creased like a canopy of storm clouds. *Phillip.* He had been a bane to his existence for three years. Hadn't Greta invited Grandon into her home? And as the man of the house hadn't he the right to direct traffic within its walls?

Phillip! Cocky, insolent brat. And Bodie! He mouthed the word in a snarl. That strange little impostor they called the Bottle Man. Always coming up suddenly out of nowhere. And Phillip was giving him Grandon's hard-earned money. Oh yes. He had watched and watched those little transactions. They thought he didn't know.

He pocketed the quarter and glanced around the room. He spotted the Senators bat, the baseball trophy that Phillip had said was a gift. He picked it up and slapped it against his hand.

CHAPTER 17

"Where are you going?"

Uh oh. *Kate!*

"Just outside. Just for a few minutes."

"You're in an awful hurry for someone just going outside."

"No I'm not. I just feel like running, that's all."

"I'll come with you."

Patti paused. "Um… okay." *What if Kate told Daddy!* What then! Well, she'd just have to take the chance. The two girls walked briskly toward the mailbox and started to turn at the poplar tree when Patti whirled and grabbed Kate's arm, whispering her fears. "Kate, Kate! Don't tell, okay? It's for Dellie. She really needs Phillip. Please, Kate!"

Kate smiled. "I could use a bit of adventure, Patti. But just please for once let me know what's going on, will you? Nobody tells me anything."

"Oh. I'm sorry, Kate. I was going to tell you everything tonight. Honest I was!"

Kate didn't look convinced. "So where are you going, squirt?"

"I've got to get Phillip! Dellie wants him."

The two were bonded, now, with secret mission. Kate shot one last look over her shoulder, checking the windows of Greta Berning's house which seemed to glower with hidden faces.

The closer they came to the stand of trees by the sidewalk, the slower they walked. By the time they reached Bodie and Phillip, the two girls appeared to be going for a summer stroll.

Patti would always remember the way the earth smelled in the glade of maples that morning. Pungent with sassafras, cool and damp and as still as a photograph. Like entering a different world, one of secrets and intrigue.

Phillip saw them first. He nudged Bodie, who turned and regarded them with polite reserve and a nod of his head. Phillip's smooth face was streaked with purple near his left eye. A shock of dark hair lay against one eyebrow. His crooked little smile, so endearing in happier times, was forced and rigid.

"Phillip. Please come," Patti whispered. "Dellie is asking for you." Phillip looked long and hard at Bodie, who raised his right hand in a little gesture of permission. "We are finished, ladies, and we wish you a gracious adieu." He bowed once again and arranged some scrap metal in his wagon.

Patti grabbed Phillip's sleeve and they hurried toward the house.

But Kate did not move.

Bodie and Kate regarded one another in appraising silence. Bodie spoke first. "You are the lead musician in your household, am I right?

Surprised, Kate was flattered but guarded. "No. No, I would say that my father is the more talented one."

"Yes. Yes, perhaps. His woodwind abilities are smooth and pleasant. Yes." He bowed his head in thought, then stood straight and held her eyes. "But you have a certain flair, Miss Kate. What the French call *élan*. And leadership." He turned to go, then lifted his eyes to meet hers. "Take care of your sisters. They have great need of your music." Swiftly he pulled the wagon into place and once again the morning was filled with the familiar tink, tink, tink as he receded down the walkway.

Kate turned toward the house, changed her mind, and plunked down on the lower step. She would just sit. Yes, she would not do anything for awhile but just sit. And she would do it with *élan*.

CHAPTER 18

Patti dragged Phillip upstairs past her mother's quizzical stare. "Dellie wants to see him," she shouted.

Clumping into the bedroom, she gasped, "Here, Dellie. Here's Phillip!"

O'Dell stared through red, swollen eyes at her friend, saw the purple welts near his eye and hid her face in the sheet. Phillip stepped back. "What's the matter? What did I do?"

"Nothing! Just nothing, Phillip. But Dellie's really upset and she told me to come and get you!"

"Dellie... Dellie," Phillip whispered. "It's okay. Just stop crying, stop crying." He sat on the bed and was nearly knocked off his perch when O'Dell lunged at him, grabbed him around the waist and began wailing. "Oh Phillip I didn't mean for you to get hurt, that quarter was just a... it was a... oh Phillip, oh Phillip! He hurt you just because of my dumb old quarter!"

She lifted her eyes to his face and suddenly she knew that she must tell him where that quarter came from. "That was the quarter I stole, Phillip! Yes, I stole it from a kid at school, and I put it in your pocket, and you're not going to like me anymore, and you won't be my friend." She collapsed against her pillows and renewed her crying in real earnest now, bringing her mother bounding up the stairs.

Olivia took in the scene. None of it made sense. "What is this? O'Dell, what on earth is the matter?"

"Oh Mother! Phillip is not going to like me anymore. He's not, he's not! And I stole that stupid quarter and I'm never going to do it again, and that lamb in Dr. Nabor's office can fix it on his big blackboard but I can't find him. I can't, I *can't!*"

Olivia rounded on Patti. Maybe she had some idea what in the world was going on. "What lamb is O'Dell talking about, Patti?"

"I thought she meant Phillip, Mother. But maybe it's what Dr. Nabor said yesterday. She said O'Dell saw a picture in her office, and there was a lamb in it and it made her happy and then we got in the taxi and… I just don't know anymore," Patti finished lamely.

Olivia turned abruptly and marched to the door. "I'm going to make a phone call. Someone knows what this is all about and that someone is going to tell me once and for all!"

Olivia nearly crashed into Thomas in her rush to the telephone.

"Olivia! What?"

"Hush, Thomas. Wait." She dialed, each rotation pushed heavily by a strong, purposeful index finger. Spinning, spinning. Five digits. Then she stood still, breathing heavily. "Miss Preston, I need to talk with Dr. Nabor. Yes, right now." She straightened, gripping the phone in an effort to clasp it to her will.

"Yes, Dr. Nabor, I need some answers. When O'Dell was in your office you talked to her about a lamb and a blackboard — something about a picture. Would you please explain that to me?" Her voice was staccato and tight. She stood rigidly, listening for long minutes. "I see. Yes." She softened and sank into the chair that Thomas offered. "Yes, Dr. Nabor, if you would, please. That would be much appreciated."

Slowly she put the black receiver onto its cradle and looked at Thomas for a moment without speaking. "Dr. Nabor is coming. She is bringing a *picture*."

Enough resting. Kate felt it her duty to return to the house. But it was nice to just move slowly and not be responsible for anything. She took one last look across the street at Madeline and Lydia's place, with its curving walkway and tiny doll-like home with a rounded door that always made her think of the Raggedy Ann house in O'Dell's storybooks. She tilted her face to the sky and closed her eyes. She could drink up the sunshine, let it caress her face. She was in no hurry. She opened her eyes and turned her head a little to the left. Her eye caught movement in the Berning house. Upstairs. A curtain flipping. Not a gentle closing, as Olivia would have done. It was a yanking — softly violent.

Now. Quietly get up, move toward the poplar tree at the bend in the sidewalk. When she reached the mailbox, she ventured another glance at Phillip's house and yard. Someone was moving their back door. She could just barely see the edge of it, as it slowly opened all the way. Kate positioned herself closer to the tree and was mostly hidden by the foliage that surrounded three sides of the mailbox. Now she could see who it was — Mr. Tolson, head bent, limping toward the edge of the lawn and the steep wooded hill. If he headed straight up through the brambles, he would soon be at Upton Street in the Porros' back yard.

Kate would not wonder until later, as she replayed the mental snapshot of those moments, why her next-door neighbor wore a bulky jacket too warm for a summer day.

Just as Kate entered the house, a 1940 gray Chevrolet coupe stopped at the curb. Kate could hear the driver lock the parking brake. *What's Dr. Nabor doing here*, she wondered. "Mother, it's Dr. Nabor. She just pulled up."

"Thank you Kate." Olivia hurried to the door, calling instructions over her shoulder as she went: "Oh, and Kate, please boil some water for tea. Let's have some real tea. And I think we can use some sugar this time." She turned back to the door, then made a final order. "And put it on that ceramic tray."

"Sugar. What's going on," Kate mumbled. "Daddy, why is…"

"Not now, Kate." Thomas was already at the door and greeted Dr. Nabor. Then the three of them started up the stairs. Under one arm the doctor carried a large flat parcel wrapped in brown paper.

Upstairs, O'Dell could hear the familiar slow, heavy footsteps which she identified as *Dr. Nabor's Visit*. There was a certain way the good doctor climbed the stairs, hesitated on the landing, all the while conferring in hushed tones with her parents.

O'Dell was getting that old prickly feeling. Did they think she was sick? Would she get the thermometer and chest-thumping treatment? She scootched farther under the covers. But wait. The footsteps had stopped. Now they were retreating. Then, the heavy footsteps belonged to the doctor alone! Then it was quiet for a moment before the door was pushed open and the doctor's smiling face peeked in, almost childlike as if harboring a secret. Dr. Nabor took in the assembled children and invited them to sit on the end of the bed. Patti and Phillip gave O'Dell sympathetic glances.

"Now. Here." Dr. Nabor peeled back the paper from the picture frame and propped it on the dresser. She let her hands fall to her side as she watched her little patient. The only sounds were Dr. Nabor's heavy breathing and the faint chirrup of robins in the maple.

"O'Dell, I have brought you the picture you liked so much. I think lots of people wanted to sit here with us and find out just what this picture is all about. But this is your special moment, and you are the only one who can decide how much to share with others. Would you like for Patti and Phillip to wait downstairs?"

"Please they can stay," O'Dell squeaked in a small voice.

Dr. Nabor pulled up the only chair in the room, carefully removed the pair of socks dangling from the knobs, and eased her heavy frame onto the wicker seat. "Now. I think you were a bit sleepy in my office and it's very important that you know what it's all about." She patted O'Dell's hand. "You may keep the painting for a few days, and you are the only one who may decide what to do with it while it is here."

At this, O'Dell propped herself up. She was beginning to feel guardianship of "the secret of the picture," as she would later call it, and sat very solemnly against the headboard, legs drawn up, hands clasped around her knees.

Phillip frowned in deep concentration, staring at the lamb. He had been wounded, too, in fact so badly hurt just a few days ago that he had been lying on the kitchen floor in his mother's arms. But no one was looking at him, so no one saw how brightly purple the welts had become in contrast to his white face.

Dr. Nabor was determined not to do all the talking. This was O'Dell's moment. The settling on the bed and in the chair had its quiet muffled symphony, then all grew quiet. The picture spoke to each of them with a soft intensity. Even the birds in the maple seemed to be listening. From downstairs they could hear muted murmurs and porcelain clinking as Kate made tea. Someone opened the screen door, let it gently close with a thud.

When Dr. Nabor finally spoke, her soft voice was like the hum of a low piano note. "O'Dell, do you know who that Lamb is?"

"Well, I don't know," she said. "He's a lamb and he looks very strong."

"Yes. That Lamb in the painting is Jesus. Do you know why he has blood on him?"

"Someone hurt him, I think… and… and I think you said he died."

"Yes. He died so that you wouldn't have to."

All three children wondered at this. In the picture the lamb looked so strong, like nothing could hurt him ever again.

"He came alive again, O'Dell."

The room was quiet and no one felt like moving.

Suddenly Dr. Nabor spied a bit of fluff on the dresser — O'Dell's woolly lamb. Reverently she picked up the smudged animal and turned it over and over in her hands. She did not know the story of *this* tiny lamb, but a quiet voice whispered in her heart: a*sk O'Dell.*

"Tell me about this little lamb, O'Dell."

In the living room Thomas and Olivia waited near the window. It had been a long time since they'd just stood side by side like this, looking at the street, taking stock of who they were and where they lived. Olivia was always moving the muscles she'd honed since childhood. Thomas, never one to waste motion, would hold a sheaf of reports from the office or thumb through one of his medical dictionaries while relaxing in the green chair. After all the running and worrying and fretting about the war and about their children, this newfound quiet and lack of movement was like a shield. It seemed right, somehow, to have nothing to do — to just let their minds rest. They were so very tired of trying to protect their little family.

They were almost surprised to hear Dr. Nabor begin her slow, heavy descent. She huffed toward the living room and sank into the green chair. Her smile was that of a child who has just found a secret. Olivia and Thomas waited expectantly as she found the breath to speak.

"O'Dell is a strong and honest little girl. You can be so very proud of her." Dr. Nabor took several more deep breaths. "She wants to share her thoughts with you, but perhaps it will take some time. She asked me to leave the picture. But a picture is not all that she needs. She needs the whole story." She looked at them both in turn. "And she needs the two of you to share it with her. That would be the best way." She rummaged in her purse and pulled out a pad, wrote a brief note and handed it to them. "This is where you will find it in the Bible, the story we talked about upstairs."

Olivia murmured, "Thomas, where is that Bible your mother gave you?"

"I have one." All turned to look at Kate, who had emerged from the kitchen with the tea tray. "Maggie Hardesty gave it to me." Kate looked timidly around the room, wondering why everyone was staring. "We've been reading it together." She stood a moment, set down the tray, and turned back to the kitchen. "I'll get the sugar."

"Well! I must hurry back." Now Dr. Nabor's childlike expression had changed to doctor-in-charge. "Miss Preston will not take kindly to my being late for Saturday clinic."

Thomas opened the door and watched their good doctor make her purposeful way to the car. He surveyed the neighborhood and sniffed the air. It smelled of damp earth and pine. It was eerily quiet. Everything seemed to be on hold. Even the Bottle Man was somewhere else.

♪

Olivia and Thomas would not have to climb the stairs to hear O'Dell's story. Their youngest girl was on a collision course, barreling down the stairs like a derailed train, her woolly lamb waving like a signal flag.

"Oh Mother, Mother! I took the quarter, I did and I wouldn't tell and Phillip got in trouble and he said it was all right and he's still my friend and this little lamb did it all." But the next words were buried in Olivia's blouse as O'Dell blubbered and laughed and reached her arms around her mother.

It took Olivia a moment to decide how to complete the embrace. Theirs was not a hugging family and the last time she'd held this little girl in her arms for any extended time had been three years ago in their last rocking chair session — which had ended with, "Now then O'Dell, you are getting too big for this, don't you think?" And of course O'Dell had obediently agreed, as her mother smoothed back her hair and straightened her barrettes and suggested she go outside to play.

But Olivia's day had been all about discovery and she was finding that a damp blouse and a drippy-nosed child was powerful balm to her soul. In muscled arms she lifted her daughter and walked to the rocking chair. The wide tapestry seat was a cradle they could share together. Olivia raised tear-stained cheeks to her husband and smiled in the way that had won his heart sixteen years before.

CHAPTER 19

Thomas started toward the bedroom stairway, then changed his mind and headed for the basement. Whatever was in that picture was something he wanted to see by himself. Surely something had happened in O'Dell's heart and he wanted to be a part of it. But he would get there by his own clock. No family meetings, not now. In the meantime he yearned to fix something, and the basement was a good place. He passed through the kitchen and saw Kate cleaning up the tea party that had never begun.

"Dad, would you like some tea?" Kate offered a steaming cup, glad they could finally use Irish Breakfast tea instead of the wartime "white tea" of hot water and milk. "Mother said it was all right to use sugar."

Thomas was about to wave the offer away when he hesitated. "Yes, Kate. Yes, I would like that very much. Please pour a cup for yourself and come out to the back porch with me."

The two settled companionably on the back stoop, sheltered by a cedar-slatted overhang that sported a family of hungry robins.

"Dad," Kate began. She had experimented with this short moniker, thinking that age fourteen was a bit too old for "Daddy". After all, they'd called Olivia "Mother" and not "Mommy" for as long as she could remember. Sometimes she wondered why, but deep inside she knew the answer.

Kate sipped some scalding tea. "Dad, can you tell me more about what's happening to O'Dell? Everyone, I mean everyone except me, has some part in it and today is just... is just one huge *enigma*."

Thomas cleared his throat, took another sip of tea. "Well, Kate, the surprises just keep coming, don't they. But today, there is something that feels kind of like a clearinghouse." He straightened his shoulders and looked around at the flat lawn that ended abruptly against wooded hillsides on the north and east, taking careful note of a patch of lawn that could use some grass seed.

"Kate, have you ever watched a magnet pick up iron bits?" He set his cup on the concrete, stretched his arms a little to both sides and looked intently at his oldest girl. "You can scatter those filings onto a flat surface, then..."

"Oh yes! Yes! Our science teacher showed us that!" Kate gestured with her hand held high. "Then you take a magnet and hold it above, and watch all the little filings come into a pile!"

Thomas smiled. He was beginning to enjoy this grownup relationship with his daughter, and relaxed into the peace that settled over them both. "That's how it seems today, Kate. We've been covered in filings for months, trying to brush them off a little from time to time, but somehow they don't seem to leave."

Kate stared at her father. She had never seen him so vulnerable. Always cool and serene, the quintessential attorney, his conversations centered on methodical discovery, analytical questions and calm deliberation. It was nice, just sitting like this. They were quiet a few more moments. Then they could hear the faint echo of the front screen door thudding closed, and soon they spotted Phillip striding across the lawn, head down, aiming for his back door.

Thomas drained the teacup and bowed his head a moment. He turned to study Kate's expression, and decided to respect her judgment. "I'm worried about that young man."

Kate looked into her father's face. "I am too, Dad." Both sat still, wondering what to do with this grownup bond. Then Thomas stood, gave back his teacup, and headed for the cool basement.

Upstairs, Patti was alone with the picture. It was strange to be in Dellie's room by herself. Even the birds near the screens sounded different in here. Patti frowned in concentration. Her dog bite had begun to sting a bit, where the bandage competed with healing skin, and she reached down to rub it — an action she knew would not help — but she did it anyway. She sat on the bed, smoothing her hand over the bandage, and stared at the painting in its gilt-edged frame. There was something she was trying to remember. Something that was voiced while Dr. Nabor was beating up on her leg (or at least that's the way it had felt, and it was good to put it into words at last).

Patti plopped herself against the pillows and tried to imagine that strong lamb lying weak and helpless and covered in blood. Her mind flashed back to their little beagle and the horrific mangled mess after the car had hit him on Thanksgiving. There was plenty of blood then, all right, and it had smeared all over Dellie's pinafore and dripped into her socks. Patti shuddered, remembering.

But no, that wasn't quite it. That wasn't all she was supposed to remember. There was something else — something so different from the way she had always thought about wounds and injuries.

Oh, oh, *oh!* Yes! That's it! She could almost feel the digging into her leg and the voice that accompanied it: *There is no healing without blood.* Patti drew in one long breath and stared very hard once again. But as she remembered she thought it strange, very strange. Because if Skippy was all covered with blood, and this lamb supposedly was covered, and they both died, how could the lamb come to life again? But she really didn't feel like asking anyone. Not now anyway. She'd had enough exhausting thought for one day. This was a little puzzle she would tuck away and try to solve by herself. But not on an empty stomach! She scooted off the bed and sprinted down the stairs, hoping to find Kate's cookies.

"Kate! Got some cookies? I'm starved!"

Kate reached for the top shelf and scooped into the raisin-oatmeal treats she'd made in home economics class. She winked at Patti. "Don't spoil your lunch, now."

"You're not my mother," Patti called over her shoulder as she fled into the living room. "Mother, okay if I run over to Madeline's?"

Olivia paused in her rocking. "Sh-h-h. O'Dell's asleep." She repositioned her little bundle. "Well, yes, all right, Patti. But don't stay long."

"Mph. Okay. Bye!" Patti's mouth was full of cookies, her feet full of adventure. Fresh air, freedom, a new destination! Too much to think about inside this house, and she didn't want a bunch of questions about her feelings or her dog bite or *anything!* She opened and closed the screen quietly, then clattered down the front steps to the sidewalk.

Olivia scooted toward the end of the cushioned rocker seat, lifted her daughter to a new position and wondered just how her little girl had grown so big in such a short time. She padded across to the sofa, laid the child against a pillow and covered her with a light blanket. Then she stretched tall, and soon her mind buzzed with plans for making lunch and doing laundry. Time to take command. "Kate, come and help me fix some sandwiches."

Kate paused. Was there no end to *Kate do this* and *Kate do that?* Well, it wouldn't do any good to complain. The sooner she helped in the kitchen, the sooner she could bike to Gretchen's. She'd made plans for her Saturday afternoon and hoped Mother remembered. And then, maybe sometime this evening, she would steal another peek at the mysterious picture. But not now. Not now.

♪

O'Dell snuggled into the sofa pillow and opened one eye. She was beginning to waken and she heard bells. Tiny bells. Ringing ever closer. Then stopping, then starting. The same little tune over and over again. Had she heard them before? She rubbed her face and called for her mother. Olivia appeared, wiping her hands on her apron.

"Mother, who's ringing the bells?" Olivia stood for a moment, listening. She went to the window and looked up and down the street. From all over the neighborhood, children poured onto the sidewalks, yelling.

"Girls, girls! It's the Good Humor Man! It's his first trip to Arlington! Oh dear! Where's my *purse!* She darted into the closet. "It was in Sunday's paper but I didn't think they would come this soon! Oh, where is my purse!" She was a girl again, caught up in the chase. "Hurry, Kate, O'Dell! I think it's time for a party, don't you?"

Outside, Vermont Street had come alive. Patti and Madeline were laughing and jumping up, trying to see over the taller children's heads, hoping to be the first to find the gleaming white truck as it slowly made its way north from Old Dominion Drive.

"Am I too late?" Veronica came running up the street with her Scotty dog in tow.

O'Dell pulled her into the circle with the other children. "No, it's just by Kiplingers'. Here. Stand by me." Gratefully, Veronica clung to O'Dell's hand, trying to spot the truck. Her little black dog sat still as a stone, frightened of the pressing crowd.

Kate leaned toward Veronica. "Do you think Mother Kiplinger bought anything? Wouldn't it be fun to see her eating ice cream on a stick?"

Veronica widened her eyes and pursed her mouth in a big "O". Kate chuckled at the thought of Mother Kiplinger. The old woman always sat erect and queenly, hair the consistency of spun sugar, complexion like the insides of those half-ripe persimmons she snookered the neighbor children into tasting. And always, a rose in her jacket and a kindly smile as she offered pink lemonade and delicate meringue cookies to the little guests she treated as royalty.

Mother Kiplinger would almost certainly stay on the veranda, sitting erect on her porch swing, smiling and nodding. But quick as a rabbit, little Riley Bascomb darted out from Mother Kiplinger's basement apartment and held out his nickel to the patient driver, who reached into the frozen cavern of his truck for a double-flavor Popsicle. Immediately Riley tore the paper from his frozen treat and began licking first the raspberry side, then the orange.

The bells jangled once again as the driver inched down the street. Closer and closer crept the white charger driven by his noble knight, fairly magnetized into motion by all the coins held aloft by thirteen children. *Where did they come from,* Kate thought. *I didn't know the street had that many kids!*

The truck slowed and the driver was nearly mobbed. Although most of the neighbors had tasted Good Humor ice cream in the District of Columbia, the menu had to be patiently explained at each stop. Finally, Patti and O'Dell settled on coconut covered ice cream. Olivia asked for a Toasted Almond bar, and Kate knew instantly that only the plain chocolate-covered ice cream was what she wanted. Already she felt the thin coating crackling in her mouth.

Veronica hung back, fascinated by the clamor, the bells and the tinkling fairyland of opportunity. Timidly she approached the sweating bear-like man in the white coat. "I will have an orange covered ice cream… thing," she said in a small voice. "If, if that's all right." Everyone laughed as the driver whipped out the frozen Creamsicle and extended it to his little customer with a knightly flourish. "Here you go, my lady fair."

But Olivia was not finished. She fumbled in her apron and whipped out two dollars. "Here! I'd like a dozen more chocolate-covered ice cream bars." She stood silently as the driver reached into the back of the freezer and brought out a full box. She pocketed the change, set the package at her feet and began working through the Toasted Almond bar.

Kate, O'Dell and Patti watched their mother eating her ice cream. But they also kept a watchful eye on the curious box of frozen bars.

Veronica had stopped eating, absorbed in the spectacle of all that chocolate covered largess sitting on the curb. Her ice cream dripped along her hand, then into the waiting mouth of her dog. She glanced down in alarm, took some sloppy swipes of her Creamsicle and unwound Scotty's leash. "Oh dear, gotta go! Bye!"

Olivia waved to Veronica, finished the coconut bar and wiped her mouth on a corner of her apron. She picked up the box of chocolate bars and smiled mischievously at each of her daughters. She opened her mouth to say something, changed her mind, and headed for the house.

The three girls studied their mother's brisk walk. Silently they worked their way to the wooden sticks inside the ice cream. Their mother had stayed for the brief roadside picnic, and for now, this sweet, cool pleasure was enough.

CHAPTER 20

"Last day of school!" O'Dell and Patti flew down the stairs in their pajamas and scooted onto their breakfast chairs. No piano practice on Wednesday, June 6, the sparkling last day. No lessons or homework or sitting in rows. There would be races and special treats, speeches and the solemn crowning of "Miss Scholar" and "Master Scholar" for every class. It would be "just so *allegro*," Patti announced over her scrambled eggs.

Kate had fled the merriment a half hour before, hoping to meet Gretchen at the bus stop. The final day for her was not met with the same joy of freedom shared by her younger sisters. Summer loomed open before her with a new paper route and the burden of added household chores. Olivia and Thomas had just announced their bold plan to raise chickens in the backyard. Not a half dozen cute little fluffy things, but *fifty* of the peeping pests! Gretchen dramatically described the smelly brood next to their family garage and the extra work of maintaining their Victory gardens. But Kate wasn't about to claim victory if it meant gathering eggs and cleaning out the laying house.

It wasn't that Kate did not want to help her mother. It wasn't that she did not have the extra strength. Indeed, she was endowed with well-toned muscles, lightning-fast reflexes and a quick mind for detail. But at nearly fifteen, blossoming youth yawned before her: friendships and the girls' club called Jibbers, freedom to take the bus into the city, and... *just leave me alone*, she would think far too often.

She had studied the painting of the Lamb. She had read the story about Him and shared it with Maggie Hardesty. She knew deep inside that there was power and love just waiting to be tapped. But where did she fit into all this? There didn't seem to be any seismic shifting of pain or releasing of fears or confessions as there had been with Dellie, who was practically sizzling with freedom, she noted with envy.

In the meantime, she would just keep plugging away.

♪

"Race ya!" Patti flew out the door, nearly slamming it in Dellie's face.

"Hey! Wait up!" O'Dell grabbed her book bag, changed her mind and threw it into the living room. "I'm coming, *I'm coming!*"

It wasn't until they merged onto Vernon Street that O'Dell missed her friend. Stricken, she wheeled around. "Stop, Patti, stop! Where's Phillip?"

"I think he went on ahead. I thought I heard his door slamming just before we went out."

"Oh. I just thought… I thought maybe he would wait for us."

"It's okay, Dellie. Last day, remember? Everything's different." Then Patti spied Madeline, Lydia and Veronica. "Wait, you guys! We're coming, we're coming!"

But for O'Dell, what should have been a joyful parade had discordant tones and mismatched steps.

♪

Safe in her pocket was a Seated Liberty quarter. O'Dell had asked her father where she could get one, and he had gallantly taken her on the bus to the Washington Numismatic Society

Clubhouse and treated her to a chocolate soda on the way home. And there at the Club, with her hard-earned money plus generous loans from Patti and Kate, O'Dell had bought an 1870 Seated Liberty quarter for five dollars and forty cents. She had heard somewhere that when you borrow money you must pay it back with interest, and so with the quarter carefully wrapped in tissue paper, O'Dell had written a hasty note to Ricky:

I am sorry that I took
your lunch money resently
it was an awfull thing to
do and I hope you will forgive
me. I talked to the lamb
and he said this is what I
shuld. I am your intrested
frend (I hope). O'Dell Farnsworth.
Anuther thing this is the
same kind of quarter you had
but it is werth more than
25 cents it is very old
and I had to spend $5.40 on it.

She had just slipped the package to Ricky when Mrs. Foster's voice rang out. "Class, eyes front! Today we have something to celebrate." She smiled brightly scarlet. "I have looked at the grades, I have looked at your conduct record and I have chosen two outstanding students to come up here and let you applaud them. Please come forward, Miss Scholar — Gracie Manson!"

The clapping and the cheering! And O'Dell was one of the loudest, which thoroughly surprised her because a week ago she would have burned with envy. She and Gracie had always vied for first place. But now it was good to give way to noisy affirmation, and no one thought anything about being little ladies and little gentlemen. This was the last day — the *last day* of school. They would push the envelope, do what they liked, because in just a few minutes they would be high and mighty third-graders!

"Children! *Children!*" Mrs. Foster frowned and smacked the desk. "Class, I know you are excited, but please remember that you are still in school! She paused, giving the children a slow, appraising look. "And now, Master Scholar Ricky Stoddart will please come forward."

O'Dell clapped and stomped her feet! This felt like redemption, reward and payback all rolled into one. She'd wanted to do something extra for Ricky, and paying back the debt had just not seemed enough. As the clapping died down, she turned to see Brownie glancing into the room with his sweet, tired smile.

She went into this room every day, to find laundry, retrieve dirty dishes, check the wardrobe, and get a sense of what her youngest daughter was up to. But today Olivia felt like a trespasser, almost guilty as she pulled up a chair and sat in front of that picture. She darted quick looks at the door and started at every little sound. "Olivia, you are ridiculous," she said aloud. "No one's in the house." What was it, then? What made her tingle inside her soul, waiting for something?

Waiting for what?

The Lamb was looking at her. But no, he couldn't be. It was just a picture. *All right, all right, I'll look back and look hard. So be it.* And the more she looked, the more she saw. The boulder on which it lay so serenely was much too large for the terrain — sticking up out of the ground almost as if daring other rocks to come forth. She sat quietly studying it. Now she saw. It had a crack running down the center. She hadn't noticed that before. Barely discernible, it traveled straight underneath the Lamb's side and continued toward the ground. You'd think a crack would be bold and random, not precisely cut as with a surgeon's knife. Not absolutely plumb with the ground.

"Oh Pfaw!" she muttered. "You're making too much of it, Olivia! Stop examining." But she didn't. And what she saw sent a plumb line through her heart.

"No more pencils, no more books, no more teachers' dirty looks!" O'Dell raced by the chanting sixth graders, surprised at the disappearing figure of Phillip Berning, who had slipped out of the schoolyard ahead of the pack. She disentangled herself from babbling friends as quickly as she dared, hoping to snatch a few moments with Phillip and find out for herself just what was going on inside that frowning head. Unencumbered from both book bag and coat, O'Dell ran down the highway's narrow shoulder but Phillip was already at the corner of Twenty-fourth Street. A whole block ahead! Feet pounding, heart racing, O'Dell gasped and willed her wobbly legs to push faster. With relief she noted the crossing guard at the intersection. Phillip would have to slow down!

But no! Phillip darted across Old Dominion Drive against the guard's outstretched arms, dodging cars from both directions. He'd have an angry blotch on his conduct record, but who would see it now? He was a graduated sixth grader, out of the reach of John Marshall School. O'Dell could be a lawbreaker too, couldn't she? But wait. There was fifth-grader Barney Todd with his canvas shoulder tape, standing guard at the corner. Sweet, thoughtful Barney, who was already smiling at his oncoming friend.

She couldn't push past him into oncoming traffic.

Or could she?

She could. And she did.

Barney yelled for her to come back, then slumped his shoulders in frustration. All that was left to this pint-sized law enforcement agent was his notepad, and he gave it a good scribbling.

O'Dell was beyond exhaustion. Her legs kept working, but they felt like they belonged to someone else. Her lungs could explode any minute, she was just sure of it. But she would not — could not — slow down. She must find Phillip!

At the rise of the hill, where he should have plunged straight into the woods for the brambly shortcut, the whizzing figure veered left, down the hill, down that mysterious hill to the settlement of unknown inhabitants. The steep dirt path soon swallowed him up and O'Dell collapsed onto the sidewalk. She knew where he was now. And that was both a comfort and a terror.

She longed for some of Patti's or Kate's good sense and courage. But they weren't here. She would have to brave it alone. She touched the woolly lamb in her pocket, but today she knew something different. There was something more powerful than a bit of fluff. Today she knew that the real Comfort couldn't be seen. She would ask Him for help and just keep putting one foot in front of the other.

CHAPTER 21

Betty Loman pulled back the bedroom curtains for a better look at the slumped child by the curb. Wasn't that the same little Farnsworth girl that her daughter Marilyn had lured into the house last September — had left locked in the basement for nearly an hour? She shuddered at the memory and the shame. She should never have gone back to work and left her children with that do-nothing housekeeper. Oh yes, help the war effort, wives and mothers. Go back to work! Well, she knew where her work began and ended, thank you very much!

She trotted down the stairs in a huff. *I must help that child,* she murmured. *Quick before Marilyn gets home.* It was the least she could do. But by the time she opened the door, O'Dell had already made it to the east end of the street. And wasn't she veering left, over the hill to *that* place?

Betty went to the phone.

I know Phillip went down there. Maybe... maybe I should just go home. But first just a few steps... and then home. O'Dell walked into the high grasses — thick and soft — almost like the veld in Kate's *National Geographic*. Were there lions here? No, there couldn't be. "Silly," she said, mimicking Patti's confident voice. It was just a whisper, yet it sliced through the stillness like a bullet.

A few more steps, and suddenly she was caught up in a strange excitement. She knew now that she really *wanted* to keep going on the sharp downward slope of the hill — the one that always hid "those people" from view. And now she was there.

Out of sight. Alone.

It brought her into a new place of hiding, but she did not know how to deal with it. Neither did she know what to do with the quiet. It was a heavy silence, damp and confining. Mosquitoes hummed, and somewhere a dog barked. She kept walking. The grassy slope thinned to a rough path.

"What ya doin' in my backyard?"

O'Dell froze. "I… I'm sorry. I didn't know this was your place. I thought it was just the path."

"Well it ain't the path. And you're steppin' all over m' soldiers."

O'Dell looked down. Little wooden sticks lay in rows. "You mean these?" She stooped to pick them up.

"Don't touch them!" A big voice from one so little. "Let them die where they falls!"

"Oh."

What should she do now? She looked at the boy and waited for him to speak again.

"Wa-a-ll… guess it don't matter." He looked at her sharply. "You wanna play?"

O'Dell studied her little adversary turned ally. He couldn't be more than six, with olive skin and a wild mop of black hair. His oversized shorts hung on tiny hips. He had no shirt.

"I can't. I mean, I'd like to, but I'm looking for my friend."

"You mean that big boy that allus comes down here? Look like he been knocked in th' face?"

"I think so. Maybe. It sounds like him." She waited for further information. The pint-sized owner of the backyard poked his thumb toward the bottom of the hill. "Down yonder. Place with th' mean dog." He started to walk away, then fished in his pocket for a sticky piece of taffy. "Here. Take this. Tho it at that dog when he come at ya. He likes it when ya feeds him. An' if ya wants ta find me again, ask fer Champy."

The rest of the downward trek was like a dream. Through waist-high grass one moment, bare pathway the next. Now the sound of chickens and the smell of something cooking. Then a hut emerged, its chimney pipe emitting a lazy smoke. Now another hut, and O'Dell could see Phillip. His back was to her, and he was gesturing with great force to a tall man in bib overalls who faced him with folded arms, bowed head. Suddenly a large peppery-gray mongrel stalked toward her on stiff legs, ears flattened, lips peeled back in a snarl. O'Dell stopped, uncertain. She fingered the taffy.

Phillip glanced back. "O'Dell! *What?*"

"Back, Goober!" The Overalls Man shouted one staccato command and the dog flopped to the ground, head between his paws.

"Kate!" Olivia clunked down the receiver and yelled again. *"Kate!"*

"I'm here. I'm here, Mother. What do you want?"

"Oh Kate! I need you to go find O'Dell! She might be in big trouble! Mrs. Loman saw her go down that hill from Wakefield. She was way ahead of the other children and going like the wind! Patti came home forty-five minutes ago and went to Madeline's house. She hasn't seen O'Dell since this morning."

"But what do you want me to do?"

"You remember how to take that shortcut through Vernon Street. Go! Go as fast as you can. I don't know those people down there, Kate! Anything can happen, anything can happen! Just go!"

Olivia slumped into the green chair while Kate ran to get her shoes. But Olivia had no sooner settled than she leapt to her feet again. "Kate! Stop! You can't go down there alone! I'm coming with you!"

♪

"You shouldn't have come! What'd you want to come down here for, anyway!" Phillip's contorted face put his purple welts into sharp relief. He gripped her shoulder.

"Ow. Phillip, you're hurting me! Don't!"

Phillip dropped his arms, slumping in defeat. "I'm sorry, Dellie. I'm sorry!" He turned his face to hers, looking intently into her eyes for a long moment. He sighed deeply and took her arm more gently. "Come over here with me, Dellie. Sit down."

O'Dell worried that the dog or the man would follow, but a quick glance told her that both had stayed rooted like stumps. O'Dell was glad to sit quietly in the thick grass, where she spread her rumpled dress around her in a circle.

"I don't like it when you shout at me," she whispered. "And I'm sorry I ever came down here!" Angrily she wiped hot tears from her face.

"Dellie, Dellie don't. Here." He fumbled in his pocket for a wrinkled bandana. "It's okay. It's okay." He wiped her face tenderly. "Gosh, don't you look like a muddy toad!" He giggled and punched her arm. They sat comfortably silent for a few moments.

Finally Phillip whispered, "We can't find Bodie."

O'Dell drew in her breath sharply. *"Bodie?"*

"He was living down here. But I think you kind of knew that, didn't you?" A slight nod encouraged him to continue. "Now he's gone and his wagon isn't anywhere. I know because we've looked." He jerked his head toward the big man down the hill. "Reuben lets him stay down there. Said it's been four days and no one's seen him." He buried his face in his hands. "And Miss Bestor wanted me to give him another note." He hesitated, scanning her face for marks of trust. "And some more money."

"Notes and money? Why? I thought he just collected bottles. How come he goes… ?"

Phillip sighed. "Okay, Dellie, it's… look, you can't tell anyone, not *any*one, you understand?"

O'Dell nodded, eyes wide.

"Bodie writes things."

A tiny whispered *oh* from O'Dell.

"Miss Bestor pays him for that."

"Do you read them?"

"I can't. Well, I mean I can, but I don't know what they mean. I just know Miss Bestor's always happy to get them."

"What kind of things, Phillip?"

"Sometimes it's just alphabet letters. And tiny letters sitting on top of them."

"What do the letters say?"

"They don't really say anything. It's just a jumble of letters and boxes with lines in them and one time there were odd shapes with little letters inside… and sometimes *largo* or *rit* or *arp* — things like that. But sometimes Miss Bestor gives him bigger envelopes and I don't open those."

"And Miss Bestor gives him money?"

Phillip turned sharply. "Quiet… I thought I heard someone."

O'Dell looked behind her. "I don't hear anything."

They sat still, listening. But the only sound was the hum of mosquitoes and the distant drone of traffic from Old Dominion Drive. Goober barked once.

Phillip looked at O'Dell, frowning. I have to go now. Remember, Dellie… don't… tell… *any*one!"

"I said I won't. She grabbed the bandana out of his hands and wiped the tears from her face. "And I *won't!*"

"I know… I know you won't."

O'Dell gripped his hand. "And don't worry, Phillip. I think the Lamb will find him."

"Who?"

"You know, the Lamb in that picture. Here." She fumbled in her clean pocket, the one without the sticky taffy. "This lamb's not… you know… the real Lamb, he's just my woolly toy. But it reminds me of the Lamb and Dr. Nabor said if I ever got into trouble I was to ask the Lamb for help." She could see that Phillip was not buying it. "You know, the one in that picture in my room."

"Guess I didn't look at it very long, Dellie." He grimaced, remembering. "I had other things to think about." He stopped, seeing the disappointment in her eyes. "But you ask him, Dellie. You ask him. Okay?" He stood abruptly, checking his watch. "Uh oh. Gotta go. It's almost four o'clock and I told Miss Bestor I'd come after school."

O'Dell scrambled to her feet. "I hafta get home too! Mother's gonna be really mad!" She scrambled up the hill, careful not to step on the dead soldiers.

Phillip raced past her and reached the road first. He nearly collided with Eddie Johns, who was rounding the curve toward home. O'Dell saw his hunched shoulders, the clipped swagger of his walk. She quickly darted into the brambly path before he could turn around and investigate the sound of her footsteps.

"Where ya goin', big boy," Eddie sneered. "Running back to that old lady and her night caller?"

Phillip paled. "Night caller?"

"Yeah, I live right behind her house, remember? Sometimes I see 'em talking in the dark, on her back porch. Once it was midnight." Eddie snickered. "Yeah, and they do some of that piano stuff too." He laughed and sprinted for home. "See ya, Mister Messenger Man!"

O'Dell plowed through the prickly undergrowth, scratching her arms and legs. "I don't care I don't care I don't care!" Her head was too full of hurts and questions and adventure and alarm. She just wanted to get home and find someone to take care of her for awhile.

Kate emerged, panting up the hill. "Here she is, Mother!" I found her!" Kate glared at her little sister. "Where have you been! How could you do this to us? We've been out looking for you! All you ever think about is yourself!"

O'Dell buried her head in her sister's blouse and began wailing. Shocked, Kate put a tentative arm around her shoulder. "I… I'm sorry, Dellie. We… we were really worried."

Olivia panted into view, breathing heavily. "Kate… Kate, thank you. If you want to go home now, please just do your homework or piano practice or reading… or… no… no… *wait!*" She stopped and leaned against a sycamore. "No, Kate, here's what I want you to do: I want you to just — do — whatever — you — *want!*"

There, she'd said it, and heaven help her if she ever thought of saying it again.

Eddie slipped out of bed and tip-toed along the dark hallway to the back door. Rusty's sleepy face was furrowed in questions as he tapped along behind, hoping for an invitation. "C'mon then," Eddie whispered.

Eddie knew just how to open and close the screen door so it would not squeak. First, he opened it partway in a quick jerk. Then slowly he swung it the rest of the way. He opened the door for Rusty and stepped onto the porch with him. Both settled themselves on the top step and waited. Night breezes ruffled the trees. Eddie shivered and put one arm around his furry friend.

This little sanctuary in the darkness helped him remember Pa and how it used to be, a home filled with music and laughter and hugs. Maybe he would hear that song from Miss Bestor's piano again —a strange rippling melody that danced across the yard to his house. Sometimes it lasted until just before dawn. Eddie had waited that long, once, and had been severely reprimanded when he was late to breakfast and late for school.

He and Rusty sat listening for a long time. It had been nearly a week since the nighttime music. But still, they waited.

He did not hear the screen door opening behind him. He did not know anyone was close until his mother put her hand on his shoulder, and with a softness Eddie had not heard in a long time, she asked, "May I sit and listen with you?"

CHAPTER 22

The wings of Arlington Hospital sprawled in their suburban neighborhood like well designed dormitories. Quiet and unassuming, their myriad windows were comfortable and beckoning. No one seemed afraid of entering, or even of staying, in their spacious, sun-soaked rooms.

In the critical care wing, Dr. Miller Brayden checked on Patient Number Six. "Male Caucasian, late twenties." This name was bestowed temporarily because no one knew who he was, and there were no calls to report a missing friend or family member. Taxi driver Marge Newsome had found him lying near the highway at the end of Upton Street, had somehow managed to drag him into her cab and deliver him in a veritable flood of chattering sympathy. She had come to the ward each evening at 7:30 to check on her "mystery man."

It had been four days, and still the pale young man with straight blond hair had not fully wakened. But he had spoken, and several nurses along with Dr. Brayden conferred endlessly over the possible clues in those six words.

"Crush," he'd mumbled over and over. The next day he'd no longer repeated this puzzling word, but was calling for someone named Leon.

Next, in great agitation, he'd wailed: "Nine! Nine!"

The fourth day he was deathly quiet until evening when he had suddenly sat up and whispered through cracked purple lips: "AHN-yoo! AHN-yoo! Grahss!" The effort had clearly exhausted him and he'd been unconscious ever since.

Dr. Brayden suspected a military connection. His shorts and

T-shirt were army-issue tan, stamped with "Appalachian Mills" above numeric and lettered glyphs. But while the underwear was obviously a couple of sizes too large, his trousers and shirt were superbly cut remnants of curious vintage, appearing to have been part of an evening wear ensemble. This assemblage looked decidedly at odds with his ancient work boots.

Each garment had been gently cut away to better treat the severe wounds of trunk, arms and face. X-rays showed three arm fractures, one an older break. The classic "ring finger" of the left hand was missing near the second joint, and it too was an old wound.

Thomas was weary. Meetings and more meetings. Foot and Mouth Disease risks to Mexican cattle had everyone in the Bureau of Animal Industry writing reports and more reports. No one wanted to be the one to inform the Mexican government that a string of newly imported and probably infected prize bulls from an island near Vera Cruz heralded the possible forced destruction of thousands of Mexican cattle. The possibility of infecting American meat during this last wartime push in the Pacific loomed dark and foreboding. All Thomas wanted right now was a quiet corner where he could lie flat on a cool floor. Then supper, then time with his daughters. Maybe. He stepped away from his carpool ride at the head of Vermont Street and breathed deeply.

"Thomas, my good neighbor, a word with you please." Clarence Porro was also walking away from his carpool at Old Dominion. He jogged the few yards from the juncture of Upton Street and shook Thomas's hand. "I'm jiggered if I know what to do about that wagon."

"Wagon?"

"Oh. Sorry. Let me explain. This could take a few minutes. Would you rather have me call you tonight?" Thomas sighed and motioned Clarence to a large tree off the side of the road, where a fallen branch provided the perfect bench.

"It's like this," Clarence began. "It's about the man... well, I guess the only name I have for the man who searches for scrap is the "Bottle Man."

Thomas's shoulders slumped. Would he never be rid of that nuisance?

Clarence continued: "For several months I've let him kind of camp out in the woods at the back of the house. Well, I don't mean camp out exactly, but I told him that if he just wants to rest he can sit a spell under the trees. Often he will have a sandwich or some such and then be on his way. He's always quiet and never any trouble and never stays long. Sometimes he does odd jobs for us after he takes a wagon load of scrap metal and other odds and ends to the collection depot in Cherrydale. Occasionally he would leave his wagon parked for a couple of days. Not sure where he went those times."

Thomas sighed, thinking of that cool, hard floor.

"Well, last night just before dark, our boy Franklin found the wagon hidden behind a clump of brush in the woods. It had apparently been there several days because that's when we last saw him. Franklin rummaged around to see what was in it. Then he showed me what he'd found." Clarence turned his face away and whispered. "There was... there was a bloody handkerchief all wadded up among the bottles. I mean, it wasn't just a little blood, Thomas. It was soaked. Well it *had* been soaked. It's dry now."

He paused, looking searchingly at Thomas. "It scared Franklin. It was really hard on him, after losing his brother Davey and all."

Thomas nodded in sympathy and waited for Clarence to continue.

Clarence pulled out his handkerchief and wiped his eyes. "Thomas, I was wondering, your being an attorney and such, if you have any suggestions about what I should do. After all," he finished, "we're practically backyard neighbors."

Thomas bowed his head in thought. "Well, I would start with a call to the Arlington police, Clarence. Yes, I would start there, in case someone has reported him missing. You said five days?" Clarence nodded and Thomas continued. "After five days the possibility of severe injury or even foul play is pretty apparent." He paused, eager to end the conversation. "And please, would you let me know how this comes out?"

The two neighbors stood, brushed bits of leaves off their trousers, and turned to walk home.

But no. Thomas couldn't just walk away. He gripped Clarence's elbow, his mouth quivering with fatigue and a new sense of shame. "You were kind to him, Clarence. Not many of us were."

The men parted slowly, each to his own road, each with his own thoughts, each to his own family.

CHAPTER 23

Patti peeked into O'Dell's room. She wiped her mouth and held out something gooey that smelled of raspberries. "Want some toast and jam? Here. I brought you a piece." Patti licked her fingers while O'Dell sat on the bed and started working through her toast.

"Dellie, what in the world were you doing in that awful place? Mother was real worried." More munching, wiping of fingers. "And I was too."

O'Dell snorted, scattering toast crumbs on her blouse. "Aw, you didn't even know I was down there until Kate told you!"

Patti shrugged and flopped onto the bed.

"Oh, Patti, it was so scary! There was this little boy who thought I was killing his soldiers and a huge dog that looked like it was going to eat me up!"

Patti's eyes widened. "Phillip was there, wasn't he? I'm sure he wouldn't have let anything happen to you!"

"He wasn't there at first. And Patti..."

"Mmmm?"

"I wasn't really as scared as I thought I'd be." She looked down at her bare feet and wiggled her toes. "I dunno, it felt like a cloud or something was all around me."

"Yeah? Did it rain on you?" Patti gave a little half-smile and raised one eyebrow.

"No. Not like that. It was just okay to be there."

"Well, that's good then. And Dellie?"

"Yeah?"

"I'm glad you're not so afraid of stuff anymore."

"Me too. But Patti, I think Phillip is scared. He can't find the Bottle Man."

"He can't? Not anywhere?" Patti turned to her sister. "Yeah, I wondered why we never heard him this week!" Both girls were quiet as they pondered this. "But he couldn't just disappear, Dellie! He hasn't got a car!"

"Patti."

"Huh?"

"Did you know the Bottle Man lives, you know, down there?"

"Really? He does?" Patti reflected, brushing crumbs off her shirt. "Well yeah, I kinda thought he might. Oh, Dellie! Daddy wouldn't like to think of him down there. And I'll bet he's really mad that you went there! He doesn't like the Bottle Man."

"Yeah. I know." They sat swinging their feet.

O'Dell grinned at her sister. "Got any more toast?"

Dr. Brayden was an old hand at working with law enforcement. It was a simple routine: Call and they came and they checked. But this was something new: a U.S. Army captain, a lieutenant and a plain-clothes police officer wanting some time in his crowded office. Head nurse Dora Sanchez had started this, he mused, with her keen detective work. She'd rummaged through the mystery man's clothing and taken a second look at the French cuffs. "We used to hide notes in our cuffs when I was in high school," she explained. "So when I saw that tiny slit I poked through there and came out with this."

Her discovery had brought both military and police scurrying to Brayden's office. The content was difficult to explain over the phone. The wrinkled paper was a jumble of alphabet letters, circles, numerals and cryptic sequences. But it was the nearly complete sentences which had guaranteed visits from someone as high up the chain as a captain and a lieutenant.

Intelligence Officer Roger McCauliff frowned as he read the crumpled note: *Largo still best? 4 July comes soon. Who complete circle? Title? Agneau d Grace.*

And then, the series of alphabet letters topped with smaller ones. Could they be map coordinates? An encrypted code?

Am F C
G A A C E

And what about those circles placed in a ring? Each contained an alphabet letter: V, V, C, P, B.

Of particular interest were the words "Largo" and "Agneau" and "Grace." Hadn't the patient in Bed Number Six mumbled something like these very words? And here they were scribbled on a blood-smeared note with the statement: *4 July will come soon.*

4 July. Independence Day. Captain McCauliff knew the penciled order of the date was typically European: the numeral first, followed by the month. Could there be a last desperate assault by a renegade Nazi faction on Florida's west coast near the small town of Largo? And what better timing than July Fourth when the entire nation would be celebrating the supposed end of the war in Europe and the almost inevitable capitulation of the Japanese!

"Captain, look at these strange shapes," said the lieutenant. "Might those be some kind of amphibian craft?" Roger McCauliff didn't like to be one-upped by a junior intelligence officer. He shook his head. "No. No, the shapes are all wrong." If there was any glory to come out of this investigation, he wanted it all to himself. Three years of war had failed to give him the promotions he deserved, and here was a chance at something big.

Frèr-e Jacques, frèr-e Jacques, dormez-vous? dormez-vous? Marge was quietly singing a little song her brother Donny had taught her. It was soothing the way those French words rolled off her tongue. She was singing because she'd tried talking with her mystery man, so proud of herself that she'd not babbled. But there was not a whisper of response or a flicker of eyelids. One night she'd even held his hand, closed her eyes and imagined she was back in New Jersey sitting with Donny at the piano. But Donny was somewhere in the Pacific, while she was in the hospital singing to this little man who was lying so still and helpless.

She was startled when he began to speak. Marge opened her eyes to find Patient Number Six looking straight at her. "Merci," he whispered. "Merci." His eyes closed again.

Dora poked her head in the office door. "Excuse me, Dr. Brayden. Our mystery man is mumbling again. Marge thinks he said *mercy*."

Like tumbleweeds in the wind, four men whisked out of Dr. Brayden's office and gathered speed toward Patient Number Six.

"This had better be something worthwhile," Captain McCauliff muttered, waving the note. "Something more significant than saying *mercy!* Somewhere this has to start making sense!"

Marge didn't need to be told. One look at the dark frowns on the uniformed officers and she quietly slipped out of her chair. It was best to just follow Dora and call it a night. But before she could turn toward the door, a flicker of white caught her eye and she watched a slip of paper spiral to the floor behind the men. Marge picked it up, ready to hand it back, when her eye caught the capital letters in the middle of the paper. It wasn't hers to read. She knew that. But the pull of those letters was like a magnet sending her straight back to the piano bench with her brother Donny.

"Oh," she whispered.

Dora had caught Marge's movement, the quick read, the little startled gasp. She beckoned to Marge and hustled her into the hall. "What is it?" she mouthed.

"I know what this is, Dora. These are piano notes."

"You can read those, Marge?"

"Yes, I think I can."

"Then come with me."

CHAPTER 24

What is it, Thomas?" Olivia wiped her hands on a dish towel, wondering why her husband stood motionless, the telephone receiver clasped to his chest.

He turned, dreamlike, toward his wife. "Miss Bestor is coming. She wants me to go with her to the hospital. It seems we were not only misguided about the Bottle Man — we were guilty of a colossal blunder. In short, Olivia, we failed our neighbor at the most basic level." He straightened, strode purposefully to the hall closet and donned jacket and hat. Thomas may not be guiltless, but by golly at least he would not be shabbily dressed.

"What in the world? Thomas?"

"The Bottle Man has a name, Olivia. He is Emile Françoise Bodrienne from Lyon, France. He is the son of Eliza Bestor's niece, who lived here when Emile was a child. This little man is a violinist of the first order, Olivia! The first order!" He paused, his eyes filling with tears. "He is in the United States illegally. But I, for one, will do all in my power to see that justice is done."

Olivia watched Thomas stride to the curb to wait for Eliza Bestor. Then she closed the screen door and walked to the phone. *Alexander! Maybe he can make some sense out of this!*

The 1927 black and gray Ford sedan chugged to the curb muttering *parupata-parupata* and gasped to a halt. Thomas tipped his hat to the tiny woman at the wheel. Miss Bestor could barely reach the pedals but somehow had tamed her father's vintage car into obedience. Thomas slid onto the passenger seat and steeled himself for the ride.

The car sprang to life with a howl of protest. Thomas winced at every stop because this meant shifting gears. Eliza never managed to press the clutch and release the accelerator at the same time. Still, he reasoned, if Eliza could get three young girls to practice the piano for an hour each day, perhaps she could also get the ancient little car all the way to the hospital.

"Dr. Farnsworth, you know the law, and that is why I want you to accompany me." Eliza lowered the window and hooked her arm in the letter "L" to alert two lines of traffic that she meant to turn right. "Dr. Brayden sounds like a reasonable man, but I think he is at the mercy of those military officers. Yes, I told them that Emile is my great-nephew, but I have no documents. His entire family was killed last summer in Lyon when their house sustained a direct mortar hit."

Eliza stretched her feet to the pedals and prepared to stop at the traffic light. With a series of little jerks, the car settled as she continued talking. "Shortly after they died, Emile joined the French Resistance. And when you do that, you don't put identification tags in your pocket!" She slid forward on her seat as the light turned, and launched the car into the intersection. Another two blocks, then Eliza shot her arm out the window to signal left, whipped into her turn, and ground the gears. "Well, there's a lot more to this. A lot more. But let's just take it a measure at a time." Thomas smiled at the musical term.

"Dr. Farnsworth, I am truly worried." Eliza busied herself with more shifting, then began anew. "Emile was very badly hurt a few days ago and is just now beginning to talk. They fear he has internal injuries." Her face bunched into a frown. "I just wish he had stayed at my house!" She banged the steering wheel and jammed the accelerator as traffic thinned. Thomas clutched the seat. "But it was his decision to live in the Settlement with Reuben. He did not want to cause me trouble."

Thomas turned to her with raised eyebrows. "And Reuben is..."

"Reuben is a man who keeps his own counsel. I'm not sure where he's from, or why he lives where he does. But he is trustworthy and generous and does odd jobs for me from time to time." A little smile worked its way across her mouth. "And believe me, Dr. Farnsworth, that big man is able to handle himself in a crisis."

The hospital loomed into view and Eliza tamed the hopping Ford into the parking lot, lined it up and set the brake. Thomas hurried from the car and trotted to the driver side. With a gallant flourish he helped the piano teacher unfold from her seat.

Generous windows framed the twilight, with sleepy bird calls heralding the end of another healing day at Arlington Hospital. A few ambulatory patients sat swaddled in blankets while nurses wandered in and out of the Third Floor Patient Lounge, tending to their own.

In the southeast corner of the lounge, Marge and Dora huddled at the ancient grand piano. Marge sounded a few tentative notes, her left foot pressed on the una corda "soft" pedal, then began to play. "Oh, I'm so rusty, Dora. But here. See, this little Am means A minor and I'm to play that chord with these notes. Okay. Here!" She played the chord, and the notes with it. "Now the F chord with this." They both relaxed and began to smile as the notes started to make sense. Marge worked into the melody and began playing a bit faster.

"*Largo!*" The silvery voice startled the two women. A tiny gnome-like figure strode briskly across the room. "Slowly! Slow-*lee!*"

Marge froze. She was alarmed by this feisty little woman who approached at allegro tempo. She rose, gave a tiny half bow and motioned with her hand to the keyboard. Eliza Bestor took command of the piano, one lone wisp of gray hair springing loose from her bun.

Most of the patients in the sunroom had also looked on in amazement and soon a shambling little group of convalescents approached timidly. Eliza Bestor was impervious to the gathering audience. She was cocooned within this melody she'd known since Easter, and as she poised her bony fingers over the chipped keys her eyes began to close.

It was indeed largo… dreamy. Quietly her fingers swept away thought, replacing it with something that felt like hunger. The gathering arpeggios rumbled their A minor ascent while a single flute-like note pulled them forward. Soon three more notes joined the high A, pushing and prodding the arpeggios to switch to F major.

Ten-year-old Francine Herndon fluttered her hands. "Oh… oh… *oh,*" she breathed, as her mother watched in amazement. The child had not spoken since the accident, had not smiled or seemed to want anything further than just to hunker low in the bed or the wheelchair. Now her eyes flickered with delight and Francine's mother hoped the rest of her body would follow.

O'Dell stood behind the mailbox at the old poplar. She could feel the firestorm from next door, her body tingling with the heat of Mr. Tolson's rage. That blaring brutal sound could only have come from a cave, from some wild beast's lair.

The roaring, growling anger slamming from the garage next door was like a blast of fire hurling Phillip down his driveway. "And don't come back! Defy *me* and get away with it? I will hunt you down like the cur that you are! Thief! Robber! Imbecile!"

Every word propelled the bicycle onward. Phillip knew he could not stop until he reached the hospital. He would go to his friend. He would find Bodie.

Tears poured down Dellie's cheeks. "Oh Phillip," she breathed. "Don't come back. Don't come back." She squeezed the lamb in her pocket and whispered a plea.

"Mother wants you, Dellie." Kate put a gentle hand on her sister's shoulder. "We can't help Phillip right now."

O'Dell turned, sobbing, toward the house. Kate lingered, watching, feeling. This very spot, this very tree. Something flickered deep in her consciousness. "What is it?" she murmured.

CHAPTER 25

"Excuse me, Dr. Brayden." Nurse Dora Sanchez waited at the door of Room Six. When every head had turned her way, she spoke again. "Will you come to the patient lounge, gentlemen? There is something you need to hear. Nurse Hannah will sit with this patient while we are gone."

Dr. Miller Brayden never doubted the motives or the good sense of his head nurse, and often let her take the lead. Dora never commanded, yet her suggestions yielded their rewards in patients who actually recovered, and in peaceful activity for an overworked staff.

"Gentlemen, please follow me."

As the assortment of military and medical personnel turned left at Wing B, they followed another leader, one that issued a summons as old as the world, as sure as language. Music. Music like they'd never heard. Melody that went where each of them longed to go, without having named the destination.

The closer they came to the lounge, the more they were swept into a tide of ambulatory patients, along with nurses, doctors and desk personnel who could safely leave their posts. All were on the move, almost magnetized, and in a clinic where "must do" was the order of the day, this was beyond "must do." It was life itself.

In Room Six a smiling, weak patient listened with his heart.

"Aahn-yoo," he whispered. "Gra-a-h-s-s."

At the Washington Numismatic Society, Ruth Blankenship studied the coin collection she'd been assigned to evaluate. She gripped her magnifying glass, moving it slowly up and down, back and forth, matching one of the coins to her faithful numismatic encyclopedia. "Classic!" she muttered. Ruth rolled her chair across the room and yelled down the hallway. "Maynard, come look at this collection of Tolson's. I've never seen anything like this 1870 Seated Liberty quarter!"

"Sorry Ruth. Got a meeting." Maynard adjusted his tie and glanced at the clock. "Just put your evaluation in writing and mail the album back to Tolson. You should be able to make today's pickup."

♪

It came in a rush. Straight down. Black as ink, cold as winter mud. No lightning, no warning bird calls. Just rain, and lots of it. Olivia hurried the girls to windows and doors, slamming them shut, wiping sills, leaving a backyard clothesline of laundry to wait out the night.

On Glebe Road Phillip answered the onslaught with a scowling welt-lined face and storm-washed tears. He would keep going. He must. He *must*. Sixteenth Street, he remembered. Turn there. But where? The deluge obscured the signs.

Just turn. He felt the command, not the words. Dodging a bus and a coupe, he leaned into his new direction. George Mason Drive and Arlington Hospital. He would find it if he had to swim.

He didn't know how he dodged a giant Doberman, a taxi and numerous cars of assorted sizes. They loomed up without warning and Phillip would come up on the image, gasp for breath, start to break away sideways, then somehow slide through with no dents in his hide. He was quite sure, however, that a very surprised Doberman was nudged to the curb before she could rally her instincts.

Finally, there it was. Arlington Hospital, its gently lighted exterior barely visible through a wall of rain. He did not know how he got to this building. It just rose up behind a dark curtain.

Parking was easy. He simply abandoned his bike and ran for Wing A's utility entrance. A dark and dripping figure slid along the wall, sloshed to the freight elevator, rang it open and disappeared before anyone could identify him.

Miss Bestor had told him Wing A, visitor-restricted Third Floor. Once he reached hospital corridors, it would not be easy to hide this twelve-year-old portable fountain. When the freight doors slid open he darted out and wedged himself between a pillar and a wheeled laundry basket just in time to avoid two doctors in deep consultation. He lowered himself inch by inch, gripping the edge of the basket for support. The doctors did not notice the growing puddle under the cart.

Now, he thought. *No. No, wait.* His wet clothing was a dead giveaway. There, in the laundry. Towels. A lab coat. He grabbed a small terrycloth and rubbed down his head, trying not to think about the yellow stain on the towel. His wet shirt stuck like molasses. With both hands he gripped the lapel, yanking and popping little buttons like tiddly winks. In seconds he had the lab coat in place, and was turned to the wall when someone called his name.

"Phillip! Phillip Berning, is that you?"

Prickles of fear shivered down his back. He turned and faced Millie Tompkins, trying to remember where he'd seen her.

"I'm Freddie's big sister. Remember me from John Marshall three years ago? Hey, squirt, what're you doing here? And why are you wearing that lab coat?"

He grabbed her arm, pulling her behind the post. "Shhh, Millie. I'm not supposed to be here. But I really have to see someone.

Really!" She began to squirm and he loosened his grip. Both just stood, not knowing what to say next.

Beginning to relax, now he was curious. "What are *you* doing here?"

"Oh," she giggled. "I'm a Candy Striper."

"A what?"

"It's brand new. They're just trying us out here. See, this pinafore has stripes like a candy cane so we're called Candy Stripers. We help the nurses. We don't get paid," she laughed. "And I'm really too young but my mother's a nurse and she got me in." She turned quickly. "Whoops, hold on." She nudged him farther behind the pillar. A maintenance man trudged by with a tote of tools.

"Look, Millie. Maybe you could help. Do you think you could just take a look into Room Six and see if anyone's there?" Millie lowered an eyebrow as Phillip continued. "I mean, I just want a few minutes with him. He… he's a friend of mine. I just want to see if he's all right."

"Room Six? From what I hear, he's in pretty bad shape and no one knows who he is." Her eyes widened. "You mean you *know* him?"

"Please. Please just do it, all right?"

"Okay. Don't move. I'll be right back." Millie raised her clipboard and pretended to be studying her next move as she slid out of her hiding place and walked down the hall.

Phillip was wet in all the wrong places. Water oozed from his shoes, and his wet trousers were beginning to leak through the lab coat, not to mention down his pant legs. *Oh please Millie hurry up!*

♪

Was it the crowded physician's office that was making him sweat, or was it a flashback to being unprepared for his lesson in third grade? Captain Roger McCauliff straightened before this tiny wisp of a piano teacher with the waving pencil. Lieutenant Hugh Sumner had the strangest desire to pick his nose, and held his hands together in tight obedience.

The Arlington Police contingent had signed out, saying they'd be back the next day. Now it was just Dr. Brayden, two army intelligence officers wishing they were somewhere else — and Eliza Bestor. Her bony fingers traced on the stained paper each alphabetic piano note with accompanying mini-lectures on their suitability to the largo piece she had played in the lounge. In this tiny doctor's office her piercing dark blue eyes riveted each in turn.

"Look here," she said, tapping her finger against the penciled shapes. She smoothed the wrinkled note. "This represents the piano quintet." Her dark eyes searched the assembled men, all of whom wondered whether their ties were straight. "And what is a piano quintet?" she asked. None could answer but felt ashamed of this little slip in their knowledge. "It is a quintet for piano (she tapped the outline), and four other instruments or voices. And here we have a violin (again a tap), viola, cello and double bass." *Tap... tap... tap... tap... tap.*

Brayden, McCauliff and Sumner felt sure there would be a test before they were allowed to go home.

CHAPTER 26

A screen of rain. Moving curtains of water that swelled and receded with little rushes of wind. Now and then the watery curtains parted in the near darkness to reveal glimpses of the back yard and its bordering woods. Kate was fascinated by the power of this sudden storm and stood shivering with the instinctive knowledge that it would tell her something. She had been unsettled all day, trying to figure out what it was.

Now. A movement. Not like the rolling sheets of water but something smaller that moved along the wooded boundary of Phillip's yard. It was hard to see what it was, exactly. But it moved steadily until it had nearly disappeared into the woods, just over the Farnsworths' property line.

She continued watching. Slowly the figure undulated, then dissolved around O'Dell's "hunnerds year old" tree. The ghostly shadow blended with walls of dark rain, and melted back toward Phillip's house.

Kate stood a moment by the living room window, running her fingers through the hanging lace. She was trying to remember what she saw last Saturday. Was it just a week ago that Bodie had said *take care of your sisters?* Just a week since she had stolen those sunshiny moments before going back up?

Back up, to the mailbox.

Now she knew what she was looking for. It was the memory of a man with a jacket too warm for a summer day.

"The nurse is just ready to leave, I think." Millie's whisper was hurried, pushy. "Just a minute. I'll move around the corner and wait for her." Millie disappeared, then hurried back, turning for one more look. "Go, Phillip. *Now!*"

It wasn't easy to sneak down the hall with squeaky wet shoes and his pants full of water. But no one saw Phillip. Better yet, no one heard him. There were more important things to hear in the Patient Lounge.

Phillip came abreast of Room Six right after a tiny nurse bolted from the door with a tray of bottles and a pencil between her teeth. Phillip turned his face to the wall and waited until she'd propelled herself down the hall on rapidly churning legs.

A quick scan of the hallway, then Phillip walked into Bodie's room. It was dimly lit, smelling faintly of alcohol and iodine. The patient seemed too small for the bed. He was not the wiry little man Phillip remembered — the friend who braved snow showers, muddy roads and miles of trudging the sidewalks of Vermont, Vernon and Upton Streets. He did not move at all. Phillip thought for one heart-stopping moment that he was dead, and that maybe the nurse had whisked herself down the hall looking for help.

"Bodie?" he whispered. The sound of his own voice startled him and he looked around in alarm.

Nothing. No movement, nothing.

Phillip cleared his throat and moved closer. "Bodie it's me, Phillip."

A flutter of eyelids, and Emile's face turned toward him. Phillip was rewarded with a weak smile and a faint *merci*.

Footsteps, a clatter of bottles. "Visiting hours are over, young man." The tiny nurse took one moment to glower, then turned her back and waved a curt dismissal to the young intruder.

Phillip had just turned to go when a silvery voice rang through the room like a call to arms. "I see that you have come, Phillip, and that you have brought the weather with you." Miss Bestor's smile was mischievous.

The nurse at Emile's side turned, ready to command this newcomer from her domain. But what came out of her mouth was totally unbidden. "You are very welcome, Ma'am. Let me get you a chair." The little nurse had a sudden desire to curtsy. "I'm finished here. I'll just leave you two alone with the patient." She smoothed the sheet around Emile's arms, bobbed her head in obeisance, and sailed out of the room.

"Don't go, Phillip. Take that other chair. Please sit with me."

The hallway lights had dimmed by the time Thomas Farnsworth shadowed the door, silently surveying the three good friends. Phillip sat quietly, nodding his head now and then, while Miss Bestor wrote in that ever-present notebook of hers, stopping now and then to ask a question. Thomas would not go in. Not yet. He would drink in the little picture of contentment as a reminder of what he had missed. The smiling face of the Bottle Man would stay with him for a long while.

Emile was awake. And he was talking. Thomas held his gaze for a moment, bowed his head, and left the room.

Jimmy Zaputa leaned on his crutches. He'd made it all the way to the mailbox at the end of the quarter-mile driveway. Each day he and Banjo had walked just a bit farther, seen more of the farm, and last night he'd even helped his father with a puzzling engine problem.

Once again Jimmy waited. The mail truck should be on time. It was always on time. But the hoped-for letter from Emile never came. They'd said goodbye in New York more than seven months ago, and surely by now he would have heard.

Perhaps he should just let things go. Emile was somewhere in Virginia — and Jimmy was in Ohio without his army buddies. And without his brother Wally. "Just let it go," he murmured.

Jimmy missed Wally with his mousetrap quickness, the way he had always whistled his way through anything this hard-scrabble farm could throw at him. He knew his father missed him too. Wallace Quentin Zaputa would have taken over the farm, would have known just what to do. Wally could "sell you the shirt you're wearing and make you grateful to buy it," everyone said. Jimmy didn't talk much, and he never got tired of listening to Wally's quick banter. And now here was Jimmy, by himself. His silence seemed to make everyone uncomfortable, as if they were waiting to see whether he had anything to say. Which he didn't.

But Wally was not here. He had died in France in those strange row-house hallways the French called *traboules*. In one last check of hallways, Jimmy and Wally had found the wounded Emile in a dark corner. The scuffle that followed was a quick exchange of bullets and shouts. Jimmy got it in the leg, The German took a bullet through the head. And Wally — precious Wally — got it in the back.

The dizzying action that followed was too fast for wise choices. When the smoke cleared, Emile was in Wally's uniform and dog tags — rumbling with Jimmy over bomb-cratered roads to the

Army Surgical Center. After three months of medical transfers, Jimmy and Emile had sailed unchallenged to America.

Jimmy had spent long afternoons in those three months of rehab designing their next step. Emile had no family. No place to go. And Jimmy's brother was dead. It began to make perfect sense to bring Emile to Ohio.

Jimmy frowned and smacked his hand against the mailbox. How stupid he'd been, to imagine that just because Emile had taken Wally's uniform and dog tags, he could suddenly be Jimmy's big brother.

Banjo whined. Jimmy balanced the crutch and rubbed behind the ears of his faithful dog. "You're my buddy, Banjo. You know that, don't you. Yes, you know."

Mom and Dad knew about Wally. They knew Emile was Wally but not Wally, that he had come across the Atlantic in their son's uniform. Mom cried when she thought no one was looking, cried when she visited the family grave that would have held her son. She tried so hard to be cheerful, tried so valiantly to make sure Jimmy was not the "leftover" son. The son with the missing leg. The son who could never be the dutiful brother who would take over the farm.

Well, at least I can hobble to the mailbox. And open it. And take the mail back to the house. "That's something, right Banjo?" The bluetick pranced close, licking his hand. Jimmy leaned heavily against the mail post, waiting for the truck that always came at 11:30. Each day he'd hoped for word from Emile. "Send me a post card," he'd said as they parted in New York.

But the card never came. Emile had been blessed with a destination, somewhere to pin his hopes. And it wasn't in Ohio with Jimmy.

CHAPTER 27

Alex was troubled. There was no way he should get mixed up with Military Intelligence. It wasn't his department. But his sister's urgent call had moved him to action. He lifted the receiver and dialed.

"Roger! Alex Fielding! Heard you were stateside. How do you like the stuffed shirts at the War Department?"

"Alex! Last I saw you were clinging pretty tightly to a little French gal from Lyon. You bring her over?"

"You'd better believe it! She's my wife! We're in Brooklyn at the Army Terminal."

"If you're in New York, you didn't call to invite me to coffee. What's up?"

"Well, I'll be leaving in a few minutes for Arlington." Alex cleared his throat. "Roger, my sister's family is friends with Eliza Bestor." A strong intake of breath from the Washington line told Alex that his longtime friend Roger McCauliff, now an Intelligence captain in Washington, would have preferred a cup of coffee to this conversation.

"Roger, is there someplace we can talk? Like, at the Arlington Hospital? I've got a lot to tell you, and maybe it's best for two old buddies to hash it out before it gets sticky."

A heavy silence. Alex wondered if he'd been disconnected.

"I'll come, Alex. But this is just between you and me. Nothing official."

"You're on. Tonight suit you? Patient Lounge third floor? I hear they're giving free concerts."

"1830 hours. I'll be there."

Alex put down the receiver and smiled at Danielle. "Just wait until Roger sees that I outrank him."

♪

"Girls, I haven't heard you practice that new trio. The recital will come before you know it!"

"In a minute!" Patti hollered from the stairwell, then clattered the last few steps into the hall, with O'Dell crowding close behind. Kate, already poised with open sheet music, sat cool and orderly in her place to the far right. O'Dell plunked herself down in the middle as Patti shoved from the left.

"You stink," Kate muttered. "Go and wash!"

"I did too wash! Go and wash *yourself*." O'Dell wiggled for more room. "Patti quit squeezing!"

"Girls, girls, *girls!* What is all this!" Olivia stood in the hallway, wiping her hands. "I don't want to hear another word! Kate, it's up to you to get them organized!"

Kate mumbled her objections. *Take care of my sisters, eh? I'll take care of them all right!*

"I cannot invite any grumblers to visit Bodie."

The three girls froze, afraid to turn and face their father's frown.

"Visit?" Patti squeaked in a small voice.

"Yes. Visit. Mother told you he was in the hospital." The three girls nodded. "We cannot stay long. The doctor said five minutes for the three of you. But I will not take anyone who does *not* know how to behave."

"We know how." O'Dell nodded emphatically and poked her sisters for agreement.

"I'll take care of them." Kate's plans included plenty of whispered instructions and a few well-timed shoulder grips and pinches.

"Good. I am counting on you. Six O'clock on the dot. Uncle Alex is picking us up."

"Uncle Alex, Uncle Alex!" The two youngest girls forgot their promise to behave, squealing and laughing with delight until their father's shadow darkened the piano bench.

"I am in the mood for *Stars and Stripes Forever*," Thomas declared. "I am in the mood for it to begin right *now!* Any of you girls know how to play that?"

Conspiratorial smiles, fingers poised to strike the keys, then "clappity-clang" went the firecracker eleven-note entry to John Phillip Sousa's famous march.

Phillip watched from his bedroom window as the Farnsworth girls ran for the army staff car. Alex grabbed them in a bear hug and the ring of their soprano and baritone voices floated to the top of the house. The rescuing Uncle Alex held the door for Olivia, Thomas, and his three princesses. The Farnsworth family was free, but Phillip felt very much like a captive prince in the tower.

Kate lifted her eyes for a parting look at the Berning home, catching one fleeting glimpse of a young face behind a sliding curtain. Her neighbors sent messages from behind glass, she thought. A Morse code of pleading.

Dora Sanchez could set her watch by Marge Newsome. But here was Marge at six o'clock. Dora smiled a greeting as the little taxi driver peeked in the door, hoping for a nod and permission to sit a few minutes with her mystery man. "Hope I'm not too early," Marge said.

But now that Marge knew his name, it was a whole new relationship and she was strangely shy. She didn't know how much to talk, how long to stay, or even whether he would be glad for the company.

"*Merci.*" The little wave of Emile's hand told her all she needed to know. A few minutes would be welcomed. She would stay. Dora motioned to a chair, signaled "ten-minutes," and left the room.

Marge had seldom sat quietly with anyone. And here she was tongue-tied. She knew what to sing and what to say to a comatose patient. Now here he was with eyes open, expectant.

But before she could frame her greeting, Emile spoke. "Please. Sing *Frère Jacques* again."

"Oh. Of course. I… yes… all right then." Marge cleared her throat, leaned back, and soon the folk song drifted across the room in her soft clear voice. *Frère Jacques, frère Jacques, dormez-vous? dormez-vous? Sonnez les matines! Sonnez les matines! Ding, dang, dong. Ding, dang, dong.*

Marge was hoping the song would soothe and perhaps open the door to conversation. But what happened next was totally beyond her control. She began to giggle. Just thinking of the word "dang" plopped right into the middle of a French song had completely unraveled her sweet composure, which, even at the best of times, was not exactly Emily Post.

"Oh, dang it! I mean… no, that's not it!" Giggles again, mostly ending in little snorts. "Oh I'm so sorry! It's just that…"

A light chuckle from the frail little man on the white sheet sent Marge into new paroxysms.

Dora glanced in the door, then saw her duty. "Marge, let's go for a walk." She winked at Emile and he understood. Internal injuries do not lend themselves kindly to a body in motion.

"Marge," she whispered in the hallway. "Soon, this will be the very best medicine, this marvelous laughter. But until he gains more strength, it is best to wait."

Marge smiled, wiping joyful tears from her eyes. "I hope that will help him, and not do any harm. Dora don't you think... don't we all need to laugh right now?"

"Yes, Marge. Yes, we do."

CHAPTER 28

It was one thing to ride like a princess in the olive-drab car "with a great big ole white star on the side" — and quite another, thought O'Dell, to emerge, walk across the tarmac and be swallowed up inside the cavernous Arlington Hospital. The trio of girls had seemed invincible as they nestled into the spacious back seat singing *You Are My Sunshine* and *Row Row Row Your Boat* while under the protection of the United States Army. Now the little retinue felt smaller and smaller as they were guided by their parents and Uncle Alex to the elevators. Alex took a detour and found his way to the patient lounge and Captain McCauliff.

O'Dell tried to keep her clomping shoes from echoing against the hospital walls. Little girls' oxfords weren't made for tip-toeing. She stroked her woolly lamb and remembered her talk with Patti. They'd decided that Bodie would like Patti's pure white lamb better than her dingy one. But both of them would offer their lambs and let him pick which one he liked.

"Patti, got your lamb ready?"

"Uh huh."

They kept walking. Would these hallways never end?

Patti stopped suddenly. "Dellie! Oh Dellie, what if he just thinks these lambs are dumb! I mean, here he is practically dying and we should have something really expensive like a dozen roses or maybe a box of chocolates. Something like that!"

O'Dell frowned. This trip was not at all the way she'd imagined it an hour ago, full of knights in shining armor (she and Patti), with maybe an announcement, like, "Here they are, Mister Bottle Man, the little girls you like so much."

Kate, keeping step with her parents, turned with a meaningful frown. "This is a hospital," she whispered. "Just be quiet, you two!"

"Who put *you* in charge," O'Dell muttered.

Olivia stopped abruptly, herding the family into a circle. "All right," she whispered. This is Room Six. Daddy and I will go in first. Kate, you see that they keep quiet. When we are finished, we will come and get you." A concurring look from Thomas sealed the instructions and the dimly lighted Room Six swallowed them up.

Captain Roger McCauliff didn't know whether to salute or shake hands. But there was that pair of gold oak leaves staring him in the face.

"Heavens, Alex! You're a major." It was more of a declaration than a compliment. Roger hadn't figured on being outranked. But it shouldn't matter. Given the disparity between their duties in military intelligence and matériel, the two friends weren't likely to cross paths. He hoped.

Alex launched the opening salvo. "Roger, let me tell you a story."

All right then. Hope it's clear-cut and clean. Captain McCauliff had spent many late hours trying to figure out what to do with the stowaway in Room Six, but all of his so-called legal solutions had too many loose ends.

Alex leaned forward, his voice intense. "France! Last August!"

Roger grimaced. *"Lyon!"*

"What a mess! Trucks buried in mud! I thought I'd never get all those supplies to the front."

Roger leaned back and folded his arms. "And the French Resistance! Alex, we couldn't have won that town without them! Those

French laid some pretty sophisticated traps in those..."

"Traboules!" Alex made it sound a bit like *bouillon*. "Lyon was famous for them."

Roger piped up. "Started about the fourth century, didn't they?

Alex nodded. "You're right. Lyon wasn't much of a city back then but one thing they knew — somehow they had to get down to the river — and years later, how to keep their famous silks out of the rain!"

"The Rhone was their major source of fresh water and shipping — something you matériel guys would understand!"

"Pretty good motivation for their first tunnel, right, Roger?" And to think that turned into whole systems of tunnels, bridges, hidden courtyards and underground passageways going through entire streets of shops and homes."

"Worked great in this war. They used those connecting passageways to snipe at the Krauts."

Alex chuckled. "Can you believe those tunnels! And the bridges! Going from one shop to another — some of them a couple of stories up."

"And some of them deep underground."

Alex pointed his pencil at Roger. "After the shooting stopped, did you get inside any of them?"

"Just one. Looked like a medieval path to a dungeon, twisting in and out, parts of it going upstairs, some down."

Alex smiled. "Yeah, those hallways were tailor-made for the Resistance. The Germans had to be pretty brave to go in there. Cleaning out the French took a lot of guts."

Roger leaned forward. "But the biggest surprise — French Resistance headquarters was smack in the middle of them!"

"Sure ticked off that German bigwig. What was his name?"

Roger frowned. "Klaus Barbie."

"The 'Butcher of Lyon.'"

"Gestapo. SS man. He wanted those Resistance guys taken alive so he could hang them publicly!"

"But torture them first, right?" Alex waited a moment, taking the measure of his friend across the table. "Roger, I know you're suspicious of Emile Bodrienne, but you need to know why he fought for the Resistance — and why he came here. The Germans killed his parents and sister, and maybe that's why he just kept fighting like a wild man. A couple of our guys found him in a traboule — wounded. Strange, isn't it, that we were both in Lyon while all this was happening!"

Roger had been leaning back, but in spite of his intention to stay cool, he stretched forward expectantly as Alex thumbed through a small notebook and jabbed at a page. "Emile came over in a hospital ship wearing a G.I. uniform and dog tags. How he got them is what I'm going to tell you."

Roger and Alex kept quiet as a patient wandered into the lounge and made her way to the opposite side of the room. After she'd found a seat, Alex continued.

"This next part gets kind of complicated. Two privates — Wally and Jimmy Zaputa from Ohio — are pretty much the key to everything I'm going to tell you." Alex waved his little notebook. "It's Jimmy's story that makes sense of all this. But let me back up a bit. I first heard about Emile's connection to these brothers from a piano teacher — from Eliza Bestor. She is Emile's great aunt."

Roger straightened and checked his tie. "Really! That's hard to believe." He folded his arms, turned to the window a moment. "But Alex, wouldn't Eliza have all the details of this story? Makes sense for me to interview her first!" Roger was talking big, but the last thing he wanted was to sit across the table from Eliza Bestor's tapping pencil.

"Just some of it. She saw Emile only briefly when he first arrived — before he made his home with others. I got the rest from Jimmy Zaputa. Eliza told me he lived in Ohio somewhere.

"Man! I can't believe how many Zaputas there are! I finally got hold of Jimmy and he told me all about the battle in Lyon." Alex flipped another page. "I wrote down as much as I could, but the phone line wasn't clear some of the time. So bear with me."

Alex poked at a page, changed his mind and flipped to the next one. "Okay. Okay, here we go. You and I reached Lyon about the same time as the two Zaputa brothers. Their company was assigned to the older part of the city near the river and of course that meant fighting in those traboules. The Germans didn't make much headway in there, but a few of them managed to hide out — and that's all it takes to cause trouble."

Roger nodded.

"Well, in any event the Germans had to be cleaned out. The shooting had stopped, but just to make sure all was clear, Jimmy and Wally were ordered to check the far end of the row of shops. They'd just gone in — started around one of those sharp corners with pistols ready — and then they saw Emile crumpled on the floor against a wall. Half conscious, left arm bleeding. Plain clothes, probably Resistance. Could be a trap, though.

Alex drew a deep breath. "And here's where the real action starts. Jimmy kept his gun raised while Wally opened the medical kit and knelt beside Emile. That's when a German soldier leaned around the corner and shot Wally in the back. I had to wait a couple of minutes for Jimmy to calm down. It was hard for him to go through this again."

The sun behind the lounge windows was dipping low. Several

of the wheel-chaired patients were ushered out the door. Nurses came and went.

Alex watched them leave, cleared his throat and looked intently at Roger. "When Jimmy got started again, he talked non-stop. I gave this pencil a good workout! Now it gets kind of unbelievable, but we have Jimmy's word on what happened."

Roger narrowed his eyes. "In our business one person's word isn't always enough."

"Okay. But just listen. Then you can weigh the evidence."

"I'll give you that."

"Everything seemed to happen at once. When Wally was hit, he fell onto Emile. That woke him up! Then Jimmy dove for Wally's gun just as the German fired again, this time catching Jimmy with a 9 millimeter slug to the leg. By this time Emile was coherent enough to grab Wally's gun and finish off the kraut with the Colt .45."

Roger's eyebrows shot up. "So how did…"

"Hold on… let me finish. Jimmy's thigh was bleeding but he and Emile scrambled to help Wally first. They patched him up and gave him a syrette of morphine. Then, with a little help from Jimmy — and Emile's one workable arm — they tied a tourniquet around Jimmy's leg, and bandaged Emile's other arm. After that, they looked for a way to sneak Wally out of there."

Roger was shaking his head, eyes closed.

Alex continued. "They dragged Wally into a small storage area but he didn't last more than a few minutes."

Roger grimaced: "Stories like this don't have pretty endings."

"You're right. It gets even more complex. Jimmy and Emile heard gunfire and shouts. But who was shooting? Then, everything was eerily quiet. And in those few minutes Jimmy knew what he had to do. If Emile was caught by the Germans — well, an

American in uniform *might* be taken captive, but a Resistance fighter would be shot — or tortured and hung. That's when Jimmy urged Emile to take Wally's uniform and dog tags. Emile didn't hesitate. He changed clothes while they planned their next move.

"More shots. Shouting. Screaming. Emile supported Jimmy with his good arm and they staggered to the street.

"And just in time. A German flamethrower team came around the corner and started spraying. Jimmy and Emile barely made it to the street."

Roger leaned forward. "And Wally's body…"

"Gone. No way to recover it after that flaming oil torched the traboule."

Alex tried not to think of the infernos he'd witnessed. Three years of injured soldiers, screaming children. His shoulders drooped. He pulled a handkerchief from his pocket and slowly wiped his face.

"So now there's no way to identify Wally's body." Alex closed his notebook with a snap. "A medic put both guys on a field ambulance. Lots more details, Roger, but here's the bottom line: To the medics, Emile was Wally Zaputa — uniform, dog tags, the works. No one had time to double-check the records.

"Confusion. Delays in medical treatment — and unfortunately Jimmy's leg couldn't be saved. Both of them were treated at several aid stations down the line, and finally they were sent to New York on the same ship. Now that was a miracle and a half. Getting ships across the Atlantic was still pretty dicey — the Germans had those new acoustic torpedoes."

"Our guys called them GNATS, remember?"

"Yep — hard to swat."

Alex pocketed his pencil and notebook. "Well, here you have it, Roger. Next stop for Jimmy — Ohio. And for Emile — his great aunt in Virginia. It's been eight months since Eliza Bestor spoke with Emile about the fighting. But she urged me not to disturb him now." Alex looked meaningfully at Roger. "And that's why I called Jimmy."

"So now perhaps he's claiming Virginia as his rightful home?"

"Seems natural enough. Emile's father was a French violinist. The way I understand it, he met Eliza's niece in Lyon at the end of the Great War. She was a nurse, but also a musician. They married and settled in the Washington D.C. area. Had a couple of kids — Eliza loved those children — taught them piano. But France was always the final aim for the Bodriennes. So back they went to Europe. Both parents taught in the Société des Grands Concerts de Lyon. Yeah, I know — how can I pronounce all that stuff!" He winked. "I've got a French wife, remember?"

Roger's face softened. "Eliza never married?

"Never did. But she adored her sister's family, always stayed in touch. It gave her peace to know that Emile's parents did the same work in France they'd done in America — the music they loved most."

Roger sat frowning, arms folded. "I need to talk to Jimmy."

"You won't have long to wait. His train gets into Union Station day after tomorrow— 0800."

O'Dell and Patti watched their parents come out of the Bottle Man's room.

"You three can go in now," Thomas whispered. "But remember to keep it short."

"Okay." Patti clasped hands tightly with her little sister and entered Room Six. Kate followed a few feet behind, then hung back with sudden shyness.

The dimly lit room smelled like Dr. Nabor's clinic and for a moment O'Dell panicked. Her hand on the dingy lamb was moist and hot.

"My young musical artists," Emile whispered. "You came."

O'Dell fished in her pocket. "It's awful bad that you got hurt, Mister Bodie. *Here,*" she said as she dumped the lamb onto his chest. All the graceful speeches she'd rehearsed tumbled to the floor in silence.

"Me too," said Patti. "I mean, I'm sorry too, and I guess maybe, like Dellie said, you could choose which lamb you like." Unceremoniously, Patti set her spotless white lamb next to O'Dell's. "You can have them both if you like."

Kate squirmed. She had hoped her instructions in the hallway would result in something more ladylike, more *proper!*

Emile carefully braced his bandaged arm and lifted the two lambs tenderly, holding them side by side. "I do want to keep them both," he said softly. "Do you know why?"

Both girls shook their heads vigorously. Words somehow got swallowed up in this somber sickroom.

"Because they remind me of what the real Lamb came to do. I was gray and dingy like this little one. Now I am clean like the other one." A paroxysm of coughing shook Emile and for a few panicky moments it looked as if he would choke and they would not know what to do about it. Kate moved forward. To do what, she hadn't a clue, but whatever it was, she was ready.

Emile lay quietly after his siege and they thought he might be sleeping, or worse. But he turned his head toward Kate and beckoned with his hand. "Kate, I have an assignment for you."

Startled, Kate swallowed hard and croaked, "Assignment?"

"Yes. A Magnum Opus." He took a moment to recover from this short speech. "Miss Bestor will instruct you." Another fit of coughing brought Dora on the run. She motioned to the three sisters that this visit was over. They trooped out, wondering what had just happened.

CHAPTER 29

Patti and O'Dell walked carefully away from Room Six, hand in hand, then down the halls quietly, exhaling the last whiffs of iodine and alcohol. They'd seen the Bottle Man in a way they'd never seen him before, and this sobered the family as they returned to the army sedan.

One rain-washed street after another filled Kate's view from the front seat. She was squeezed against the passenger window. Her mother spoke softly with Thomas, who was enjoying the surprise offer to take the driver's seat — his only chance to do something military in this never-ending war.

Kate was quiet, pondering her mystery assignment. Something to do with music. She knew that much. But what was a Magnum Opus? Was it Latin? She would ask Maggie Hardesty, who had suffered three years of that ancient language in high school. It was very important to Kate that she know where she was going with this project before she met with Eliza Bestor. She needed time alone to make sense of it all!

In the back seat Alex was exactly where he wanted to be — near the two youngest girls. Always, their squirrelly cheerfulness blotted out those painful years in Europe.

Patti hummed something she'd learned in school. She, too, was mystified over the afternoon's events. Why did the Bottle Man want both lambs? What did he mean? She sighed. Then she jiggled her foot up and down. She wanted to move, get out of this seat, do something besides trying to be a little lady.

Alex turned to Patti. "You gave Emile two lambs?"

"He wanted them both. We thought maybe he'd want just the

clean one, but…"

"Yeah," O'Dell interrupted. "He said it was important to remember how dirty he was before he got clean."

Alex rubbed his chin. He smiled, remembering the wilted crowns O'Dell had given her lamb. "Did he say anything more?"

"No," Patti chirped. "But he seemed so-o-o-o happy about it!"

"Like he really *wanted* the dirty lamb," O'Dell whispered, her eyes wide. She patted Alex on the arm. "But you could ask him. I'm sure he would tell you!"

The wheels had barely stopped turning when the younger girls tore from the car, scampered up the sidewalk and into the house, then squashed each other against stair railings in their race for a quick change into their play clothes.

From the top window next door, Phillip watched the procession.

Kate clicked the screen door and headed for the living room, opened the window and collapsed onto the sofa with her new book: *Gone With the Wind.*

Olivia heard the girls chattering. She smiled as she cut generous slices of her famous apple pie, something special for her little brother Alexander. She paused for a moment, listening to her children's voices floating down the stairs.

"Patti, wanna squeeze under that big tree? Betcha can't fit!" O'Dell taunted.

"Can too!"

Olivia leaned around the corner. "If you're going outside keep it to a half hour! It's getting dark!"

"Yes, Mother." Peals of laughter and another thumpity-clump, this time down the stairs and out the back door for a race up the slope. Alex grinned, settling back with a plateful of cream-smothered pie. Such a joy to hear children laughing.

Once outside, O'Dell shivered with hidden secrets. "Over here, Patti. See that hole?" She brushed away the wet leaves and twigs, finally getting to some damp dirt. "All you hafta do is stick your legs in there. No, not that way. Turn on your stomach and lie down first!"

"Did you really go in here, Dellie?" Patti wasn't going to be outdone by her little sister, but lowering herself into that earthy, dark cavern? "Dellie, I'm too big. *You* show me!"

"Okay pudding face, if you can't do it, *just watch!*" O'Dell flattened against the ground, crunched herself backward and closed her eyes. The insect and leaf and mold fragrance filled her nose as she worked her way down. Then, a faint clinking made her pause. "Did you hear that, Patti?"

"Yeah. I think it's just like you said. It's some kinda glass in there."

"Something else, too. It's hard and it's big. Wait. We need a big stick."

"The hoe, I'll get the hoe!"

Kate, intrigued by sounds of adventure, got up from the sofa and stood at the living room window, watching her sisters. Two days ago she'd been rooted to this same spot, tracking the rain with its hazy shadows sweeping across the lawn to the old tree. Suddenly Scarlett O'Hara wasn't at the top of her list anymore. Through the kitchen and out the back door, Kate sprinted up the hill to join the action.

"I found something!" Patti pulled gently on the hoe, reached down with her hand and clutched an empty Johnny Walker Red. All three stopped to examine the strutting little man on the label.

"What's it for?" Patti asked.

"It's a whiskey bottle." Kate turned it to the fading light. "Look. It's got a few drops in there." She tilted it up, poured the drops on her finger and touched it to her lips. "Ugh. Don't know why people drink this."

Patti and O'Dell looked at her with new respect.

"I think there's more stuff in there." Kate prodded with the hoe and was rewarded with another clink. "I think we have another Johnny!"

"Let me! Let me try this time!" O'Dell lowered the hoe but there was no clink. Just a dull thud. "There's something else. Wait. Oops, I can't. Oh dear!"

"I can do it!" Patti grabbed the hoe, wriggled on her belly closer to the opening, pulling and losing her quarry and pulling again, this time more slowly. "Ooh," she squealed. "Here it is! Here it is! It's a long black wooden thing."

"It's a bat!" The three girls stared. But they didn't have to ask where it came from. It was Phillip's trophy bat. The one with the jagged splinter near the top.

"What's it doing in there? We gotta tell Phillip!" O'Dell took it from Patti.

Kate touched O'Dell's shoulder. "No, wait. Let me talk to Dad first. Please wait until I show it to him, all right?"

Dellie sighed and released her grip. Waiting. Always waiting.

Thomas turned the bat from end to end, holding it under the lamp. He ran his hands over the smooth black paint, pausing at the Senators logo. Gingerly he pressed the little splinter at the blunt end, holding it closer to the light.

"Where did you say you found this, Kate?"

"Under that big oak tree between our house and Phillip's.

Dellie was in that hole when we played kick-the-can a few weeks ago and she thought she heard bottles clinking. Oh, just a minute, Dad." Kate opened the paper sack at her feet. "There were two of these."

"Johnny Walker Red. Common brand." Thomas gripped the bat and swung it gently from his shoulder. "I'll give this back to Phillip." He stood silently as if listening for direction. "You did well to bring it to me."

Kate knew the signals. Her father wanted to be alone. Alex and Mother were in the kitchen, her sisters were splashing in the bathtub. Now. Finally. *Gone With the Wind.* All by herself. Just Kate. Alone with Scarlett O'Hara and Rhett Butler. She slipped quietly upstairs to her room and shut the door.

♪

Thomas headed for the basement. He'd seen something on the bat, but he needed his workshop to examine it further. He could think best in this sanctuary of coolness, where massive quarried stones separated him from the world. Best to hold the bat under the bare light bulb hanging above his tools.

He was tempted to give this bat a good cleaning. He always did his best work scrubbing and oiling and keeping everything in its place. But no. Not today, although everything within him rebelled at leaving the bat dirty. He knew that washing would remove… something.

But what was it? A stain of some kind? And something was caught in a little crack. He would try the tweezers near the top where the splintering had occurred last year at the Senators game. He smiled faintly, remembering how proudly Phillip had beamed as he talked of the gift handed to him by the first baseman.

In that little splintered crack, something like a tiny hair was hanging out. Two hairs, maybe three. Hair. Real hair. Was it Phillip's? He took a damp cloth and carefully wiped off a smidgen of mud, then looked again. No, it wasn't Phillip's dark wavy hair. It was straight and nearly blond.

Someone else should see this. He called up the stairs. "Alex, would you come down here a minute?"

CHAPTER 30

Each step toward his neighbor's back door was unlike any that Thomas had ever taken. What in the world had he gotten himself into! How foolhardy to walk right up to the house and begin accusing a man with whom he'd rarely spoken. He was thankful to have Alex at his side, intimidating in his major's uniform.

The newly washed grass lay like a thick carpet, muting each footfall. Yet Thomas was sure each step thundered their approach. It was dark beyond the circle of light at the Bernings' back door, with barely a breeze to stir the drooping branches of the nearby woods.

"I'm armed with a bat," Thomas whispered. "How appropriate."

"I've been armed with less," Alex muttered.

Even with Alex at his side, Thomas dreaded facing the ever-glowering Grandon Tolson. But his neighbor shortened the trouble. He was waiting in the lighted doorway, arms hanging loosely, defeat in his slumped shoulders. Mr. Tolson's lips wobbled as if groping for words. But there were none.

The two men locked eyes. Alex hung back, waiting.

Thomas held up the bat. "I brought Phillip's trophy. I want to show you what Major Fielding and I found. Here, at the blunt end." The word was carefully chosen. *Blunt:* a legal description.

Silence. Each man took measure of his neighbor. Thomas squeezed the bat more tightly. Then — Grandon Tolson, proud, muscular, sinister — crumpled like a tossed gum wrapper. "I… I don't. I can't…"

And then the sobbing began. In great heaves the big man seemed to grow smaller with each breath. His shoes scraped the sill while one hand squeaked against the jamb. He sank to his knees on the doorstep. Thomas had expected many things, but not this. He lowered the bat to his side and took a deep breath. "Mr. Tolson, the only reason you have not been arrested is because the Bottle Man does not wish to bring charges." He waited. His neighbor remained slumped on the door sill, head lowered.

"But Major Fielding and I will keep this bat." Still no movement from Grandon, who slumped on the sill, choking with quiet sobs. Thomas turned to Alex and raised an eyebrow. Alex closed his eyes, shook his head slightly and remained firmly planted, silent. Thomas was not ready to touch his neighbor. Comfort was not his to give. Not at this time. He waited one long moment, then he and Alex turned for home.

Phillip and his mother sat huddled at the top of the stairs, waiting.

♪

Eliza Bestor wondered how it would work. But Emile had insisted with rare strength for one so weak: *Kate would play with the quintet!*

But July 4 is too soon. Too soon. Sundays were not her favorite days for recitals, but she would try to move the performance to Sunday, August 5, and pray that Emile would last that long. He was not doing well, Dr. Brayden told her. An old injury must have suppurated — something deep inside. From what? No one knew. And X-rays were not clear.

♪

The train was right on time. Jimmy Zaputa felt the rumbling vibration of its iron body as it echoed into Union Station at precisely 0800. The jolting trip from Ohio had kept him awake for most of the twenty-four hours. Somehow he'd managed to make a couple of trips down the aisle, one hand on the crutch, one arm for balance. But most of the time he'd just stayed put. For one sweet hour he had slipped into dreams of home, of the childhood he'd shared with brother Wally — with the sheep and old Banjo. The rough awakening came at Pittsburgh, where some passengers left, and others — mostly servicemen — came aboard in a noisy cacophony of tossed duffel bags and a scramble for seats.

What a relief to get off this train! But where should he go now? Perhaps just follow the kindly porter who carried his suitcase to the cavernous concourse. He walked a kind of hop-step, balancing on one foot and one crutch, mesmerized by the mixture of sounds. Train arrival and departure announcements floated upward, lost in a droning, echoing togetherness. Cathedral-like archways framed the ceiling, and Jimmy nearly lost sight of the porter as he gawked like a schoolboy at the statues of legionnaires thirty feet above his head. "Could have used a few of them in France," he murmured.

"Sir, this way please, sir." The porter smiled and shook his head. "Which street would you be needing, sir?"

"Well, I don't know, I…"

"Jimmy? Are you Jimmy Zaputa?" A merry bubbling voice rose near his elbow.

Jimmy whirled, balanced on his crutch and nodded.

"I'm Marge. Emile sent me. Said you'd have a crutch. I'm right out front. Boy, it's hard to get a parking place here, but I have a taxi and howdy-do I just zoomed right up front and got in line with the others! No one bothered to check the Virginia license plate. Only D.C. taxis allowed in that lane, ya know? Well, you just follow me and we'll have you in Room Six with Emile in no time!"

The porter chuckled.

Marge, face flaming, led the way. Her babbling had begun and she'd vowed not to do that again. Their footsteps were not in rhythm and Marge was continually slowing down, then speeding up. She was relieved to be in charge again at the door of her taxi.

She turned to the porter: "You can just put that suitcase in the back seat. Here, this is for you." Marge thrust a fifty-cent piece into his hand. "We thank you!"

She beamed up at Jimmy. "You can sit in the front. I'm the driver so why not!"

Emile had told her to take good care of Jimmy, and oh boy, she hoped she wouldn't botch this job!

Jimmy backed into the front seat, then pulled his one good leg into position while Marge laid his crutch in the back.

"There now. All set? Hold on now! Off we go!" Marge put the Plymouth into gear, hit the accelerator and zoomed ahead of a long string of Yellow Cabs.

Jimmy looked with wonder at his driver. "Oh my," he mumbled. "Oh my. If Wally could see this!"

Nurse Dora quietly cradled her cup of tea. Finally. A break! She needed to just back off a few minutes and think about the patient in Room Six.

But he was not *the patient* anymore. He had a *name*. She must get used to calling him Emile. Not like some of his visitors who had no names. Like the towering giant of a man who'd come silently with a skinny black-haired waif in tow. He had a kingly air and a subdued kindness and his visit had made Emile happy. Dora was glad for any spark of cheer surrounding this mysterious man who'd been carried through the emergency entrance by a taxi driver and the hospital guard three weeks ago.

And the children. How Emile loved them! From the water-soaked boy with the pain-etched face to the three sisters too shy to know what to say, Dora had seen their healing effect on Emile's fragile body.

Dora frowned, remembering the irritating presence of those military men, obsessed with finding a conspiracy. But her favorite — *ahh* — she sighed at the memory. Her favorite was the tiny piano teacher who'd transformed this very hospital into a symphony of hope and peace.

Dora hoped with all her being — and she prayed — that somehow Dr. Brayden would be able to locate this new trouble in Emile's body, could miraculously bring him to health and re-birth.

Re-birth. Why had she chosen that word? It seemed everyone who surrounded Emile had changed somehow — the hopeful into more hope, the hopeless blessed with a glimmer of direction.

And the angry and the resentful? Perhaps there was hope there, too. How strange had been the report of an encounter with the gaunt shadowy man who'd breached security and suddenly appeared by Emile's bedside last night. Hannah, the night nurse, had come upon the intruder with the wild, agonized face and had sped for help.

But whatever had begun in wildness was surely softening by the time Hannah returned with the third-floor watchman. The strange tall man was kneeling, his face pressed against the bed, Emile's gentle hand resting on the trembling head. Infusing the room was a soft tune — a child's lullaby. Emile was singing a benediction, his voice breaking with love and anguish:

Unto thee this child I bring
To the Lamb, the King of kings.
Sing to him throughout the night,
And bring him safely to the light.

Hannah had stayed in the doorway until the man rose, looked about with haunted eyes, then dutifully followed her and the watchman down the hall, down the stairs, and out the door.

♪

Dora took one last sip from the cooling tea, remembering. Suddenly she glanced at her watch. Was it really the middle of the morning? Did that really happen last night? Surely Hannah, sensible Hannah, had not imagined it! *Oh Emile, Emile. Please live. Please live!* She sat very still. Then, briskly, Dora brought her cup to the corner sink. Two more hours until lunch. She hoped they would be quiet ones. She glanced at her clipboard, then strode to Room Six.

Laughter. One softly baritone voice, one bubbly giggly one. *Marge,* she thought. *But who's that with her?*

"Meet Jimmy," Emile whispered. "My army brother."

Jimmy ducked his head in a slight bow. "Ma'am," he said quietly.

"Oh. He's from Ohio. I just brought him from the train station. Isn't he just wonderful?" Marge blushed. "I mean, isn't it just wonderful that he could come all the way here? He and Emile were in France together but they couldn't meet again until now.

I'm going to take him to Eliza Bestor's house to stay awhile." She paused a moment to let that sink in. "And I'm going to take him back and forth."

Dora smiled. "You are most welcome, Jimmy. This will be a blessing to Emile. He has spoken of you. But please remember our strict guidelines for intensive care. You will need to keep your visits to ten minutes." She winked at Marge, then busied herself with the medicine tray and the crank at the base of the bed.

CHAPTER 31

I can do this I can do this I can do this. Kate set the carefully penned musical score on the lip above the "fall" board, rubbed her hands together and bowed her head a moment. Then she straightened and took a sounding of the first bar.

With her right hand she played the first five notes. *Hmm. Where is this going? Okay wait. What's this? Hmmm. The chords in the left hand change every single note. Resolution… resolution.*

Olivia paused, dishcloth in hand. *What's Kate muttering about. Wish she'd get going. Only three weeks until the recital.*

Now! Kate thought. *Now or never!* She plunged both hands into the keyboard. *"Slowleeee!"* Miss Bestor had said. Kate was sure that her self-assured piano teacher was more anxious than she was. Together their nerves would tangle into a regular train wreck by August 5, the new date for show time. *Oh quit it,* Kate thought. *Show time? No. This was Magnum Opus time!*

Finally, the notes began to make sense. From the kitchen Olivia heard the deep thrumming bass: *Largo, always largo!* And then, five notes climbing, pausing, stair-stepping back down.

There would be four stringed instruments added to the piano, Olivia knew. Once, as a child, she'd heard a violinist on a street corner. He had a coin box at his feet, and with sightless eyes he would smile a thank you at each clink. Over the years that simple melody had entwined itself into her soul as it dug and flitted by turns. Somewhere deep inside of her, that same melodic feeling played again, meeting Kate's tentative, tender notes. Olivia longed to be able to bring forth her own inner music, to sit down with strings or keyboard. But it was too late for her. She would let her children be her music.

♪

"Olivia?" Greta's voice was soft, tentative. "May I come in?"

"Of course. Please." Olivia strode to the back porch and opened the screen door. "Come into the dining room, Greta."

The two women pulled chairs away from the table and sat where they could view the north patio. Two squirrels frisked on the stone wall, hoping for treats from O'Dell.

Olivia waited a moment. "What is it, Greta?"

"Grandon is gone." Greta's shoulders sagged. "I think… I really do think it is for the best, Olivia."

"But where has he gone, Greta? Is he…" She stopped, waited. Olivia nearly asked the unbidden question: *What if Emile brings charges?*

"I don't know where he is, Olivia. He took some clothes and his wallet, but not the car." Greta's eyes filled with tears. Both waited. Suddenly, Greta lifted her chin. "I don't care. I don't *care* where he is! He's gone, he's *gone!* That's all that matters!" The pent up flood spilled forth. Greta bent low over the table, sobbing in great heaving gulps.

Olivia put her hand on Greta's shoulder for a moment, then pulled back. Best to just let her cry. But no! That wasn't any way to give comfort! Suddenly she grabbed her neighbor in a tender embrace, soothing, comforting, pulling ever tighter, obeying some inner urge which had long lain dormant.

"Dellie, come and look," Patti whispered from the hallway. "Mother's hugging Mrs. Berning." Both girls sought each other's fingers in a strong clasp. Kate, unaware of the dining-room drama, continued her Magnum Opus from the living room, its notes swelling in clarity and strength.

CHAPTER 31

Jimmy Zaputa wasn't used to the luxury of sleeping late. But here he was, waking to a ray of bright morning sunshine, a buzzing fly, and a stream of notes emanating from one of the two pianos in the tiny living room. Eliza's silvery voice tinkled between bars, stopping the flow here, urging more pauses there. Jimmy chuckled at the stream of instructions. They might as well have been Greek. "Largo and andante and resolution, always resolution with ritardando, Kate!"

He closed his eyes again. Should he drift back to sleep? Could he? Maybe it was some kind of dream. But his reverie turned to laughter with the touch of something wet. Eliza's lanky German pointer began each morning washing someone's hand, if she could find it, and here was Jimmy's, hanging invitingly close. With several quick swipes, her laughing mouth made sure Jimmy was awake.

"Okay, Jillie. Okay. I'm up!" He swung his good leg to the floor and reached for the crutch. It wasn't as burdensome today. Somehow his wooden appendage was okay this morning. It felt right — finally a part of him.

"Yoo hoo!"

Marge! Uh oh. Said she'd pick me up at ten. Is it really that late?

Marge continued her chatter in the living room. "Sorry I'm a little early. Traffic was light, no customers yet, and I wanted to hear Kate play. I'll just sit here like a mouse and not talk and you two just go ahead and play. Don't mind me." She cuddled herself into the ancient horsehair sofa and picked up an *Etude* magazine.

Free. Am I really free? Phillip tiptoed to the kitchen, looking for his mother. Everything looked so empty. No, not empty. Clean. It looked clean. Clear. Free. Phillip stopped suddenly. *Why am I tiptoeing!* "Mom... Mom?" A low whine came from the dining room, followed by the clicking of toenails. Beauford wobbled into the kitchen and thrust a wet nose into Phillip's hand.

"I'm going to keep you safe, Beauford." Phillip bent down, stroking the silver-flecked muzzle, then lay on the cold tiles, remembering another time when he could not get up and wondered whether he ever would.

The old dog ran his warm tongue over Phillip's face and lay quietly beside his master.

"I believe you would like to keep me safe, wouldn't you, old man... yes you would." Phillip stroked the grizzled head and reached for a towel hanging above him. Rolling it into a pillow, he tucked it under his head and cuddled closer to Beauford, entwining his fingers in the golden-gray coat.

Greta found them asleep an hour later.

Dora didn't like the sound of Emile's breathing. More oxygen had not relieved the pressure or the inflammation — or the "something else" Dr. Brayden spoke of yesterday. Every word was a struggle now, and his face had a troublesome grayness. It seemed his very essence was missing.

And there was something else missing too. The lambs. Dora knew how he treasured those tiny woolen figures lovingly given to him by the little girls last week. He was constantly holding them between his good hand and the fingers that peeked from the cast on his left arm — mumbling, even singing at times, always something about "grahss." She searched the floor, the bedside table, folds of the blanket. Nowhere.

Finally, she spoke. "Emile, do you have the lambs somewhere? I don't see them, and I know what store you set on those. Would you like me to check your blanket?"

"A gift… they are a gift. I gave them… to… my neighbor. He… needs them." Emile stopped, suddenly listening for something. Dora looked around the room, almost expecting someone or something that had not been there a moment before.

"I told him to take… them both… and… he could decide… which…" Emile gasped, struggled, lifted himself onto one elbow. "He must know… he must know… which… which lamb he wants. Dirty or clean. Dirty… or clean." Emile sank into the pillow, exhausted, his breath coming in short shallow gasps.

Dora pressed Dr. Brayden's buzzer.

The Greyhound bus idled at curbside in Rosslyn with a gentle tippy-tippy-tap. With a whoosh the door swung open and forty-three passengers marshaled themselves into an orderly, silent queue. A mother and baby boarded first, followed by three sailors and an elderly couple. Shadowing close behind was a tall, gaunt man with a jacket too warm for a summer day. One hand held his bus ticket, the other clutched a small woolly lamb in his pocket.

CHAPTER 32

Dr. Brayden tensed. He waited until the tight phone voice of hospital administrator John Stemple had droned all the reasons they couldn't hold a recital in the third-floor patient lounge. "Then will you at least grant one practice time for the piano quintet?" Brayden asked. "It shouldn't take more than thirty minutes. One of our patients composed that piece, and he cannot be moved outside the building."

There was a pause. "If you keep it to thirty minutes. And make sure it is finished before the end of visiting hours." Click.

The veteran doctor settled the receiver gently in place and bowed his head in gratitude.

Kate was beyond tired. Every day the same. Practice the quintet! Or *was* it a quintet? Miss Bestor said the gathering of piano and four stringed instruments was like an intimate concerto. But whatever it was called, indeed she must practice, practice, practice! And the last thing she needed right now was a pair of noisy sisters on the piano bench.

"Quit shoving, Dellie! I'm about to fall off!" Kate leaned into her, hoping she'd crowd her sister at the other end. O'Dell pushed Patti and got a quick shove back.

"Okay, I quit! I've got the entire quintet to practice and if you two can't manage a simple…" Kate covered her face, but not before a sharp sob had escaped. The two sisters were stunned, silent.

"Oh Kate! We'll hold still, won't we Dellie!" Patti begged Kate to perch once more at the end. She eyed her little sister defiantly. "Dellie… *Dell-eeee!*"

O'Dell sighed, hunched tightly into herself, and squeezed her arms to her side.

"One, two, three, *four!*" Kate whispered the beat, and off they flew, executing *Stars and Stripes* flawlessly.

Olivia folded the stiff rye bread dough and punched it again. She lifted her arms and tried to release her tense shoulders. Never had she known such a compaction of events. First the Bottle Man's injury, next Miss Bestor's shocking revelation, followed by digging up the assault weapon. And now, finally, watching Kate learn the most difficult musical score she'd ever attempted, and all in the space of three weeks. *Stars and Stripes Forever* should be the easiest part of this ever-increasing load, and if the girls couldn't get that right, then it seemed as if nothing would work! She dusted her hands with flour, and punched the dough with a vengeance.

"He's dying, Mom." Jimmy hadn't meant to blurt it out. But he did not have his brother's finesse.

"What — ! Who? Who's dying, Jimmy?" The voice crackled over the phone, losing timbre.

"Emile! You know, the French guy who tried to save Wally." Jimmy began sobbing. "Oh Mom. I wanted you and Dad to meet him. I wanted…"

Marge moved closer, reached a tentative hand to Jimmy's shoulder. "It's okay, Jimmy, it's okay. Just take a deep breath." Then, a sudden inspiration: "Let me talk to her."

Gratefully Jimmy handed the phone to Marge.

"Mom… I mean Mrs. Zaputa, it's Marge, Jimmy's new friend. I sort of, you know, drive a taxi and I kind of rescued Emile and the next thing I know here we are talking on the phone with you and I want to meet you sometime because Jimmy loves you so much and he's told me all about your farm and Banjo and everything. And, well, he's just so worried about Emile." She paused, listening. "Yes. Yes. Here he is again. And I am so glad I talked with you, you're a good woman, I just know it!"

Jimmy wiped his eyes on his sleeve and with a quiet smile he took the phone. Slowly, haltingly, he shared the story with his mother. Three more minutes of talk, then deliberately he clicked the receiver back into place. He shook his head slowly and turned to Marge. "She's taking the evening train and she will be here tomorrow." He paused, nearly sobbing again. "And Marge, she wants to meet *you!*"

In Room Six Emile smiled in his sleep, softly repeating *gra-ah-ss.*

Marilyn, Richard, Gregory and Lydia — the four string players on loan from Miss Bestor's colleague in Maryland — alighted from the bus at the Military Drive stop. They were eager to experience full harmony with the piano. They'd been given scant time to make this musical event work. What would they find in that special student Miss Bestor had described?

The four musicians walked toward the hospital in a tight bundle of encased instruments all tapping lightly into each other. Somehow they squeezed into the elevator and emerged near the patient lounge. Miss Bestor ushered them toward the scarred piano. With their bass, violin, viola and cello they filed in, then sat in the circle of chairs which had been set out for them. In a gentle clatter they each removed their instruments and bows.

A general murmur, like bees hovering, stopped as if switched off when Kate walked in. She stiffened, her heart beating like a bass drum. She'd never seen this room. So much *space*, and in a few days it would be filled with chairs and a crowd of people all looking at her.

Eliza called across the room: "Kate! There you are! Come, dear, I want you to meet these four exceptional players." She introduced them all in turn.

Shy smiles, a bit of fidgeting. The two boys got up to shake hands. The girls wondered whether they should shake hands, too, but chose to simply nod. They busied themselves with their instruments.

Kate sat on the bench and opened her music, almost afraid to begin.

Eliza leaned close and smoothed the pages. "Now Kate. Just do what we've been practicing and it will please Emile — and all who hear it."

Eliza nodded. Kate pressed one piano key. Then, each instrument was tightened at the pegs or loosened until a pure "A" hummed throughout the room. Eliza leaned toward the five of them and conferred in silvery whispers before retiring to the sunny windows where she sat waiting.

Dr. Brayden came last, wheeling his patient. He had hoped for a wheelchair but at the last minute opted to let his fragile patient remain in his own wheeled bed. Emile was propped with pillows that nearly swallowed him up. He smiled weakly to Eliza and raised one finger, like a baton from an ancient maestro. The violinist nodded to Kate, whose arpeggios would lay a carpet of quiet introduction.

Four patients, sunning themselves near the window, were surprised to find themselves smack in the middle of a concert.

"Largo, Kate, *largo*," whispered Eliza. Slowly, softly, the arpeggios tumbled across the room. Then, a faint vibration rose from somewhere deep within the towering double bass, whose bow, under expert fingers, filled the room with rest and invitation. Kate commandeered the primal melody of five single notes, ascending slowly, then doubling back upon themselves. The violinist lifted her bow and moved the melody from minor to major and back again. "Reso-lution. *Reso-lution*," mumbled Eliza. "Yes. Oh-h *yes*."

Emile's eyes were closed, the eyelids showing no movement. Dr. Brayden desired with all his heart to watch the quintet, but he feared that if he turned from his patient for one moment, when he looked back again Emile would be gone.

Shadowing the doorway, Administrator John Stemple stood with folded arms, a frown creasing his darkly handsome face. A quick check was his plan, then a perusal of the halls before coming back to ensure timely closure to this rag-tag rehearsal. He pulled out his silver pocket watch, glanced quickly, and prepared to leave. But he could not move. He could not sever the cord connecting him to that music — the cord which was willing him to listen with his heart.

"Surely you don't mean that, Roger. Germany's finished, and Japan won't last much longer." Alex shifted the phone and paused, listening to his old buddy Captain McCauliff.

Alex let out one long breath and willed himself to be calm. "And do you really think your legalism would make this country any safer? The scuttlebutt is that our own AWOL cases are rapidly being dismissed. Great heavens, Roger. He's dying, for goodness sakes! Just let the poor man be!" Alex fumed, gripping the receiver as if to squeeze a commitment from that stubborn friend of his. "Will you at least give it one week? My family has set great store on this recital. And the main feature is Emile's composition. In fact my niece has a major part. So please, *just wait!*"

A pause, crackling at the other end.

"Thank you. My family thanks you. Yes, one week then." Alex set the receiver on its cradle and wiped his face. Dealing with Military Intelligence in Washington was about as frustrating as moving supplies across France.

O'Dell knelt at the south side of Kate's bedroom, arms resting on the window ledge. She sat pondering Phillip's house. It hadn't shown its nice face for a long time. But it looked a little more friendly today, with some of its windows open.

Where was Phillip? O'Dell couldn't see him though she sensed his nearness. She felt that something had changed. She didn't know what it was, but she knew that it was good.

Did she hear music? Maybe Phillip was practicing for the recital. Was it Mozart or was it Bach? It was a rolling sad-happy kind of piece, room for lots of allegro. "Oh goody goody *allegro*," she said.

Suddenly the music stopped, and she thought she heard laughter. Then, the jingly piece started over, faster this time. But it stopped at exactly the same spot, like a horse galloping up to a hurdle and refusing to jump. Laughter again, louder this time.

Once more the music started from the beginning. O'Dell willed him over that hurdle but again he stopped. Now Phillip's guffaws were joined by his mother's. Both of them shouted their laughter until Phillip banged on the piano as if to smack it into obedience.

No good. He started over, and never got to the trouble spot. O'Dell giggled, then turned from the window when her mother shouted up the stairs: "O'Dell, Patti, dinner is almost ready. Your father and Kate should be home soon. Run to the living room window and see which one comes first!"

Kate had come home from last evening's practice instilled with renewed confidence. The other quintet players were orderly, well-rehearsed, and encouraging. Marilyn, the cellist, had talked with her afterward, inviting Kate to a Saturday practice in Silver Spring later in the month. Kate had resolved not to worry about the concert and for one or two hours at a time she could actually poke it to the back of her mind.

But here it was Saturday evening and it seemed that everyone was looking at her and wondering whether she would make it until tomorrow. A light rain had started during supper. She could hear the soft pit-a-pat against the window. Kate noted the gathering gloom and with it her freedom. Only a few more hours and then — Magnum Opus. And she, Kathryn Elaine Farnsworth, would be responsible for the entire climax of the recital. And perhaps the biggest performance of her life. But it wasn't just *her* performance. It was Miss Bestor's. And the entire quintet's.

And Emile's. Especially Emile's.

Absently, she twirled her fork into the spinach soufflé. But she did not eat. She could not.

The sky was darker now, and the rain was blowing in little swirls. Was it the wind that was creating that tune in her head? Someone was singing. Faintly, a familiar melody pushed against the darkening sky. It rose in volume until Kate was certain of the tune. It was *Silent Night.* Kate put down her fork. A Christmas carol. In *August*?

Quietly she rose from the table. "Mother, may I be excused?" But she did not wait for the answer. Once in the hallway she moved quickly. She was out the door and up the street before anyone could see where she'd gone. All she had to do was follow the sound.

Maggie Hardesty. Singing at the top of her voice. Kate laughed and ran to meet her, then stood under the Kiplinger persimmon tree, partially sheltered from the light rain. Soon she could make out the words. It was the second verse, one she seldom sang: *Silent night, holy night, Son of God, love's pure light; Radiant beams from thy holy face; With the dawn of redeeming grace; Jesus, Lord, at thy birth. Jesus, Lord at thy birth.*

Grace. Was it the same "grahss" from Emile's quintet?

Kate spoke. She'd come straight to the point, as she always did with her friend. "Maggie, what is grace?"

Maggie put her hands to her chest. "Oh Kate, you startled me! Let me catch my breath!" Then she laughed her melodic giggle. "Here. Sit on these steps with me. Mother Kiplinger won't mind."

The two sat on the steps. Maggie made a tarp of her raincoat and slung it over the two of them.

"Well, it's a gift, Kate. Something we don't earn. You know, like a present on your birthday." She paused. "Only this is the gift of all gifts."

"Oh," was all Kate could think of to say. But it was enough. She would think about it later and she knew Maggie would understand.

Suddenly the air was split with a sharp whistle. Thomas Farnsworth was looking for his daughter.

Kate leaped up. "Oh dear! I've got to run. I just *can't* get a cold! Not now!" She put her hand on Maggie's shoulder. "You're coming tomorrow?" And Kate knew that Maggie would. The two friends sprinted down Vermont Street, the raincoat flying behind them like a sail.

CHAPTER 33

Kate's legs felt as though they were made of wood. She might as well be a marionette. Forget lunch! The very thought of food turned her stomach. *Just move*, she told herself. Just *move*. Somehow she would get through this day. *Magnum Opus indeed!* She wished she had never heard the term.

O'Dell and Patti whisked around with chattering voices. All they had to perform were their simple parts in the *Stars and Stripes* trio, and she was convinced they would do it well. Kate willed them to keep quiet. It wasn't working.

"Alexander is here!" Olivia's strong voice jarred Kate into action. *Down the stairs. One at a time.* One at a time. But Kate had to admit that each step was easier than the last, and by the time she was in the front hallway she knew she would survive. Grace. That's what she needed now. Grace. She'd looked it up after Maggie left. It was indeed the Gift of all gifts — it had said so, right there in her Book.

Olivia held Kate's eyes, then she smiled and nodded a brisk benediction. Kate had never seen her mother look at her that way. A tingle started at the tip of her head and rippled through her body as she watched her mother corral Patti and O'Dell for one last inspection. Thomas hung back, smoothing his new black and gray tie against a freshly crisped shirt. He waited until Kate was near the door, then gave her shoulder a squeeze.

Through the screen door Alex looked approvingly at his nieces. His broad smile reassured Kate, who made one last check of her hair before beginning the little trek down the porch stairs to the waiting car. She was relieved that Alex had left Danielle at the hospital lounge. Kate had no room for kisses on the cheek and hot-house gardenias.

O'Dell waved to Phillip and his mother, who had just started down their steep driveway. "Daddy, Mother, it's Phillip! Can I ride with them?"

"May I."

"May I? Oh please, please!"

Please, please, muttered Kate. Her heart squeezed a mite as she remembered the Bottle Man's plea: *take care of your sisters.* Yes, she would. But not right this minute. *Please!*

As if on cue, Greta waved a hand of invitation. "Patti, O'Dell, come ride with us."

Olivia nodded. "All right then, girls. And remember to say thank you. Olivia patted her hair and settled comfortably into the back seat.

Patti and O'Dell tried to be ladylike in their stiff petticoats and Mary Jane shoes, but broke into a run after the first few steps, quickly tumbling into their neighbor's Chrysler with a slam and a giggle.

♪

Eliza Bestor was not one to give last-minute reminders and cautions. If her students did not know their pieces by recital time, so be it. All had been done, and now her job was to greet every family and give an encouraging smile. All she wanted was an island of calm.

She beckoned Kate with a nod of her head, her dark blue eyes sparkling. "Your resolutions are lovely, my dear. The quintet members have remarked on your amazing skill. Just do your best and we will all be proud of you." Eliza walked her student to the front row, then seated her with the rest of the string players. The five stole shy glances at one another, searching for reassurance.

Alex looked for his wife and found her near the back, kneeling by Emile's bed. Tears streaked her face. Alex waited for her to speak, which usually took no prompting. But Danielle dabbed her eyes, slowly shook her head, and moved with Alex to the second row.

Slowly the room filled. And filled. And filled. Patients who could safely leave their rooms were wheeled in. Doctors and nurses just finishing their rotation slipped to the back of the room.

Arriving just before two o'clock were Marge, Jimmy and Mrs. Zaputa. Marge blushed furiously when everyone looked her way, then smiled gratefully as Elinor Zaputa took one arm while she clung to Jimmy with the other.

There was a stir as heads turned toward the entrance. Patti nudged O'Dell. "Who's that?" A huge man in cleanly patched overalls stood at the rear, scanning the room. His black curly hair hung in a tight ponytail. Hanging nervously by his side was a small skinny boy in a voluminous white shirt and loose shorts.

"That's the man I told you about," O'Dell whispered. "I think his name's Reuben. And that boy is the one who didn't want me to trample his soldiers."

"Gosh." There was nothing more to say. Patti gulped, and with a tap on her elbow from Thomas, both girls faced the front, where Eliza Bestor waited for silence.

"Parents, friends, students, and patients and hospital staff," she began. "This is a concert like no other. Tonight you will hear an original quintet piece composed by one of the patients, as well as lovely and inspiring offerings from every one of my students. We thank the hospital administration for allowing us to convene in the patient lounge, and we thank our students for their hard work."

She paused and scanned her unconventional audience. Her gaze fell on Emile, and for a moment she fought for control. Taking a deep breath, she smiled and waved her hand over the audience. "Thank you, my friends. Let the celebration commence."

CHAPTER 34

In quick succession, five younger students came to the piano. O'Dell tapped her foot to the simple tunes. *Tum te tum tum!* She was so absorbed in the first short pieces that she was startled by a poke from Patti. "We're next, c'mon!" Both crowded toward the aisle but when they saw Miss Bestor walk to the front, Patti stopped so suddenly that O'Dell thudded back into her chair.

Eliza Bestor stood quietly for a moment. *She never does this,* thought Kate. *Not in the middle of the recital.* The tiny piano teacher waited for complete silence before announcing the piano trio.

"What you are about to hear is the famous *Stars and Stripes Forever* by John Phillip Sousa," she began. "Originally our recital was scheduled for the Saturday following Independence Day. But circumstances have changed, and here we are one month past that date with a patriotic march in our program!" She cleared her throat and smoothed back her bun. "But the truth is that we must celebrate daily, thankful for the end of the war in Europe, and the return of our brave soldiers. And I say, let the celebration continue!" The audience, as one body, broke into applause, heads turning to acknowledge Alex and Jimmy and several patients in wheelchairs.

Miss Bestor was quiet. But still she did not move. Finally, in a voice tight with emotion, she finished. "Please bow your heads with me for a moment as we remember our fighting men in the Pacific." Marge stifled a sob, and Mrs. Zaputa extended an arm of comfort.

Next to Alex, Danielle looked at her new family with shining face. "C'est mon pays maintenant," she whispered.

"Yes. Your country too, Danielle." Alex squeezed his wife's hand and held it tightly while the three Farnsworth girls trooped to the front.

Kate's eyes widened. *Oh no!* The bench for this piano was even smaller than the one at home. She approached the piano with a twinge of panic. Immediately the violinist saw the problem and brought a folding chair for Patti. A ripple of nervous laughter fluttered through the audience as the three sisters squeezed into position.

"Now or never, girls," whispered Kate. Her smile sparkled, and the two little sisters relaxed. "Ready? One, two, three four!" The opening notes took ownership of the large room. It was pure thunder and the Farnsworth girls gave it all they had for the rousing two-page introduction.

"Now. Softly, girls, softly," Kate whispered, and a vast tension was released when the airy middle portion began. The audience relaxed into the time-honored theme, some tapping their feet, the younger children clapping lightly. They could almost hear the fife and drum.

Now. The finale! Tuba, trombones, trumpets! The three children unleashed coiled muscle in the ascending finish until they heard Kate whisper, "Okay… slow down… slow down… pour… it… *on*." Patti and O'Dell could feel their older sister's summons to power. It vibrated through their shoulders, down to their fingers. During practice they knew Kate had been afraid of something, and that fear had fostered rebellion and squirming little bodies. But not now. Not now! And the tuba! That big bulbous horn came alive! In the closing salvo the audience was captured in joyous united freedom until the stunning climax. As one body they willed their stars and stripes to unfurl.

The end of the piece came so suddenly that the audience was stunned into silence, as if all the breath had been plucked from the room. Then, in a great upwelling thunderbolt of applause, the assembly in Patient Lounge Number Three stood and cheered.

"Oh, bravo, dear girls, bravo," whispered Maggie Hardesty.

In the back of the closed room, Administrator John Stemple knew it was too much noise for a hospital. But he simply did not care. He had been bound with invisible cords these past twenty-four hours, imprisoned with a new energy called music, and he meant to enjoy his captivity until the very end.

Dora scanned Emile's face anxiously. Had it been too much for him? And oh dear, was he even breathing? But though Emile's eyes were closed, he was breathing easily for once. He reached out his hand, found hers, and transferred his peace.

O'Dell whispered tightly into Patti's ear. "Look! Here comes Phillip! He's next, Patti!" The two girls watched him stride to the front. He appeared to be stifling a sob — his hands wiping his eyes. Certainly he was in some kind of distress. O'Dell breathed a silent prayer for him: *Don't let him fail, don't let him fail!* She reached for her woolly lamb, suddenly remembered she'd given it away, and gripped Patti's hand instead.

Phillip took his time at the bench — adjusting, moving — until he was finally settled and ready to play Solfegietto by C.P.E. Bach. Spritely and certainly allegro, it was even presto! Its close-coupled arpeggios romped tightly from C minor to F minor to B flat major, then E flat major — and Phillip executed the first section flawlessly. But after the tight little sixteenth notes in the third line, he landed squarely on B flat with his right hand but could not find the correct note for his left.

O'Dell stiffened. The very piece! The very piece she'd heard from the window! *Oh no, Phillip. Don't stop. Don't stop.* But he did stop. Three times, and each time, he buried his face in his hands. The third time, his body began to shake, and just as everyone was anguishing over the poor boy's dilemma, the giggling began. He stuffed a fist into his mouth, the only weapon he had for control. But nothing helped. His body burst into full-blown laughter.

"I'm... I'm sorry, Miss Bestor... it's just..." And once again the laughter — louder and with a variety of little snorts and giggles, his adolescent voice crackling and snapping from tenor to bass.

Miss Bestor, trying to keep her composure, moved nearer to the piano, then stopped. Something was different about this. She, the sedate master of her pupils, the bright star of her nineteenth century music professors, was beginning to chuckle.

Four rows back, Greta felt the rumblings too. Laughter! How cleansing it felt, after three long years in bondage. Laughter! Oh, let it come, just let it come! She glanced sideways at three of the parents, whose giggle-suppression methods varied from hand-over-mouth to hiding their faces to covering their mouths with handkerchiefs. But it was no use. No use at all.

Gentle giggles began to erupt through the room, gaining in traction like a tsunami freed from the ocean bottom. Phillip stood erect and kingly. Bowing with a low sweep of his hands, he set loose wild applause and more laughter.

Eliza Bestor did something she'd never done. She pulled Phillip toward her and hugged him tightly. And Phillip bent down and gave her a little kiss on the top of her head. By now the laughter had settled to pure delight. There was an element of satisfaction that covered each person like a mantle. Olivia felt the release, as if she had been holding her breath these forty-four long months of war, and now she could draw within herself huge mouthfuls of freedom. Thomas turned to see his wife's perennial frown disappear as her face creased into a huge grin. Olivia gripped his hand. "Oh Thomas! It's grace. It's just... grace!"

Gradually the laughter and chatting simmered to a murmur and the concert resumed — Rachmaninoff, Beethoven, Brahms

— the older students performing with more freedom than they had ever experienced.

And the audience was satisfied.

There was a rustling of programs, a light murmur. The long anticipated composition was next. One by one the quintet players came to the front, took their seats, and began tuning up. Kate need play only one note for tuning purposes. Simple enough. But as she struck that one simple *A* it startled her, resounding like a bell tolling within her chest. Yet one by one, just as they did in rehearsal, five bows crossed their strings, tuning pegs were turned, and the piano key struck once again.

She could do this.

O'Dell crinkled her program for a closer look, then whispered her question. "What's this say, Mother?"

Olivia was proud of her French, a skill fostered by her British grandmother. "Let me see now. It says *Jesu, Agneau de Grâce.*" That's the name of the piece, O'Dell."

"What does it mean, Mother?"

"It means Jesus, Lamb of Grace."

"Oh." Leaning toward Patti, she passed along her newly acquired knowledge. "It's about a lamb."

Olivia looked once more at the program. *The Lamb again. I cannot get away from him.* And perhaps, just perhaps, she did not want to. Not today.

There is a hush following orchestra tuning that is somber and inviting, like hanging branches waiting for a puff of wind.

Eliza Bestor took center stage again. "You have never heard the music that is about to be played," she began. "It is fresh and untried, waiting for you to receive it as the gift the author intended. It was written against a backdrop of pain, over a period of six months. The composer is my great-nephew." She paused, scanning her audience, as if looking for kindred spirits. "I would like to introduce him to you: Monsieur Emile Françoise Bodrienne." She gestured to the back of the room. "He is a patient here, in the excellent care of Dr. Miller Brayden."

Polite applause, gentle smiles, indistinct murmurings, shifting in seats.

"His career until last summer was with the Société des Grands Concerts de Lyon, in Lyon, France, where he was second violinist. First violinist was my niece." Miss Bestor fought for control. "I say 'was'. During the invasion to free the country, Emile's family… did not make it." She straightened, then, and opened her hands in welcome. "But this is a gladsome time, and your quintet stands ready to serve you. Please enjoy this, my dear friends."

Kate, already seated, placed her hands on the keyboard and waited a moment.

Thomas reached for Olivia's hand.

Maggie gripped her chair.

Emile struggled for breath. *Magnum… Opus… dear… Kate.*

Reuben laid his hand on a surprised Champy's shoulder.

Kate began with her soft arpeggios, then nodded to the bass player, who began a slow thrumming arpeggio in A minor. Dora felt a shiver run through Emile's hand to hers.

Next, the violinist. He was soon joined by the cellist and violist, who strung their notes in a plaintive trio, climbing, descending, sometimes meeting halfway only to rise, before descending once more. Now, Kate and the cellist played forth the dominant theme while the other string players held back.

As one body the audience sat suspended. "Oh Papa, oh Papa," murmured little Francine Herndon, as her father gripped her hand. No longer held captive by a wheelchair, she was healing now with the help of one crutch that stood propped against her chair.

The quintet paused, then plunged. Deep called to deep as the full octave ranges first pulled against each other, then coalesced in a somber largo of resolutions and cascading arpeggios. A minor, F major, E major, D minor… plunging and resolving and reaching for more depth.

By the time Kate held her last note and the string players drew four bows back into position, the captivity of the audience was complete. Kate lifted her hands, prepared to rise, then felt the tears descend. Embarrassed, she stood, not daring to look up. But she needn't have worried. There was not a dry eye in the room. Everywhere, handkerchiefs — even shirtsleeves among the little ones — were employed to staunch the flow. No one clapped. There seemed to be no need, until one child in the third row smacked his hands together in gleeful response. Slowly, others joined and began filling the room with a growing movement like gathering, healing raindrops.

And never-ending. The applause lasted through four bows, and as many attempts by Miss Bestor to speak.

Finally, just as rain gently recedes, the room quieted.

And then they heard it. A string of golden notes from the back. A simple, rich tune. "Oh," said Patti. She remembered the melody — one she had sung at camp and had brought home to teach her sisters. The deep somber melody swelled in depth and volume. All heads turned to behold Reuben, standing alone, head thrown back, pouring forth his love for Emile.

God be with you til we meet again.
By his counsel guide, uphold you,
With his sheep securely fold you.
God be with you til we meet again.

Patti felt the harmony rise within her. She hummed quietly. And Reuben heard. He stepped across the aisle, strode gently to Patti and extended his broad weathered hand. Patti, unafraid, did not hesitate. She walked with him to the front and continued with the chorus — the baritone and the sweet lilting soprano in perfect tandem.

Till we meet, till we meet,
Till we meet at Jesus' feet;
Till we meet, till we meet,
God be with you till we meet again.

The quiet at the end was as profound as the song. No one stirred. "Resolution," whispered Kate. "*Resolution.*"

CHAPTER 35

What had awakened her? The house was so still this Monday morning. O'Dell turned to the window. It was barely light enough for her to see a bluejay balanced on the maple, its head bobbing up and down. It chuckled and flitted, stared intently through the screen, and then it was gone.

But O'Dell did not need bluejays to sing to her. All the little musics from the day before were tip-toeing through her mind, replaying the mysterious joy of the recital.

She giggled at the memory of Solfeggietto. In her mind she could see Phillip again. The friend she knew and loved.

She thrilled to the replay of *Stars and Stripes*, and could feel the warmth of her sisters' arms tightly pressed together, the energy of the listening audience.

O'Dell settled into her pillow, closing her eyes to replay the final quintet, *Jesu, Agneau de Grâce.* Where was that music now? And where was the Lamb? They were still here. Always here. And she knew that deep within her where she was not yet ready for words, that the music would replay for the rest of her life.

What was it Kate had told her last week? O'Dell had come to the living room, had settled onto the sofa, watching. Kate appeared to be listening hard, as if the piano would tell her something. She was not playing the full score. Instead she slowly fingered five notes, up and down, over and over, sometimes adding a chord. She would stop, hum the notes and sometimes murmur what sounded like a question.

Kate turned to her little sister and motioned her forward. "Dellie, did you know that you can play 'grace' by itself?" It was not the usual big sister voice. It was a companionship, a type of sharing O'Dell had seldom known.

Kate put her arm around O'Dell, drew her forward. "Yes, you see, here are the notes." And slowly she replayed G, A, A, C and E. "Do you see that these are the notes for 'grace'?"

"But Kate, that doesn't spell 'grace'. And you can't play R on the piano."

"Yes you can," Kate said. "Because the letter R is spelled a-r. So you see, the quintet theme is "grace" all the way through."

Once more she played the five notes and the chords with them. "Do you hear the resolution, O'Dell?"

"Reso… ?"

"Resolution. It's when the notes make you wait for just the right ending, like they finish a very special story."

"Oh."

"And O'Dell, when you hear a resolution that gives you peace, the story will be all yours."

Remembering, O'Dell tucked the blanket under her chin against the chill of the morning. She remembered the closeness, the keening call of the notes.

"*Grace,*" she murmured. "It always… goes… up. Always… up."

She turned, snuggled deeply into the pillow, and closed her eyes.

♪

A light mist enveloped Dora as she walked toward the hospital a few minutes before six. It was not her regular shift but she had urged the scheduling nurse to put her on the docket. The need to check on Emile had kept her awake most of the night.

Quiet hung like a damp curtain. She took a deep breath and stepped into the service entrance. It would be good to bypass the elevator and get a feel for things on the stairway. A little climb would do her good. Solid, cool concrete, pale, smooth walls. Each step helped her close the door to the outside world and discern the climate of the day.

A few minutes later she emerged onto the third floor hallway.

No sound. No clatter, no footsteps. Just her own breathing. And the idea — not the sound exactly — that someone was humming. She began walking the hall. One by one she visited each patient, then stepped into Room Six to relieve Emile's night nurse and check his chart.

"I'm glad you're here," the little nurse huffed. "I've been trying to locate the radio on this floor. Someone has brought one in, and I intend to find it!"

"Please don't worry about it, Hannah. I will check it out. You go home and get some rest."

"Well, all right then! Fine thing, to have rules, and no one obeys them!" Hannah exited in a crinkly rustle of skirts.

A radio? Perhaps Dora had not imagined the humming. Yet she had not heard anything in the other rooms. Still, she would retrace her steps and listen. She could take the extra five minutes. All charts and patients were stable. Yes, she could make the rounds again.

Up and down the hallway she walked slowly, listening. The quiet was almost more profound than voices or instruments. Until she walked again into Room Six.

Then she heard it. A faint humming. Not just one voice, but many. The longer she listened, the softer it became. Softer, yet swelling with power.

This was no radio.

The door to the hallway was open. Or was it closing? Shadows softened the walls, emerging and disappearing like watercolors.

She looked at Emile, enshrouded in his oxygen tent. He was very still. But the gaunt lines around his face had softened. Peace emanated from him like a physical presence.

Dora pulled up a chair and sat quietly listening. The music had faded. She reached under the tent and took Emile's hand. It felt cool.

He was lifted slowly, powerful arms encircling him. A deep strength, an ageless one. He could not have resisted that force even had he wanted to. And Emile did not want to. A gentle tune flooded through his shoulders, piercing his very being. The sturdy muscles of his new companions rippled against his frail body, propelling him up, always upward. A peaceful swirl of music brushed aside shadows, finding an embodiment of light that was both new, yet without time. Multitudes upon multitudes of voices now joined, coalescing into many anthems, yet only one.

As his strength deepened, he found his own voice. And with it, the humble means to greet his timeless Friend face to face.

"Jesu. Agneau de Grâce.
Jesu."

ENCORE

MUSICAL TERMS

Allegro: Quick, rapid and cheerful tempo.

Alto: Second highest female voice.

Andante: Slowly, evenly.

Arpeggio: Notes in a chord are played one at a time, not simultaneously.

Baritone: Second lowest of all the voices.

Bass *(1):* Lowest of human or instrumental voices *(2):* Large stringed instrument, sometimes called contrabass or double-bass.

Contrapuntal: Independent melodies working against each other.

Discordant: A disagreeable sound — disharmony.

Fall: The piano's wooden closure to cover the keys when not in use.

Harmonic third: Third note above the main melody.

Largo: Slow, dreamy tempo.

Magnum Opus: Great Work — often the greatest work of a single artist.

Major and minor keys: Series of notes forming a scale; The third note in the scale determines the type. Music in a minor key is more solemn; major scales more bright and cheerful.

Measure: Beats contained within bars of music. Timing for such measures is described by instructions such as 4/4 (four quarter notes per measure); 3/4 (three quarter notes per measure); or 6/8 (six eighth notes per measure).

Octave: (1) Eight diatonic tones in a series. (2) The first and eighth notes played simultaneously.

Percussion: Instruments struck for sound, as bells or drums.

Pitch: The relative height or lowness of a tone.

Polonaise: A Polish waltz in moderate tempo.

Presto: Very fast.

Quarter note: One fourth of a whole note, approximately one second in length.

Quintet: A composition for five performers of mixed instruments and/or voices.

Resolution: The move of a note or chord from dissonance (an unstable sound) to a consonance (a more final or stable sounding one).

Ritardando: Gradual slowing.

Scale: A series of tones contained within an octave.

Scherzo: A musical piece in a lively and playful style.

Sonata: An instrumental composition, usually for a solo instrument, in three or four parts.

Sonatina: A shorter sonata, often written for children.

Soprano: The highest female voice among four voices.

Sotto voce: Softly subdued voice.

Staccato: Each note sharply detached or separated from the others.

Tempo: The pace at which a composition is to be performed.

Trill: A musical ornament quickly performed against a single note.

Trio: Three players or singers on one instrument; or three instruments, three players.

Triplets: A group of three notes played within the time frame allotted for two.

Vivace: Brisk and lively.

A FINAL NOTE

A quiet parade of friends, family and professionals came to my rescue at just the right time and helped me find resolution. Sometimes for just a few hours — sometimes for months.

STEPHANIE LARSON: I searched two years for the right editor. And the answer was there all the time — our own daughter. She knows my quirks and habits and isn't afraid to disagree with me.

An editor and graphic artist, she produces articles for national farm publications and helps authors publish a wide array of textbooks, scientific works and fiction.

And so began two years of being told by the child we'd raised: "Mom, you really must learn the difference between *which* and *that*." And, "How did O'Dell get from the top floor to the front step so quickly?" Sometimes no words were needed. She'd return a chapter of edits with the Ellipses Rabbit doing its thing in the margin, or the Exclamation of Doom bumping the headline.

JERRY CARLSON: My encourager. My husband. A sixty-year journalist and researcher, his quiet questions and the little red pen in his shirt pocket are amazing revitalizers. Our marriage has survived — even grown — through decades of mutual edits (some unsolicited). For three years he patiently studied every word of *The Fugitive's Concerto* through multiple manuscripts and resisted the urge to ramp up the only battle scene in this book. Throughout, he trustingly deferred to Stephanie's expertise.

ALICE stuck by me for the entire nine years of writing. She painted. I wrote.

KARLA carefully corrected my French and my music.

TOM AND QUENTIN showed Mr. Farnsworth how to clean his piano.

MARK AND SUSAN gave the book a wise, thoughtful review.

BECKY invited her author/musician friend for consultation.

ERIK walked with me into the thick of the battle chapter, and got me safely back out.

JADE, AJA AND KAYTLEN, our cover pianists, donned vintage clothing and patiently played their silent version of *Stars and Stripes Forever*.

KAREN taught me fifty years ago that the student *is* the music.

RONNIE, my first little friend, helped me remember.

FRIENDS AND FAMILY. You prayed. You encouraged. And I thanked you again and again, which is where such deeply personal gratitude belongs.

Grandkids are never too many to name:

> CHEYENNE at age four looked past the grays and browns of a bleak November landscape and taught me to see with my heart. "Purple, red and yellow, Grammy."
>
> BLAKE assembled cover photo props faster than my eyes could follow, and with his brothers had them back in place before I could look for them. In his produce business he's figuring a way to add Grandma's books.
>
> TERRY shot the cover photos but declined my offer to compose the concerto for this story. He advised me to let readers find the music for themselves.
>
> JOEY, our military man, showed me the soul inside the uniform.
>
> JACOB is the Army captain on top of the piano.
>
> JUSTUS gave me editorial advice and *parupata*.
>
> LANE helped O'Dell write her hasty note to Ricky.

89501559R00148

Made in the USA
San Bernardino, CA
26 September 2018

THE FUGITIVE'S CONCERTO

JILL CARLSON

Take a furlough from wars, fear and anxiety — and read the adventure of three musical sisters who received the *gift of a lifetime*.

See other side for ways to buy your own copy of Jill's newest novel, or to read it on Kindle.

IN THE FINAL MONTHS OF WORLD WAR II, the mysterious "Bottle Man" suddenly appears in the Farnsworths' neighborhood. Children are fascinated; parents don't trust him. Where is he from, and why is the War Department investigating him?

WHAT READERS ARE SAYING
ABOUT *THE FUGITIVE'S CONCERTO:*

"**I have never read a more beautifully written manuscript** than *The Fugitive's Concerto*. As an artist, I am fascinated with how the story creates a picture with only a few powerful words. Full of intrigue and mystery, it delivers pure delight. The author has a rare gift for storytelling."

— *Alice Dolgener, www.artbyalicedolgener.com*

"**Louisa May Alcott** meets Charles Dickens in this intriguing novel."

— *Mark and Susan Stanley, Harbor of Refuge International, www.harborofrefuge.org*

"**I lived through this time period,** and this is the first novel I have had the pleasure to read that expresses musicality so lovingly, knowingly, spiritually. It is humanity groping for a foundation of peace and purpose."

— *Martha Robinson, Wayzata, Minnesota*

JILL CARLSON is the author of *What Are Your Kids Reading* (Wolgemuth & Hyatt, 1991); *Run Baby Jake* (Merton Glenn Publishing House, 2005); and over 100 articles for national publications. She taught high school English in Pennsylvania and Iowa and coached piano students for 10 years. She and her husband Jerry live on a multi-generational farm where the family manufactures and tests non-toxic farming applications on a large variety of crops.